FANNING THE FLAMES

VECTOR CITY SUPERS
BOOK 2

KELLY FARMER

Fanning the Flames

Copyright © 2025 by Kelly Farmer

This is a work of fiction created without the use of AI technology. Names, characters, places and incidents are either the product of the author's imagination or are used fictitiously. Any resemblance to actual persons, living or dead, businesses, companies, events or locales is entirely coincidental.

ISBN (trade paperback): 979-8-9917483-3-9

ISBN (eBook): 979-8-9917483-4-6

ISBN (Kindle): 979-8-9917483-5-3

First Edition: July 2025

Edited by Mackenzie Walton (www.mackenziewalton.com)

Copyedited by Julie Cassidy (www.juliecassidyauthor.com)

Cover illustration and design by Steve Buccellato (www.legendhaus.com)

*For all the LARPers, cosplayers, fanfic authors, and people who
unabashedly love what they love.
You're awesome.*

CONTENT NOTES

This is a pretty ridiculous book, but there are a few content items to note. It has on-page sex, people with superpowers being *very* destructive to a large city, fear, violence, and discussions of past betrayal.

Also, please note that this is Book 2 in the Vector City Supers trilogy. It follows the same main couple, so you might want to read Book 1, *Secret Spark*, first.

Enjoy the shenanigans with care.

CHAPTER 1

Joan stared at the closet door and took a deep breath. This decision could make or break everything else that followed. Could set the tone for the entire day.

She opened it, revealing neatly arranged pairs of sneakers in nearly every color. Now that she was ex-Supervillain Spark, she was dipping her toes into brighter kicks. Not that she wanted to attract attention. That still felt too vulnerable. Almost risky given the fact that it'd only been six months since Vector City had been rid of Villains. Some by choice, some by force.

Hmm. The hot-pink ones with dark-blue stripes kind of went with her red-plaid flannel and black skinny jeans. And Sadie was wearing a pink sweater, so she'd think the semi-coordination was cute.

Or was that matchy-matchy in a bad way? The long aprons they wore for Hot and Cold had vertical pale pink and blue stripes. Too many shades of the same colors.

"Joanie," Sadie called from the kitchen. "Just pick a pair. We have to get going."

Joan glanced over her shoulder with a smile. She loved hearing Sadie's cheerful voice in their apartment. The home they'd created together. The spare bedroom where Joan used to keep her Villain gear and spoils of her illicit profession was now...

Well, it was kind of a mess now. When Sadie moved in, she'd cozied up the space with her colorful furniture. Which had remained neat and tidy for about three weeks before she'd started piling things everywhere. Books, paint swatches and draft menus for the food truck, off-season clothes, extra throw pillows and blankets on the purple couch...

The only clean surface was the whitewashed desk, since Joan used it more often (and thus organized it). But it was worth it to live with the woman who'd shown her love she'd never thought was possible.

She opted for a pair of reliable black-and-white shoes that would provide comfort and quieter style. Then she pulled her chin-length hair back as far as it would go. A few of the shorter dark layers in the front slipped through her fingers. This was why she didn't usually do layers. At least her undercut was freshly shaved. Ah, well. It'd be another hat day inside the food truck.

Late morning sunlight streamed through the tall sliding glass doors in the living room. One beam glinted off the metal shelving unit that showcased Joan's expensive art pieces and little trinkets Sadie had crafted over the years. They didn't exactly coordinate but spoke volumes about the merging of their lives. Like Joan's napkin doodles Sadie had gotten framed of concepts for Hot and Cold, and hearts with their initials in them.

Sadie bustled around the open kitchen in her thin pink V-neck sweater and royal-blue pants. Her damp red hair was piled up in a messy bun. A flicker of heat whispered through Joan's lower abdomen. That exposed neck, the milky skin above the twin swells of the most perfect set of breasts known to humanity...

"I should've gone with the pink-and-blue shoes," Joan said.

"There's no time to change," Sadie said before shoving the rest of her toast in her mouth.

"I can do it really quick."

"No." Sadie covered her mouth as she chewed. "We need to stop at the store. Mark will whine if we're late."

"Mark whines about everything."

Joan sidled up behind her to nuzzle her neck. Then loop her arms around Sadie to press their bodies together. She kissed the spot she knew made her girlfriend's toes curl. "You look cute today," she murmured.

"Ma'am," Sadie giggled. "What did I just say about not having time?"

"What's the point of running a business if I can't set my own schedule?" She splayed her fingers where Sadie's secret tattoo of flowers hid beneath her pants. Her internal fire responded with an excited burst of liquid warmth.

Sadie leaned into the embrace. "We already had morning shower sex. Was our quickie not enough?"

"Sweetheart, you should know by now my least favorite word in the English language is *quickie*."

Sadie laughed softly, then squeezed Joan's arms. "Okay, horndog." She hesitated for a moment. "You never answered me earlier. Are you sure you're okay?"

"I'm terrific."

"That nightmare was your second one this month."

"It's really okay."

"I hate that you get those dreams," Sadie said.

Joan kissed her cheek. "I hate that it woke you up."

The nightmares that had been plaguing her since turning on Trick, Hide and Volt had stopped for a while. Now they were back with a vengeance. She really didn't want to worry Sadie with how disturbing they were.

Sadie eased away to grab her ceramic coffee mug and down its remaining contents. Joan's fire kept bubbling, needing to go somewhere. She willed it toward her heart, though a lot of it stayed south. Extra fire lingered everywhere in her body lately.

Sadie set her mug and small plate in the sink. Now the fire flattened in irritation. "Babe," Joan said.

"Hmm?" Sadie slid her phone into her back pocket.

Joan just looked at her.

Sadie swiped her usual cherry-red lipstick on before tossing it in her rainbow-striped tote bag.

"Babe."

"What?"

Joan gestured at the sink.

"What?" Sadie looked around, then understood. "Oh my lord."

She huffed back to the sink and picked up her mug, then wrenched the dishwasher open and set it inside.

"Thank you," Joan said with more patience than she felt.

"Mm-hmm." Sadie put the rest of her dishes in the washer.

"I appreciate it."

"I know you like a clean kitchen."

"Happy home, happy life."

Sadie closed the dishwasher door, then looked up with a small smile. "Happy Joan, happy Sadie."

Ugh, harping on her felt equal parts asshole and expressive. But a clean kitchen meant more than just a sink without dirty dishes. An orderly home had been one thing in Joan's chaotic life she'd been able to control.

She followed Sadie to the door. "Are you making Mexican hot chocolate again today?"

"We should have enough ingredients left," Sadie said.

"Cool. It pairs perfectly with the Tequila Sunset sandwich."

As they exited their apartment and headed for the elevator, they discussed the day's menu. In the three months since opening Hot and Cold, they'd made quite a few changes with Mark. Tweaked the menu, added more sides, started selling Sadie's specialty drinks like hot chocolate and apple cider for the cooler winter months.

The biggest change was very quickly realizing none of them enjoyed getting up early to shop and prep to be open for lunch. So they'd found a perfect weeknight dinner crowd location outside several towering office buildings. People liked to grab something quick ahead of their evening plans or commute. There was less competition too, so it was a win all around.

After stopping at a nearby grocery store, Joan drove to where Mark had already parked the truck. She found a spot around the corner and eased her black sedan into it. Sadie hopped out to get the groceries as Joan fed the meter. The sun had dipped behind some clouds, making the breeze in the January air chillier. She slid her Wayfarer sunglasses to the top of her head even though it felt strange not wearing them in public. Old habits died hard.

Sadie handed over one of the reusable shopping bags so they could hold hands while walking. They passed the husband-and-wife duo who ran Cajun Soul also unloading supplies for their truck.

"There's the cutest couple ever," Tenia said with a warm, toothy grin.

"You mean you and Morris?" Sadie replied. "For sure."

They all laughed. The middle-aged Black couple were so giving with advice and helpful suggestions. They were also enjoying this later-in-life food truck endeavor.

On Crawley Avenue, a few late-lunch customers stood in line for Powered By Plants' amazing vegan dishes. Beth-Ann was writing something on the truck's menu board. Her white jacket and platinum-blonde ponytail were almost as bright as the yellow truck.

"You guys have that warm beet salad today?" Joan asked.

"We only have a few left," Beth-Ann said.

"Ooh, you won't regret ordering that," Sadie told their customers. "It's perfect on a day like today."

"And then stop by Hot and Cold to get some of Sadie's spicy apple cider."

"Aw, thanks. We'll be open in just a few."

Joan shared a nod with Beth-Ann. She spied Wren's jet-black ensemble inside the truck. Beth-Ann's tatted, shaved-headed best friend was her total opposite on the outside, but both were all kindness inside. The supportive community of food truck owners was not something Joan had expected when they got into this business venture. A happy surprise.

This walk with Sadie was her favorite part of each workday. It was so normal. Two people greeting other people they'd befriended doing something they loved. Something good.

They reached where Hot and Cold was parked just north of Allegria Tower. Its deep-pink-and-blue logo popped from the light-blue background. Sadie grinned up at Joan, warming her in that pure way. How had a former Supervillain gotten lucky enough to find a woman who loved her for being boring old Joan Malone?

They shared a quick kiss before opening the side door. The lingering scent of pressed sandwiches mixed with a slight tinge of all-natural cleaning products hung in the truck.

Mark was efficiently dicing an onion at the prep counter. His sandy-blond hair stuck up and out in bedhead chic. "Did you get my tomatillos?" he said.

"Yes, chef," Sadie teased. She set her shopping bag on the small stainless-steel worktop.

Joan set hers down and began to unpack the fresh veggies her brother needed for his cold topping creations. "Gruyère cheese was on sale, so I got extra."

"We don't buy ingredients because they're on sale," Mark said. "We buy them because they're high-quality."

"It's the kind you like, not a bargain item."

Sadie stepped back from where she stashed her tote bag by the driver's seat. She paused beside Mark, eyebrows knit. "Isn't that what you were wearing yesterday?"

Mark glanced down at the gray, short-sleeved polo and jeans that actually yes, he had worn yesterday. "It would appear so."

Sadie shook her head, though she was smiling. "And what was this gentleman's name?"

"Uh... Eddie? Drake? Orlando?"

"Markie, you said you'd at least remember their names."

"I probably remembered it last night."

"Maybe," Joan snickered.

"I'm pretty sure there was a D in it," Mark said.

Sadie giggled. "Oh, there was a D in it all right."

Mark burst out laughing and gave her an elbow bump. "Nice one."

"Next time, will you at least remember their name?"

"I make no promises."

Joan chuckled at them. She snagged a clean apron from one of the low metal cabinets as the two most important people in her life joked about Mark's romantic escapades.

Prep work zipped along smoothly—a well-oiled machine at this point. She got the flat-top and fryer going, Sadie started on her hot chocolate, Mark got the toppings in order for the day's chosen sandwiches. A comforting routine.

She adjusted her trusty black-and-red Vector City Vultures baseball cap in place. Always a funny coincidence that her favorite team and her Spark suit had the same colors. Only that suit was now the property of the Superheroes. She kind of missed it. Or at least the anonymity it'd provided. This hat was her Food Truck Joanie persona. Like it would somehow shield her warming proteins and melting cheeses with fire from her bare hands.

"Hon, back me up on this." Sadie bumped Joan with her hip.

"Always," Joan assured her.

"You're not even paying attention," Mark said.

"I back Sadie up no matter what."

"Ugh. Gross."

Sadie grinned and leaned into Joan's side. "Aww, thank you, honey-woney sweet potato blossom," she cooed.

"*So* gross," Mark grunted.

Joan wrapped her arms around Sadie's shoulders from behind, squeezing tight and kissing her soft cheek.

"That's unsanitary."

She kissed Sadie's cheek several times, making her laugh.

Mark rolled his eyes. "Your girlfriend is so clingy, Sades."

"Your girlfriend knows how good she has it and doesn't take that for granted," Joan said.

"Good," Sadie said.

She patted Joan's arms before pulling away to measure the milk. Beautiful, sweet, kind, endlessly forgiving Sadie. Yeah, no way was Joan gonna do anything to mess up this perfect life they'd created.

Classic rock echoed through the warehouse as Sadie checked the inventory inside the ancient, cranky fridge. The small kitchenette was really just a sink and a bit of counterspace.

What had once been a secret lair for Villains was now where they kept the food truck. Joan's sedan was parked by Mark's sporty blue car in the mostly empty space. The only things that remained from the old days were a worn folding table, some plastic chairs, and workout equipment in the far corner.

She made a note about excessive arugula on one of the many handy sheets Perry had prepared to keep them properly stocked. Cloud cover had made for a dreary night with low foot traffic, so they'd decided to close up a bit early.

Mark stepped out of the truck munching on his own personal version of the Harvest Moon sandwich. Extra turkey and provolone bulged out between untoasted slices of sourdough bread.

"You're eating your profits again," Sadie lightly teased.

"Shh. Don't tell Perry." He licked homemade ranch dressing from his index finger.

"He already texted about us closing early."

"Why do we have the end-of-day reports sent to him again?"

"Because he's the one who pays attention to them."

Mark shrugged and took a huge bite.

It wasn't that he and Joanie didn't care about watching their budget. They'd just never been held accountable for expenses.

Perry trusted Sadie to keep them in line as much as she could. And Perry trusted very few people, so it was a duty she took seriously.

Her position at Hot and Cold had expanded from being the people person and public face to also being the go-between whenever the other three resorted to witty remarks and the occasional use of superpowers instead of just listening to one another.

Ah, Supervillains. They still had a ways to go but were being more responsible every day.

"We got too much arugula at the farmers market," she said. "Can you incorporate some into a recipe?"

"Sure," Mark said as he joined her. "I'll take some off your hands now."

He reached into the fridge and pulled a few leaves out of the bag, then opened his sandwich and placed them on top.

"That's coming out of your paycheck," Sadie said, closing the refrigerator door before he could steal more items.

"Fine with me. I don't have taxes taken out when I'm paid in food."

She stopped the music on her phone. No notifications on her lock screen. There were almost never any from the SuperWatch app since setting it to high alerts only. Just the occasional Superhero activity involving regular citizens. Like when Catch moved some downed power lines from a storm, her ability to absorb energy keeping her safe.

Sadie chuckled to herself. A year ago, she'd have swooned over Catch's brave heroics. But the woman behind the navy-blue mask—Darlene—was pretty dull. All of Vector City's Superheroes had visited Hot and Cold as their true selves. Checking up on Joan and Mark for sure. Darlene couldn't hold a candle to Joan. Well, she could literally, but Joan would melt it just to spite her.

Speaking of Joan… She was finishing up the dishes in the truck, so this was a good time to catch Mark alone. "Hey, I wanted to ask you something," Sadie said. "Joanie had another nightmare. It's her second one this month."

Mark's eyebrows met in concern.

"She keeps telling me they're nothing to worry about, but I know there's more to it. Can you talk to her?"

"Of course."

"I think… I mean, they started after the incident with Trick. I think she hasn't dealt with what happened, and it's coming out in other ways."

Like how it was coming out in Mark by how he spent more and more nights on the town or at Sadie and Joan's place. Like he didn't want to be alone with his thoughts. But that was a conversation Joanie needed to have with him.

"I just know it's easier for her to open up about that part of her life with you," Sadie added.

"She worships the ground you walk on. That's why she doesn't like bringing that crap up around you. But I'll ask her about it."

"Thank you."

Mark nudged her with his elbow. "Are you still doing okay after getting Trick-napped?"

"Oh, I'm fine," Sadie said. "It was weird being under mind control, and I definitely needed Joanie to drive me to and from work for those few weeks afterward. But it got better. Knowing Trick can't hurt anyone anymore really helps."

"Good."

Joan exited the truck, fitted flannel sleeves rolled up, hair tousled from wearing her hat. Her glorious forearms glistened with drops of water. Ungh, she was so hot. Literally, figuratively, and all points in between.

Dampness seeped through the cement floor and walls. Sadie went over to the long table to grab her magenta fleece off one of the plastic chairs.

"Are you cold?" Joan asked.

"A little."

"Here." She wrapped Sadie in her arms. A moment later, her body heat radiated out.

"Ahh. Thank you." Sadie nestled closer and rested her cheek in the crook of Joan's neck. The faint odor of canola oil from the flat-top and fryer clung to her shirt.

"We've got a lot of arugula," Mark said around the sandwich in his mouth. "I was thinking of using it for pesto. Mashed chickpeas and shaved parmesan for a vegetarian option."

"With sliced Roma tomatoes?" Joan nodded against Sadie's forehead. "Sounds good."

"I'll see what's in season at the farmers market on Saturday. I want fresh tomatoes."

"Keep our standards high, chef," Sadie said. The cherry tomato plant on their apartment balcony was not a fan of the cooler winter weather.

Mark started to say something, then cried out as a glop of ranch dripped onto his shirt. He swore and rushed to the sink.

Joan tilted her chin down. "So we've got some extra time this evening," she murmured.

"We could watch the news and go to bed like a proper old couple," Sadie joked. Though that sounded pretty good.

"We could. Or…" Joan's hands slid lower. "We could use the bed for some different activities."

"We'll see when we get home."

"I can thoroughly warm you up." Joan squeezed her butt cheeks.

"You always do."

"Uninterrupted private sex time."

Sadie laughed and de-nestled from Joan's chest. Her girlfriend's bright amber eyes glimmered with intent.

"I promise to make it worth your while." Joan waggled her eyebrows. She was so ridiculous.

"I'm kind of not in the mood, babe."

Her face contorted like not having sex was the single most painful event in history.

"We had morning shower sex," Sadie reminded her.

"That was *hours ago*," Joan moaned. She went in for a kiss that Sadie dodged.

"Joanie."

"Sadie."

"You've been so horny lately. What's up with that?"

"I don't know." Joan scratched at her hair. "I'm just feeling…" She flicked a few tiny sparks off her fingers. Something she had to do when she had too much fire built up. "Itchy. Like there's a backload of fire I need to release."

"You need to do something about that."

She raised her eyebrows like *Sex would help with that*.

"You have to get that out of your system." Sadie waved toward the kitchenette. "Mark does, too."

"Mark does what now?" he said, blotting his shirt with a wet paper towel.

"You both have been total horndogs lately."

He nodded in agreement, then frowned. "Okay, but ew. Please don't ever tell me how horny my sister is."

"You know she is," Sadie said.

"I don't want that in my head, Sades."

She stepped away from Joan. Her body heat was getting too warm. "You don't release nearly as much fire or ice as you used to. It's probably all backed up in your bodies."

"Probably," Joan said.

"And it's coming out in other ways." Sadie pointed at Mark. "You're hooking up way more than ever. And you're…" She touched Joan's shoulder with a finger. "A lot."

"You're right. We need to get it out."

"Make use of the extra time we have tonight."

"Yes, dear." Joan gave her the grin that dissolved any lingering annoyance. She couldn't help being born with the ability to conjure fire. And her internal warmth was usually great for their sex life.

"We could go down to—" Mark wiped at a glob of ranch dressing near the hem of his polo. "Seriously?"

He strode toward the small bathroom, pulling his shirt overhead.

Joan plucked at Sadie's fleece, loosely pulling her back into her arms. "I'll make you a deal. I'll get rid of this extra fire if you use tonight to work on your plans for Sadie's Café."

An uncomfortable squish twisted Sadie's gut. She avoided eye contact and mumbled, "It's pretty late for that."

"Honey, it's time to move forward."

"Hot and Cold is still in its early stages."

"We're doing fine."

Sadie glanced up, grateful but uneasy from the genuine support softening Joan's face. "But you need me."

"I appreciate every single thing you do," Joan said.

"And I really like working here. We have so much fun."

"I love working with you. But the food truck was *my* dream, not yours."

"It's not the right time," Sadie insisted. "I'm the face of the truck so you and Mark can lay low."

"Mark and I can be less in the background. Enough time has passed. The Supers have seen we really did go legit."

"I'm still the best for customer service and dealing with people."

"I'm not bad with it," Joan said.

"Hon, you were fired from a customer service job for melting your desk after a difficult phone call."

"That was a long time ago. I've matured."

Sadie stepped out of Joan's arms. "Who are you gonna get to work with you? It's not like you can hire just anyone with your unique cooking styles."

"That's not your concern."

"Everything about the truck is my concern."

"We can find a norm who got out of the criminal life," Joan said. "An old associate who wants steady employment and understands keeping our former identities quiet."

A shadow crossed over her face that she quickly shook off.

"Remember our deal, Sadie Eagan. You helped me get on the straight and narrow. I help you open your dream café."

"I'm just…" Sadie gave a weak shrug. "I'm not ready yet. And whether or not you want to admit it, you need me to keep eyes on the money and things for Hot and Cold."

"That's what Perry does."

"Yeah, but you two don't listen to Perry."

"We do. We just pretend like we don't."

That was pretty doubtful. Even with all her hang-ups and fears and anxiety about opening her own café, the biggest factor in not pursuing it was the need to make Hot and Cold stable and profitable.

Joan tilted her head. "Per said he's been waiting to go over the research he's done for you."

Sadie uttered a sound she hoped sounded like words.

"He'll meet you anytime." Joan smirked. "It's paperwork. His favorite."

"Some other time. I just want to go home, have a warm cup of tea, and relax."

"All right, but meet with him soon, okay? He keeps bugging me."

Mustering up a smile, Sadie said, "I will."

Joan enveloped her in a comforting hug. "I'll be the first person in line when you open your doors. I'll be so proud, I'll tell everyone, 'This is my girlfriend's café. She's amazing and can do anything.'"

"That's sweet and slightly annoying."

"I'll be so obnoxious with my support."

"Well, I can't wait for that," Sadie giggled.

Joan tightened her arms, filling Sadie with love. Sadie did the same. She adored Joan and so appreciated her unwavering encouragement. On one level, it made Sadie's Café something within reach. But the onus was still on Sadie to like, do the work, and make the big boss decisions, and have all the responsibility, and…

And what if I fail?

"I'm gonna go lock the truck," Joan said. She dropped a kiss on Sadie's lips.

Sadie wandered toward the window, suddenly chilled without Joan's heat. The thick curtains that once blocked everything out had been replaced with less severe off-white drapes.

A strange green glow briefly lit up the outside. She pulled one of the curtains back to see if it was lightning.

Nothing shined through the overcast sky. She started to let the curtain fall, but it happened again. A pale green shimmer dancing through the clouds. Huh. Weird.

Well, it wasn't Villain activity. Vector City had no Supervillains anymore. Three of them were imprisoned, however the Supers properly secured people with superpowers. And the other three were running an up-and-coming food truck. It was nice not to worry all the time about potential destruction.

Things were comfortable. Easy. Uncomplicated. Maybe even a teensy bit boring. But boring was good. Boring was what Joanie had wanted for a long, long time. Boring was...

Safe. And it was good to be safe.

CHAPTER 2

Joan formed another large fireball between her hands. She lobbed it into the night sky over the river. Mark shot a big, icy ball at it, dissolving it on contact.

They'd been at it for a good ten, maybe fifteen minutes. Every blast of fire brought relief, like her body was grateful for the release.

The row of riverfront warehouses provided coverage from prying eyes. A good place to discharge built-up fire. She'd never gone so long without using it to fly or fight.

"Are you almost out?" Mark asked, shooting little ice pellets into the cracked blacktop.

"Not yet." Joan wiped rogue hair off her slightly damp forehead. "You definitely let the Supers know we're doing this?"

"I texted Zee to let them know there was no cause for concern."

A slow smile pulled at her lips. "You *texted Zee*. I didn't realize you had Race's number."

"It's for shit like this so the Supers don't freak out."

"Mm-hmm."

Mark crossed his arms. "Don't start with that."

"Just saying you two have this very entertaining flirty repartee."

He sprayed her butt with a snow shower.

"Which I get to witness once a week when they drop by the truck to get dinner because we have—" She made air quotes. "Good hand-cut fries."

"We do have good hand-cut fries."

"That you personally serve."

Conjuring up a big block of ice, Mark said, "Focus on the task at hand, nosy."

Joan shot a streaming flame at it, melting it to a pool of water in seconds. They did it twice more, each time with a little less oomph.

"Whew." Joan exhaled a deep breath. "That does feel better. I'm glad Sadie suggested this."

"She's the best," said Mark.

"She *is* the best."

"Are things good between you two?"

"Everything is perfect."

"Other than you wanting to get with her like a rabbit in heat?"

Joan laughed. "Yeah, I guess she had a point."

Mark stared out at the dark water. "She mentioned you started having nightmares again. I thought they'd stopped."

With a vague shrug, Joan said, "I've had a few random ones."

"Sadie said it's been two this month. She's worried."

Shit. She hated to worry Sadie.

Glancing over, Mark said, "Were they like the other ones?"

"They're always the same. Some variation of Melvin, Irving and Ethel yelling at me. Staring me down or holding me so I can't escape."

"What are they saying?"

"I'm not sure. It's not really words." Joan rubbed at the tightness building in her chest. "But they're mad. They're so mad, I can feel it. I wake up wanting to run and hide."

"Damn."

She sat on the concrete barrier separating the riverfront from the warehouses. "I'm freaked out that what happened to them will happen to us."

Mark dropped beside her. "That the Supers will change their minds and say, 'Just kidding. We're gonna lock you up, too.'"

"Yeah. One misstep and this could all be gone."

"I get it. I worry about that, too."

Flashes of her former cohorts' angry faces played in her mind. "It's not fair. What went down."

"They were going ahead with their half-baked plans no matter what we did."

Joan shook her head. "What happened *wasn't* fair. They got life in prison. We got to walk free."

"They made their own choices. They wanted to be Villains. They enjoyed it." Mark rested his arms on his thighs. "We didn't actively choose that life. I don't think Perry did either. He had his cagey reasons he never tells us."

"He had to have been double-crossed by the Supers. We know he once trusted them, and now he acts like they're mortal enemies. I mean, he gave his Breeze suit and computer crap to *us* to give to the Supers so he wouldn't have to face them."

"Yeah, Per's got secrets, but…" Mark raised his eyebrows. "Maybe he's freaking out, too. He's been betrayed before. Who's to say it won't happen again?"

"Exactly." Joan's heartbeat thumped from the realization.

"I wouldn't worry too much. We're making amends. We've always tried to do some good. Melvin and Company were selfish assholes who never thought about anyone but themselves. They liked being the bad guys."

"We sometimes liked being the bad guys," Joan admitted.

Mark nudged her knee with his. "We were pretty good at it. We also gave a whole lot of apology money to people and businesses. The Supers know that."

"Yeah, but do they care?"

"No, but it's further proof we don't suck."

A heavy sigh brushed past Joan's lips. "We turned on our friends, Mark. Turned *in* our friends. We're persona non grata to everyone we used to associate with."

"We're building a new life."

"I know, but…"

He nudged her knee again. "I know, sis."

They sat in understanding silence. They'd stayed ultra busy over the past few months to mask the pain of giving up the life they once knew.

"Why dwell on what's done?" Mark said. "We have the food truck we always wanted. You have the girl you always wanted. Per likes being a not-so-silent investor in Hot and Cold."

"We *think* he likes it," Joan corrected. "He doesn't tell us one way or the other."

"I think one of his superpowers is masking his true emotions. So I assume he's happy to keep my conscience clear."

She shook her head at how easily her brother could rationalize something. "How are you *really* doing? I know you're avoiding being at home."

"'Cause it's boring."

"Your hooking up more is only partially from the excess energy."

"It's also my abandonment issues, Joanie." He said it flippantly, gazing at the gray clouds, but real pain pinched his eyes. Mark always left someone before they could leave him. But lately, it'd been more like running away before he even learned the guy's name. Running away from potential hurt.

Thanks a bunch for kicking us out, Mom and Dad.

Joking was the only way to get him to open up. "How can you have abandonment issues when your wombmate hasn't left your side in thirty-five years?"

Mark cracked a grin. "Present company excluded."

"And Perry and my very patient girlfriend let you crash at our respective homes whenever you feel like it."

"Which I do appreciate."

"Greta still talks to you."

"Greta's your friend."

"But she talks to you."

Not that she saw Greta much lately. Their usual *Let's break into the mayor's office for funsies* hangouts had been replaced by her old friend stopping by the food truck once in a while. Leaving the criminal element had put a strain on their relationship, mostly because the Supers knew where to find Joan. She couldn't lurk in the shadows anymore.

"Maybe we need therapy," she said, not entirely in jest.

"Oh, we definitely need therapy," Mark laughed.

"Good luck trying to find a shrink who specializes in super-powered issues." She tried a new approach. "You can hang out with me and Sadie's friends if you want."

"You said you have a hard time relating to them."

True, their normal lives and problems sometimes made Joan feel out of place. "It's getting easier now that I have regular people issues to talk about. The price of gas, taxes... And they're nice. They seem to be happy."

"I *am* happy, Joanie," Mark said. "I don't regret what we did. I love finally being able to cook every day. And we're making new acquaintances with the other food truck owners and vendors. Things are great."

Joan smiled. "I'm happy, too."

"Good."

"I hope Perry's happy. We foisted this on him."

Mark set a hand on his chest. "I like to think we put him on the path he always wanted to be on."

"He wanted to work in the art world."

"He technically worked in the art world for many years."

"I don't think stealing works of art counts," Joan said.

"He always knew which ones were worth taking."

She dug the toe of her shoe into the ground. "I just hope he's not struggling too much with the adjustment."

Mark snorted and said, "If he was upset, he'd let us know. Irritation with us is the one thing he's never had a problem expressing."

"True."

A whiff of mucky river water floated past on the breeze. Sadie liked to say it smelled like fish poo. After working at a fish-and-chips cabana on the upscale riverwalk to the north, she'd stopped eating anything that came out of water.

"Sadie needs to meet with him to talk about her café," Joan said. "She's dragging her feet. It'll be good for both of them to have something to focus on."

"Why do you think she's stalling?"

"I think she thinks we can't run Hot and Cold without her. And I'm kind of worried she's putting aside what she wants for what I want. She has a history of going along with whatever her partner wants."

"Ah. I can see that." Mark cringed and added, "But we do need her."

"We don't need her to work for us with no ownership interest. Which yes, she doesn't want because of the stolen money we used to fund the truck. She deserves more. She can have more."

"But like, who's gonna tally up our expenses at the farmers market to keep us on budget?"

"I can operate the calculator on my phone," Joan drawled.

"And she's so great with the customers."

"We'll hire someone who's great with customers."

"But what about her—"

"I don't want her to give up on her dream," she stated. "Not when she refused to give up on me, even though I *really* didn't deserve it."

"Okay. I get it." Mark twirled his hand, spraying ice shavings into the air.

She really didn't deserve Sadie. But every day, she worked hard to be worthy. Maybe that was why the fear of getting locked up for past crimes was so sharp. Her amends might not be enough.

"Ugh, that's enough feelings." Joan stood and cracked her knuckles. "I've got a little more in me."

"Sweet." Mark hopped up. "We haven't lit it up in forever."

"Okay."

They held their palms out and blasted equal streams of fire and ice. Steam rose at the point of contact. One of their favorite tricks to create cover as Ice and Spark.

The connection went on until Joan's flames began to sputter. "Are you good?" Mark yelled over the hiss and pop.

"I'm good," Joan yelled back.

They waved out the remaining flames and ice shards. A cloud of thick air hovered just overhead. "I figured we should stop before that got any bigger," Mark said. "Don't want to attract attention."

It was a bit of a gamble doing this in their street clothes. No Supervillain outfits meant no protection, either from their powers or hiding their true identities. "That's smart," Joan said. "Otherwise, someone would report it on SuperWatch, and you'd have to text Zee again to tell them—"

"Oh my god, you're the worst."

"Though maybe you want Race to come running down here so you can—"

"The literal, actual worst."

Joan cackled and took off in a sprint, calling over her shoulder, "I'll text my bestie Darlene so we can have a party."

"I hate you," Mark shouted.

"Love you too, buddy."

CHAPTER 3

The Saturday morning farmers market hummed with a pleasantly chill vibe. Sadie stifled a yawn behind her hand as Joan chatted about winter squash with a vendor. The market was smaller and less crowded than in the summer and fall, but still had good seasonal selections.

Across the blocked-off-from-traffic street, Mark geeked out over freshly ground specialty spices while Perry hid behind his sunglasses despite the overcast sky. Not that he blended in all that much in his tailored charcoal-gray overcoat and stylish chestnut-brown wingtip shoes. And, y'know, Perry was a good-looking guy. Grumpy and oblivious to anyone who flirted with him, but that was part of his charm.

Sadie returned her focus to the acorn squash conversation. Joanie was so cute and content in her element. She got such a kick out of thinking up new recipes, and Sadie got a kick out of Joan's childlike grin and enthusiasm. It'd be nice when the weather warmed up to get back to their balcony garden.

A familiar figure dressed all in black hustled by with overflowing bags of kale: Wren grabbing essential ingredients for Powered by Plants.

"Did you run out already?" Sadie said.

"We're doing kale chips today," Wren said, her Scottish lilt coloring her words.

"I love your kale chips. I'll be over in a minute."

"If you see my wife, tell her no more scented candles."

Sadie giggled as Wren rushed toward where her food truck was parked outside the market entrance. Ah, morning people. They got the market crowd. Hot and Cold got the night owls out and about on Saturdays.

Joan looked up from a curvy butternut squash. "Was that Wren?"

"Yeah. She said to keep an eye out for her wife buying another scented candle."

"That woman is obsessed."

"You're lucky making candles isn't one of my hobbies."

"We don't have room for another one of your hobbies," Joan laughed, though she probably wasn't joking.

Living together was amazing—wonderfully amazing. For the most part. Joan was a lot more particular than one would think for someone who'd lived her entire adult life as a free-wheeling Supervillain. She got this little pinch of annoyance between her eyebrows when Sadie forgot to put her dirty laundry in the hamper or left one of her craft projects sitting out for a few days.

She was trying to be more tidy, so Joan had to cut her some slack. It wasn't like Joan didn't leave scorch marks on the kitchen sink or shower tile whenever she drowned out a particularly strong fireball. Those were hard to scrub off.

And she definitely didn't complain whenever a craft project involved something for Hot and Cold. That was… Okay, that was a little irritating.

At least she was sleeping better since talking to Mark the other night. He'd told Sadie, "It's all good," which hopefully meant fewer nightmares.

Sadie's phone buzzed in her back pocket. The vendor's phone chimed. Beeps and bleeps came from all around her. Only one app went off with simultaneous alerts like that.

SuperWatch.

The woman next to Sadie studied her screen. "There's Villain activity going on at Century Plaza."

Sadie's blood froze. Joan stood tall and fisted her hands, visually sweeping the area.

Murmurs of mild concern surrounded them as people read the news. Sadie pulled out her phone with a shaky hand.

> High Alert: Reported Villain activity near Century Plaza shopping area. Unknown who it is but they are causing damage to cars and parking lot.

Someone had posted a blurry photo of a huge man in burnt-orange spandex holding a compact car over his head. Another person posted a video of the same guy banging his meaty fists on hoods. He punched through a windshield, shattering glass into the minivan.

"Joanie?" Sadie looked to her to see if Joan knew who it was.

Her mouth twisted in thought. "I think that's Smash. He's a Villain from some small Midwestern city."

"What's he doing here?"

Joan shrugged.

Mark hurried across the street, Perry following close behind. Sadie and Joan met them halfway. "Isn't that Smash?" Mark said, staring at his phone.

"I think so," Joan said.

A live feed went up on SuperWatch. Smash jumped onto the roof of an SUV, caving it in. "I'm *The* Smash!" he roared. "I'm coming to Vector City!"

"Aren't you already here?" the brave smartass behind the camera said.

"Aren't you just Smash?" a woman offscreen said.

"*The* Smash!" The Villain jumped up and pulverized the SUV upon landing.

"Yeah, okay."

He stomped the vehicle into a flat metal rectangle.

"Not this again," said a tall white man walking past Sadie.

"I thought we were done with Villains," the woman with him said.

Other comments floated by:

"Great. Another one of these jerks."

"Does this mean the Villains are back?"

"I told you Spark and Ice were still around. They're working with whoever this is."

Joan shared a look with Mark. In tandem, they pulled their Wayfarer sunglasses from their jackets and put them on. Perry adjusted his aviators.

"Well, this isn't good," Mark muttered.

The video got shaky as Smash picked up a motorcycle and compacted it between his hands. He threw it toward the row of shops, narrowly missing the front window of a shoe store.

Frightened screams and people running away made Sadie's heart lodge in her throat. "He's gonna hurt someone."

Onscreen, the video grew even shakier. "I'm outta here," said the guy behind the camera.

The feed ended. Joan continued to scan the market crowd from the middle of the street.

"So, what?" a person behind Sadie said. "Are we getting Villains from other cities now?"

Oh, shit. Were they?

"He's a low-level Villain," Perry said. "Probably wants to make a name for himself."

"Yeah," Mark said. "Get his fifteen seconds of fame where there's no competition."

"Should we…" Sadie lowered her voice. "I mean, should you be concerned?"

"Nah. Lunk's a brain surgeon compared to this guy. The Supers will handle it."

"I meant having Villain activity in the city. Could that…" *Could that put your deal with the Supers in jeopardy?*

Joan touched her arm. Her fingers burned hot even through

Sadie's lavender cardigan and long-sleeved white cotton tee. "I don't think there's too much to worry about. We're nowhere near there."

Mark gave his sister a look. "You know that was one of our favorite diversions."

"This guy's not a threat. Lunk can take him out in no time. But, uh, just in case, we should probably…"

"…let people know you're here," Sadie finished. "Definitely." She tapped on her phone's camera. "Let's get a pic for Hot and Cold's socials."

She huddled close to Joan and Mark. Perry stepped to the side because he never wanted his picture on social media. Making sure vendors were visible in the background, Sadie took a snapshot. It wasn't the greatest pic—they looked like they were being forced to smile for the family Christmas card photo—but it'd be good enough proof.

"Send it to Mark so he can text it to Zee," Joan said.

"Really?" Mark said. "You're making jokes about that—"

"Send it to them so the Supers know where we are."

"Ugh, it's like checking in with our parole officer."

"It basically is."

Joan rubbed Sadie's back. While she was acting fairly nonchalant, she couldn't hide the nervous tremble in her fingers.

Sadie refreshed SuperWatch. No notifications about Supers arriving on the scene. But they would. They were still the protectors of Vector City.

"I really hope this is a one-off," she said.

"It is, sweetheart." Joan gave her a smile. "Don't worry."

"It's kind of hard not to worry." What did this mean for Vector City? For Joan and Mark and Perry?

"Stick to business as usual," Perry said. "Open the truck. Don't do anything outside of your routine."

Joan and Mark nodded. Part of Sadie wanted to run home and lock the door to keep her and Joan safe. But Perry was right. They needed to show the Supers the food truck was their priority. That they had been planning menus, not villainous hijinks.

She really hoped this wasn't a big deal.

It's not a big deal. It's nothing.

Joan repeated the mantra in her head as she tossed hot fries with Hot and Cold's signature rosemary-and-sea-salt blend in a large metal bowl.

Outwardly, she was calm. Pleasant. Just another evening at the food truck. The Supers had caught Smash. It was over and done.

She shook the fries into a red-and-white-checked paper tray, then grabbed it and the November Rain sandwich and stepped to the service window. "Here you go," she said to the guy in a knit hat and hoodie.

"Thanks," he said. "Stay safe out here tonight."

Joan wrenched her lips into a smile. "You, too."

Stay safe because there could be Villains lurking about. If he only knew how Joan had melted the cheese blend on his sandwich...

Dusk settled over the street lined with bars and microbreweries. It had been a slow day so far. Mark hummed to himself as he cleaned his mess off the prep counter. He was doing a fine job not dwelling on the bullshit. It probably *wasn't* bothering him all that much.

It shouldn't bother any of them. So there was a minor Villain who'd put on his big-boy spandex and was trying to make a go in a major city. He'd already been neutralized. They'd opened Hot and Cold and were being law-abiding citizens. Sure, there weren't as many people out and about, but that was to be expected. Things would pick up again.

Sadie fidgeted with the food order pad, unease etched on her face. She was doing a worse job of pretending like everything was fine. But she was a norm having a normal reaction to everything.

Her phone vibrated in her back pocket. She rolled her eyes. Most likely her mother checking in again. Sadie's mom had been a lot more chill until the events of this morning.

"Oh, crap," she said, staring out the service window.

"What?" Joan leaned down to come face-to-face with— "Oh, crap."

Zee and Kade stood beneath the truck's awning. Kade unsuccessfully tried to blend in with a dark baseball cap even though his huge Lunk muscles bulged out of his jacket and jeans. Zee wore a long olive-green coat and their ever-present smirk.

Mark came to see what was up. "Oh, crap. I mean, hey, how's it going?"

"We stopped by for dinner," Zee said. "And maybe a little chat."

"Sure thing." Mark grinned at Kade. "Hey, big guy."

"Hi." Kade always seemed vaguely confused when Mark flirted with him. His not-Lunk voice was much quieter. Almost jovial.

Nodding toward the rear entry, Zee said, "Can we come in?"

"So you can inspect my goods and services?" Mark said.

Zee just looked at him.

"I don't think I'll fit in there," Kade said.

Mark gave him another flirty grin. "Oh, I think you'll fit just fine."

Joan straightened, saying, "We've got nothing to hide."

"We've been here most of the day," Sadie said. "And we were at the farmers market this morning."

"Then you won't mind us hopping aboard," Zee said.

"We *are* getting food, though, right?" Kade said as they both turned.

"Yes," Zee sighed like this was not the first time they'd had to assure him.

Joan walked to the door, chugging in a deep breath. *It's nothing. It's not a big deal.*

The tight space further crowded with Zee's lean frame and

Kade's giganticness. Zee had dyed the back half of their straight black hair magenta. Kade ducked to avoid hitting his head on the ceiling vent.

"We had nothing to do with what happened at Century Plaza," Joan told them.

"We don't know that guy," Mark added. "Never met him."

"I got your text," Zee said. "I know."

Mark planted his hands on his hips. "Then why are you here?"

"We were curious about something."

Her brother was about to be inappropriate again, so Joan said, "Are you here on behalf of all the Supers?"

"Yes." Zee glanced at Kade, who was attempting to make himself smaller by crossing his arms and hunching inward. "We're here to find out if you've heard any rumors about Villains coming to Vector City. Anything from your prior contacts."

"Nobody talks to us," Mark said. "We've been blacklisted since we worked with you to bring down Trick."

"So you haven't picked up on any gossip from other Villains?"

"*No one* talks to us," Joan emphasized. "Even if we wanted to reach out—which we don't—we're known as the Villains who ratted out their own. That's unforgivable."

Zee studied the Malone twins for a long moment.

Sadie shifted her weight. "I can vouch for them because I'm with these two every day. They aren't having clandestine meetings."

"I said they wouldn't know anything," Kade stage-whispered.

"It was worth a shot," Zee said. "Of course, if I find out you're lying…"

"Why would we lie?" Joan said, flashing hot as her internal fire flickered.

"Why would we team up with Smash?" Mark pointed out.

"*The* Smash," Kade said.

Zee shrugged.

Joan curled her hands into loose fists. "You guys took him

down in five minutes. If we were planning on reentering the Villain scene, we'd pick stronger allies."

Sadie slid her fingers through Joan's and squeezed. "Not that you're planning on that, right, Joanie?"

"Of course not, but—"

"He threw a car at my head," Kade said, unfurling his arms and knocking over two mixing bowls. "It might've looked easy, but he was mean and strong."

Mark squeezed his brawny shoulder. "And we appreciate what you did. We don't want bad guys throwing cars around town."

Zee picked up the bowls. "If you do hear anything, we'd appreciate it if you told us. I'm sure you can agree that protecting our city is important for all of us."

"Important for us staying out of jail, you mean," Joan said.

"It *is* in your best interests."

Well, it was a good thing nobody talked to the former Villains anymore. They wouldn't be put in another situation where they'd have to align with the Supers.

"Do you think this was a one-off, or the start of something?" Sadie asked.

"Hopefully a one-off," Zee said. "We're monitoring the situation."

"I hope so, too." Sadie squeezed Joan's hand.

"Me, too." Kade scratched at the blond curls springing from under his ballcap. "Things are a lot better now that we're not fighting all the time."

"I am a lover, not a fighter," Mark said.

"You're hard to fight against."

"Thanks. You're hard—"

"Could we get some food?" Zee interrupted. A hint of irritation played across their face. Huh. Was that a touch of jealousy or just general annoyance with Mark?

"Absolutely," Sadie said, untangling from Joan. "We've got a new sandwich. It has pesto and chickpeas, and I know you like to eat vegetarian sometimes."

"That sounds good."

Mark pointed his index fingers at Kade. "Turkey?"

"Turkey." Kade bobbed his head and broke into a toothy smile.

They shuffled around one another to prep. "Sadie can ring you up," Joan said at the fryer. Zee always wanted truffle fries.

"Are you really not gonna give us a discount?" Kade said.

Mark pulled on a disposable glove. "We need to earn money if you want us to stay out of trouble."

"It's fine." Zee tugged their phone from a coat pocket. Their mobile payments were tied to an account at City Hall. If Joan were feeling villainous, that could be something fun to look into.

"Can I get three sandwiches?" asked Kade. "I'm starving after battling with *The* Smash."

"You bet, handsome." Mark raised a very suggestive eyebrow. "Gotta keep your strength up for other activities."

"Thanks Mark, but I'm not gay."

"Ah, well, a boy can dream, right?"

"Uhh...I guess?" Kade looked to his cohort. "Wait. We're not supposed to talk about personal stuff with them, right? Otis said not to."

That was unsurprising but still irritating. "Don't get to know your prisoners," Joan muttered.

Zee's lips quirked. "A few months ago, you were active criminals. We have every right to be cautious."

"So do we."

"But I like hanging out with you guys," Kade said. "Your food is really good."

Mark grabbed a bunch of slices of sourdough bread from the bag on a high metal shelf. "Eh, we're all friends here. What Otis doesn't know won't hurt him."

"Cool. So I'm straight. Sometimes Darlene and I hook up, but that's whenever *she* wants to."

Oh god, no. Joan held her hands up. "I did not need to know that."

"TMI, buddy," Mark laughed. "But also, Darlene's the boss, huh?"

"Totally," Kade said. "She sucks up all my strength. It's kinda weird, but not in a bad way."

"I'm sure."

"Otis has an on-again, off-again thing with Aura. She's a Hero in Destine. The one who can alter your mood if you're in her aura. Nobody's supposed to know but every Superhero knows."

"Kade…" Zee appeared to be at a total loss.

Kade looked at them. "You never talk about your personal life, so I have nothing to report."

"Dude," Mark cackled. "This is amazing."

"Zee is pansexual and speaks Mandarin because their parents are from China."

Sadie turned to Zee. "Hey, I'm pan, too."

"Gender *is* a social construct." Zee caught Mark's gaze, and they both quickly looked away.

"Well, now I want to give you a discount. But we have bills to pay."

She told Zee the total, and their smirk deepened. "I always forget how much it costs to feed you," they said to Kade. "That's the thing I can share about *you*."

Kade grinned. "My mom, who doesn't speak Mandarin, she's from a small farm town. She used to say I ate a week's worth of groceries in a day."

Everyone laughed. Everyone but Joan. Sadie and Mark had grown accustomed to being around the Supers. Joan still couldn't fully trust them. Not yet. Maybe not ever.

She busied herself shaking the fryer basket. *It's not a big deal. It's nothing.*

They were just here fishing for information. Information Joan and Mark didn't have. Greta would've said something if she'd heard anything. They just had to keep their noses clean and this would blow over.

Wait. Greta was at her newly renovated apartment in France. She tuned out Vector City gossip while over there. But still.

Kade blocked the flat-top with his bulk. Joan gestured to it. "I can't get to where I have to make your sandwiches," she said.

"Let me make some room," Sadie said. She edged around Zee to get to the rear entry.

"Where are you going?" Joan asked.

"To do my job and wrangle up customers."

"I don't want you out there alone tonight."

"I do it all the time." Sadie tucked the truck's tablet under her arm.

"Not tonight," Joan said.

"Why?"

"Just not tonight."

Sadie rolled her eyes. "Then come with me."

"Hang on. I just dropped some fries."

Mark waved a hand. "I'll get them. Go find us warm bodies." The glint in his stark blue eyes said he wanted to have some fun with his crushes.

Joan followed Sadie onto the sidewalk. Foot traffic was noticeably lighter. The gay bar that let them park in front had its usual packed house. People were getting to their destinations and staying put.

"I'm not sure we should leave those three unsupervised," Sadie said.

Through the service window, Joan spied her brother shooing the Supers away from him. "Mark's got this," she said. "Did you see Zee get jealous with how much he was flirting with Lunk—er, Kade?" She looked around to make sure no one had heard that slip.

Sadie crossed her arms. "Why don't you want me out here by myself?"

"Because there was a douchebag throwing cars around earlier. You can't protect yourself from superpowers."

She half-laughed at that. "You do know I sleep next to someone who generates fire. And spend a lot of time with a guy who can freeze something with the touch of his hand."

"That's different."

"You have the same potential to hurt me. I'm not afraid."

An anxious knot twisted in Joan's gut. "But there are people who might *want* to hurt you."

"I think you can trust me enough to know I'd get the hell out of there if someone was throwing cars."

She choked back that Sadie had been walking to work alone when Hide and Volt grabbed her. That Trick had used mind control to get her to comply. She simply didn't have the right genes to fight off a vengeful Villain.

"You know I trust you," Joan said. "It's the assholes throwing cars I don't trust."

Sadie made a face. "You sound like my mom."

"If I put you in harm's way again, I'd never forgive myself."

"What are you going to do? It's not like you can go full Whooshing Fire Lady in your civilian attire."

"No, but I know how to fight," Joan said. Even though she hadn't sparred with Mark or Greta for months.

"You're not putting me in harm's way. It's just how…" Sadie tilted her head. "I just realized you haven't been on this side of Villain activity. You've never seen it the way the norms do. It's part of our daily lives. I guess we've gotten used to it and don't put our lives on hold."

That made sense. "Huh. You're right. This is new for me."

"Welcome to being an average person," she teased.

It felt weird, being in the dark as much as everyone else. Not knowing if and when the next bad guy would strike. It kind of sucked.

"I thought you were nervous about what happened this morning," Joan said.

"I'm more nervous about what it means for your deal with the Supers. But I think as long as you cooperate, it'll be okay."

A trio of young people walked by. Sadie greeted them with: "How would you like to try the best sandwiches in Vector City?"

To which they replied, "We just ate."

"Aw, that's your loss. Stop by next Saturday night and your minds will be blown."

Joan had craved normalcy her entire life. Now that she had it, well... There was something to be said for being an active participant. Even if that thing was villainy.

Yeah, that was something she needed to unpack later.

Hugging the tablet, Sadie said, "Are you okay?"

"Always." Joan smiled.

"You look like you're thinking hard about something."

"Growing pains shifting from my old life to this one."

"It's weird, huh?"

"Very."

"The Supers came to *you* for information," Sadie said. "That has to be trippy."

Glancing at Mark gleefully teasing Zee and Kade, Joan said, "I never pictured those two inside it when dreaming about a food truck."

Sadie reached out and touched Joan's apron. "Lots of changes. I'm here for you, honey. You can be sure of that."

"You're the only thing I *am* sure of."

"Same here."

A bark of laughter came from Hot and Cold. Mark clapped his hands while Kade looked perplexed and Zee slightly amused.

"And yeah," Sadie said. "Zee was totally mad at Mark for flirting with Kade. And can we talk about the most interesting item of the day? Darlene and Kade hook up? What?"

Joan breathed out a little laugh. "I know, right?"

"And Otis has a thing with a Super from Destine? Also, I'm pretty sure Zee hasn't been keeping things strictly professional with your brother."

"Definitely not."

"So much drama." Sadie shook her head. "I'm glad to be the boring, settled-down couple."

"Me, too."

She gave Joan the smile that pinched her heart every single time. "I love you."

"I love you, too."

They leaned in and met for a soft kiss. Then grinned and kissed again.

"Yas, girls!" someone called nearby. "You get that!"

They broke apart to see a curvy Black drag queen in fuchsia sequins on the way to a gig.

"Hey, gorgeous," Sadie said. "You want to grab something before you dazzle the crowd? Our truffle fries will change your life."

"Will they get me a man and a million dollars?" the queen said.

"We can give you a portion big enough to share with a special someone. Who might be a millionaire."

"Then hell yes."

For not the first time, Joan enjoyed watching Sadie make a customer feel special. She chatted and laughed with the fabulous queen as she rang up the order.

Sadie really was the best. Nothing was going to hurt her. Not with Joan around.

CHAPTER 4

The Vector City Museum of Art had always been one of Sadie's favorite places to visit while growing up in West Vector. She'd imagine something she created in one of its collections someday.

She had not imagined spending the afternoon admiring those collections with Perry, knowing full well he'd robbed this place more than once. At least he wasn't one to kiss and tell. Joanie and Mark were out in the suburbs on a Monday supply run to Cost Club. It was finally time to give in to Perry's badgering and discuss plans for her café.

They studied a swirly Impressionist landscape of an autumnal field. One corner of Perry's mouth quirked up.

"You do love a good landscape," Sadie said. Most of the paintings in his condo were of countryside or water scenes.

"I appreciate how they capture the movement and colors of nature in a single moment."

"This one makes me want to zip up my coat and have a warm beverage."

"It's a fake."

"Really?" Sadie considered the oil on canvas. "How can you tell?"

"The strokes are too deliberate. The artist's name is visible above the frame, which is something he would never do." Perry paused. "I may also know the whereabouts of the original."

"This isn't one you…"

"I don't have it, but I've seen it. It's in good hands." Perry glanced at her, then refocused on the painting. "If it makes it any better, this has always been the one on display. It's good work. The artist should be celebrated."

"I'm not sure that makes it better," Sadie told him.

Perry simply headed out of the Impressionist gallery. Sometimes knowing about the exploits of Breeze, Spark and Ice made her feel icky. But they didn't hide the truth from her.

They walked to the café tucked in the back corner of the museum. Perry flashed his membership card to the hostess and was granted access to the staircase leading to the members-only area. She liked that he supported the museum with his membership dues. Perry understood the value of art and preserving it.

"I've never been up here," Sadie said.

"It has nice views of the city."

It really did. Tall windows brought plentiful light to the modern concept space. The sun shimmered off glassy skyscrapers and highlighted the sculpture garden below.

A handsome bearded man behind the sleek black bar smiled at Perry. "Good afternoon, Mr. Barbosa. The usual?"

"Yes, thank you," Perry said.

Sadie gave him a look. "How often do you come here?"

"Pretty often."

"Now I know where you disappear to."

She ordered a flat white—coffee was complimentary. "Wonderful," the server said. "I'll bring your food and drinks to you in just a moment."

"Ooh, food?"

"They have excellent tapas," Perry said.

"I love excellent tapas."

They settled at a small table against the windows, which made Sadie laugh. "I didn't use to like sitting next to big windows like this. At any moment, Breeze or Flight could come crashing through."

"Flight still could," Perry said.

"Did you know our city has so many buildings with glass designs because replacing panes of glass is easier than repairing structural damage?"

"That was part of the building codes they enacted after... When Friendship Park was developed."

"After Big Quake destroyed all those buildings."

He bristled at that. Nobody talked about when Big Quake took out an entire block downtown. Maybe 'cause it had been a long time ago. Maybe 'cause the Supers never officially apprehended him. He'd gone off the radar, leading most people to believe he'd been fatally wounded in the battle between him and the Supers.

"Were you around when that happened?" Sadie asked. "As you-know-who?"

"I didn't start until after that."

She'd been young—maybe nine years old—but she remembered that Big Quake was so bad, even the city's other Villains at the time had disavowed him. His ability to manipulate the earth and rocks made him incredibly dangerous. He was a truly ruthless bad guy.

"Do you want to move?" Perry said.

"Nah. Let's live dangerously."

"Let's discuss your future."

Sadie slumped in her vinyl chair. "You make it sound like homework."

He reached into his sport coat and pulled out several folded pieces of paper. "Have you visited the neighborhoods I suggested?"

"I lived in Knollwood Village for a year in my twenties. It was too neighborhood-y for me back then, but I do know it."

"It has a large population of young professionals who work from home. They spend an average of twelve to fifteen hours a week at local coffeehouses."

"I don't disagree that it could be a good spot," Sadie said. "But I think artsy, funky people are more my crowd."

Perry set a sheet filled with data in front of her. "Then there's the Jewel District."

"That's too far from home. I wouldn't want that commute every day."

"Okay." He set another demographic analysis down. "We have this, then."

Sadie glanced at the info about a different neighborhood she once lived in that she'd dubbed The Bad Place. "I have crappy memories there. I got dumped on Valentine's Day in the middle of a crowded Italian bistro."

"Was it bad enough to not consider?"

"Well, he did pay for dinner." She shook her head. "But no, I'm not vibing with it."

"Are you *vibing* with anything?"

"It sounds silly, but I think I'll know it when I see it."

Perry gave her the vaguely annoyed look he usually cast at Joan and Mark. He was trying to help. Why wasn't she more excited?

"I appreciate you doing all this research," Sadie said. "I really do. I'll take a look at everything."

"I'm seeking investment opportunities. You have a solid idea, and you've done a lot for Hot and Cold."

"But we're nowhere near a point with Hot and Cold for me to step away."

Perry drummed his fingers on the papers. "Is there a reason you're making so many excuses?"

"I'm not—" she started to debate. "I mean, I just don't think the food truck is totally stable. Are you gonna be the one who draws customers in?"

"Joan and Mark have charisma. The truck has gathered a steady repeat customer base."

"You mean Joan, whose eyes glow red when she's overly

emotional? She has to hide in the truck when there's an annoying customer."

"Mark is good with difficult people."

Ugh, why was Perry so logical? And...and...right about everything? Where were those tapas so she could occupy her mouth with food?

Two streaks of movement flew past the windows—navy blue and red. "Catch is on patrol with Flight," Sadie said, leaning against the glass to watch them fly above the street.

Perry turned back to his papers.

"I wonder if Catch has to hold on to him to maintain flying powers. How long does her absorption ability last?"

"Not long," Perry said. "It depends on how much she takes in first."

Sadie looked around to see if they were alone enough to talk about the Supers and Smash—er, *The* Smash. Two well-dressed older white women were trying to catch Perry's eye, so no.

"Those ladies are totally checking you out," she told him.

Perry sighed and rubbed his forehead. "Will you stop changing the subject?"

"No, for real. You're a catch, Perry. Do you have a social life we don't know about? Are you meeting someone here?"

"I come here for the quiet."

"And the tapas?" Sadie waggled her eyebrows. "You know tapas are meant to be shared. When was the last time you went on a date? Unless that's not your thing, which is completely valid."

"Did Joanie teach you how to avoid conversations you don't want to have?"

"No, I've been doing that my whole life."

A real interruption came from the server with coffee and wine. Sadie's phone buzzed with an incoming text. She grinned at the photo of a Cost Club receipt from Joan.

We did it! Stayed under budget!

Way to go babe!

"They stayed on budget without us," Sadie said, showing Perry.

He peered at the screen through his glasses. "How can I have a social life when I'm too busy parenting those overgrown teenagers?"

She giggled despite herself. "Cut them some slack. They've had to learn how to live in the real world."

Perry clearly wanted to say something. He picked up his deep burgundy wine instead.

"How are you adjusting?" She genuinely wanted to know. "You lived for a while not in that life. With college and stuff. Was that different than it is now? Was it harder?"

He paused for a long moment. "It was stressful. You're always worried someone will find out about your powers."

"Oh. I hadn't thought of it that way."

"I don't understand why those two are always trying to hide theirs. Accepting who you are—no, embracing it—is the way to go."

"That's definitely been my experience," Sadie said. "But like, living in the city and dyeing my hair red. Not being a Supervillain."

He paused again, considering her.

"It must make it hard to date." She snorted. "I know how hard it was for Joan to be honest with me."

"The truth inevitably comes out in the end," he said. Something in his voice…

Something told her Perry once nursed a broken heart, and it had never fully healed. Joanie thought a past hurt was what had made him so guarded with people.

Another incoming text buzzed. A photo of Joan and Mark in a parking lot with Tenia and Morris from Cajun Soul.

Look who we ran into!

Love it! Say hi from me

It had to be hard for Joan to pretend everything was ordinary —going shopping, chatting with friendly food truck folks, all while masking her abilities.

"Do you genuinely want to own a café?" Perry asked.

"I do."

"You have the opportunity, but you're constantly dodging it."

Her heartbeat swelled into an anxious pounding. "It's not that I don't want to." A ball of nerves clogged her throat. "I just…"

"If you say you embrace who you are, and this is who you are…"

Tears pooled in her eyes. Damn it, she had to tell someone. Get it off her chest. "I'm afraid I'll fail," she whispered.

"You might," Perry said. "Most new businesses do."

"But if I fail…" She cleared the lump from her throat. "Then everything everyone says about me will be true. 'Oh, Sadie followed another one of her wild whims and crashed and burned. She can't hack it and should just work for someone else.'"

"You think that's what people will say?"

"Yes. Nobody ever trusts me to make good decisions."

"It's not a wild whim if you have investors and a solid business plan," Perry said.

Her tears gathered in strength. "Then I'm letting *you* down."

"You can't possibly let me down. I don't get let down."

"Everyone gets let down."

"I've had worse things happen than a failed business venture," he said.

More truth pressed for release, and she couldn't hold it back. "I don't want to fail. I want to prove everyone wrong."

Perry leaned forward with a smile. "Revenge? That's something I can get behind."

"No, not revenge. Why do you look so happy?"

He was smiling a little *too* much at the prospect. "I specialize in revenge. Excel in it, actually."

"If you dial it back a notch and reframe it as *not* revenge, you can help me make people see I can do what I put my mind to."

"Can I think of it as slight revenge? Gentle revenge?"

"Perry," she sighed, though a little laugh escaped, too. "You're weird."

Their sizzling tapas arrived. They abandoned talking for a minute in favor of sampling the small plates of savory deliciousness.

Perry wiped his mouth with a starched cloth napkin, then said, "One other suggestion."

"If this is about revenge…"

"Indirectly. You can also *not* be what people imagine you to be."

"Like how?"

"Like not being what people think you ought to be."

"I don't follow."

He gestured at himself. "Is this what you pictured Breeze looked like under the mask and gear?"

"Not at all. I didn't think he'd be a polished, classy guy."

"Exactly." He swirled his wineglass. "It's about embracing who you truly are. Yes, I have those abilities. But I also enjoy the finer things. Both can be true."

Sadie nodded slowly, letting that sink in. "People don't expect a big-boobed redhead who dresses like a crayon box to run a successful business."

"Uh…"

"Sorry, that's probably an overshare. But I get what you're saying. The best revenge is living life exactly how you want to. No regrets."

"I'll make you a revenge expert yet," Perry said.

A glint twinkled in his gray eyes. Not vibrant like Joan or Mark's, but cloudy. Kind of unremarkable until you really noticed them.

Kind of like Sadie.

A streak of navy blue landed on a tall office tower. Catch planted her hands on her hips, surveying the area below. It still made Sadie feel protected, knowing the Supers were out and about. Catch never wavered from her goal of having justice prevail. She could barely speak civilly to the former Villains, even when ordering a sandwich at Hot and Cold. Which was pretty annoying, honestly.

Of course, justice didn't seem to translate to her wanting to pay for said sandwich. Sadie never minded taking her money.

Still, patrolling Superheroes meant Vector City was a safe place to open a business. To go after a dream. It was safer now than ever, really. Insurance rates would probably go down the longer they had no Villain activity. Maybe banks would be more receptive to loans, too.

"Okay," Sadie said. She wrung her napkin between her hands, nervous but with growing excitement. "Tell me more about these neighborhood demographics."

CHAPTER 5

Joan stepped off the bus behind Sadie. She looked so darn cute in her date night outfit of a low-cut blue dress and thick tights. Her tan overcoat covered her ass, but maybe that was for the best. Lewd acts in public could send a person to jail.

It'd be worth it, though.

Sadie breathed out a deep, contented sigh. "That ramen was *so good*," she said. She swung her small paper bag. "I can't wait to eat my leftovers and enjoy it all over again."

"And share with your girlfriend," Joan teased.

"Sorry, pal. No sharesies."

"Fair."

Sadie tucked her arm through Joan's as they strolled toward home. The Monday evening crowd moved at a moderate pace with those getting off work late or heading to nighttime activities. "I'd almost consider the Jewel District for my café, only I'd spend all my money on ramen."

"And bus fare."

"Yeah. I like it there, but it's so far south, it's practically not even the city anymore."

Joan rubbed Sadie's hand. They'd had an early dinner after checking out the Jewel District for a possible Sadie's Café locale.

The commute down there had been terrible, which was a pretty big deterrent. "I'm proud of you for taking this step."

"Thanks." Sadie's lips bobbed in a feeble smile. "I'm proud of me, too."

Talking to Perry a week ago seemed to be her catalyst to take baby action steps. *Perry*, of all people. It was good to know he wanted to pursue other legal business ventures. This needed to work for him and Sadie. Then all of Joan's favorite people would be happy.

Sadie rested her head on Joan's shoulder. She kissed the top of Sadie's head. Being so comfortable together was awesome.

"You look incredible tonight," Sadie said.

It was just dark pants and a white diamond-pattered shirt beneath a leather jacket, but Joan took the compliment gratefully. "I was just thinking how great you look. Good enough to eat."

"You're not getting my leftovers, Malone."

"I was referring to dessert, Miss Eagan."

Sadie chuckled. "Ugh, I wish I wasn't on Day Two of my period."

"I wish I had a regular cycle and could empathize with you."

"No, you don't. Menstruation sucks."

Whether it was from super genetic makeup or wonky hormones, Joan never had regular periods. Not that she'd ever been able to ask a medical professional about it. Or another super-powered individual. "I'll give you a long massage when we get home," she said.

"I'll give you whatever you want." Sadie lifted her head, beautiful brown eyes filled with intent. "*Whatever* you want."

"It's not as good if I can't pleasure you, too."

"Babe, I promise it will be better than good."

Joan squeezed her arm. "You're the boss."

"Damn right. So think about what you want me to do to you."

"Yes, ma'am." Heat rose from her core, heading down to—

A bright green flash popped in the night sky. Then a series of neon squiggles dashed through the clouds.

"What the heck?" Sadie said.

The clouds thickened and billowed, drawn together by a shimmering green glow. Eerie lightning flickered behind the cloud wall. A rumble of thunder rolled over the city.

Joan's heart skipped a beat. Oh, shit.

The clouds lit with more intense neon lightning. The wind picked up. This wasn't something that happened in Vector City. The only time Joan had seen it was in…

Oh, *shiiiiiit.*

Her stomach churned with dread. "Get behind me, honey," she said, stepping in front of Sadie to block her from whatever—or whoever—was doing this.

A series of green flashes shot into the sky. The atmosphere hummed with thick energy, like just before a thunderstorm broke open. People stopped on the sidewalk to stare.

She felt Sadie's hand on her back. "What is it, Joanie?"

Maybe it was a weird weather phenomenon. Global warming. Nuclear waste. Anything other than…

The air grew as humid as a sultry mid-summer night. A steady neon-green glow emanated from a singular spot a few blocks away.

She had to see it to believe it, even though the truth sank deep in her gut.

"Stay close to me," Joan said, taking Sadie's hand and heading toward the glow.

"What are you doing?"

"I think I know who's causing this."

"Who, not what?"

"Unfortunately."

They hurried past concerned folks wisely moving in the opposite direction. Dodged people blocking the sidewalk while recording the event on their phones. The glow intensified the closer they got, along with the humidity. Her shirt stuck to her skin, and her hair fell out of its mini bun.

The faint hum was now a loud buzz. They huffed and puffed

to the edge of a large park with an open baseball field. Sure enough, right there in center field, a man in a Supervillain outfit striped with shades of green held his hands up to the sky.

"Derek," Joan said, confirming her fears.

"Who?" Sadie yelled over the noise.

"That's Ether. He's a Villain from Oceanview."

"What's he doing here?"

That was the question of the hour.

Flight burst through the low-hanging clouds, red cape flapping in the wind. A few people cheered. An off-white streak zoomed onto the field. Zee stopped a cautious distance from Derek in their Race gear.

Joan fisted her hands, fire smoldering beneath her palms.

Derek turned in a slow circle, saying something unintelligible through the noise.

Otis leaned down mid-flight. "What?" he shouted.

Derek said something louder.

"What?"

He dropped his arms and said it again, annoyance in his tone.

"We don't know what you're saying," Zee yelled.

"Is this better?" Derek said through a muted buzz.

Zee pointed to their ear. "We literally don't know what you're saying."

With a huff, the Supervillain waved his hands. The green glow dissipated around him, as did the humming. "Can you hear me now?"

"Yes," Flight bellowed from above.

"Jesus." Derek struck a haughty pose. "As I was saying, I am Ether, and I control your atmosphere now."

A slinky figure in deep purple leapt from a tree. Oh, fuck. Not her.

She sprang onto the metal fence behind home plate, climbing to the top with her freakishly strong nails. Perching on all fours, she said, "I've always wanted to take down a city. Get ready for Prowl."

Sadie clutched Joan's arm. "That's another Oceanview Villain."

"Yeah," Joan said, only she knew her as Ricki. Which was not her real name, but hell if anyone knew her real name.

A tall, reedy man in yellow with a too-confident swagger walked out from the grouping of trees. Oh shit oh shit oh shit.

"Cover your ears," Joan rushed out.

"What?" Sadie looked around in confusion.

"Cover your ears."

Squawk let out a shrieking wail. It was so forceful, it brought everyone surrounding the park to their knees. Several car windows shattered.

This asshole was from Destine. What the hell was a Destine Villain doing with two Oceanview Villains?

Squawk introduced himself, but nobody could hear him through the ringing in their ears. What the fuck was going on?

Joan knelt beside Sadie to wrap an arm around her. "Are you okay?"

Sadie gripped Joan's jacket as several people scampered past. They helped one another stand, keeping eyes on Squawk to see if he'd do that again.

Derek gestured at the newest Villain. "That's a taste of what to expect. Your city is ours for the taking."

"Not with us here," Flight said, swooping down on him.

Ricki jumped off the fence and tackled him to the baseball diamond. Squawk directed a shrill burst at Zee that knocked them back.

Fire crackled from Joan's fingertips. She stepped into a fighting stance, itching for action.

"Joanie." Sadie blocked her with her forearm. "You're sparking. Someone might see."

Damn it. She shook her hands to blow out the sparks.

Derek raised his hands high, then brought them down. A torrent of heavy rain struck with solid force.

People shouted and ran for cover. Sadie gasped, "My ramen!" and scooped the disintegrating paper bag off the sidewalk.

Ricki sprang onto a sturdy tree branch. "We own you, Vector City!" she declared, her diabolical laugh echoing through the rain.

It was hard to see, which was exactly Ether's strategy. Adrenaline-laced fire pulsed through Joan's veins, her fight-or-flight instinct firmly set to fight.

Squawk released another piercing cry. *Motherfucker*, that hurt. She huddled with Sadie to ride out the waves of ringing.

"There's Catch!" a woman to her right said. "And Lunk!"

For the first time in her life, Joan was glad to see Darlene running toward Zee. Probably absorbing their super speed. She couldn't make out what all was happening, but activity moved around the park. It felt abnormal not to partake in it. Almost wrong.

The rain stopped as quickly as it started. The park was empty, but the sound of continued action came from neighboring streets.

Sadie cradled the plastic tub of leftovers to her chest. "Do you think there's more of them?"

"I don't know," Joan said, surveying the park. "My guess is no because they would've been a part of the splashy introduction."

Steam rose off her from how hot she smoldered. She wiped her soaked hair back. Villains from other cities were working together? To take over *her* city?

Her phone kept buzzing in her jacket pocket. Most likely Mark and Perry saying what was running through her mind: *Fuck fuck fuck.*

"Are you going after them?" Sadie said.

"Hell no. I'm not going anywhere near them. I don't want a whiff of guilt by association."

"Do you know them?"

"Ether and Prowl. I've never met that screaming asshole. I've heard he's a douche."

"Clearly." Sadie squirmed in her wet clothes. "If this is over, can we go home?"

Joan did another visual sweep of the area. "Yeah."

They squished down the sidewalk, listening to water running into the gutters and sirens and a *boom-thwack* in the near distance. She rubbed her ear, trying to rid the last of the ringing.

"I can't believe this crap is starting up again," a businessman in a ruined suit said into his cellphone as he rushed by.

Sadie took Joan's hand and laced their fingers. "It is, isn't it?" she said quietly.

"Looks that way," Joan grunted.

"I guess it makes sense. We're a whole big city without any Villains. It's ripe for the taking."

Two young women stepped out from beneath a steakhouse entrance's awning. "I've barely been here a month," one of them said.

"So much for moving to a safer city," the other said.

A strange queasiness filled Joan's body. She felt…bad. Like this was her fault for leaving the city vulnerable to interlopers. When she was a Villain—if she was still a Villain—this wouldn't be happening.

Squawk released a cry that was fortunately far enough away.

"Do you think the Supers can contain them?" Sadie asked.

"No. They're not used to fighting these Villains. These guys had a plan. They'll scatter."

"How do you know the Oceanview Villains? Did you hang out, or…?"

How to best phrase it? "Professional associates. Most Villains know each other, or of each other. Derek used to host these big beach bashes that were pretty off the hook."

"And Prowl? I've heard about how ruthless she is."

Sadie looked up with smudged eye makeup. Her poor hair and bangs were smashed flat, and it had to feel disgusting wearing wet tights.

She deserved honesty always, so Joan said, "Everyone calls her Ricki. We might have hooked up once."

"Really? The ruthless one?"

"She's very flexible."

"Joan!"

She shrugged. "I was a Supervillain. Those were the only people I could get with. Everyone got really drunk at those beach bashes. Things happened."

"Uh-huh."

"It meant nothing," Joan said, not sure if that made it better or worse.

Sadie slipped her hand free. Okay, worse.

"She literally said it meant nothing to her. I don't think she has the capacity for compassion. She eviscerates with her words as much as her nails."

"Uh-huh."

Joan started to make a joke about Ricki's nails not being conducive to certain sapphic deeds, but this wasn't the time or place.

Her phone buzzed in quick succession. She pulled it out to see multiple texts and missed calls from Mark and Perry.

"Let them know you're safe," Sadie said.

"I'm sorry, sweetheart," Joan said. *For everything.*

"It's okay. I'm just afraid of what this might mean for you."

"Me, too."

She'd worked hard to build this lovely, quiet life with Sadie, with Hot and Cold, and distance herself from villainy.

Something deep inside said it was all about to change.

CHAPTER 6

The past two days had been like the Vector City of old with news headlines filled with Super activity. Details about the trio of new Villains in town. Questions about what their Heroes were doing about them.

The last thing Sadie wanted was to pretend like everything was normal, but what else was there to do but keep on keeping on? Even Joan had encouraged her to keep her plans of visiting Vector City Coffee to see Nyah on her birthday.

So now she was standing behind the counter she used to work at with friends she used to work with, making drinks she used to make. She glanced at the wall of windows at the front. Those were in danger of getting crashed into again. The last time she'd visited, there were tables and chairs against those windows. Today, they were shoved back.

The sky was a cloudy, eerie green, the air filled with misty moisture. Where was this rain last summer when they'd really needed it?

Oh, right—Ether hadn't been messing with their atmosphere.

Sadie poured a steamed almond milk leaf design on top of a lavender latte to-go. Her former coworkers laughed at how she'd stepped right in. Amit's wavy black hair was shaggier, and Nyah had recently gotten long sky-blue braids. Both still had to wear those very drab dove-gray aprons that matched the white-and-gray color scheme of the place.

"You don't have to do that," Amit told her, as bossy as ever.

"I want to," Sadie said.

"You came here for me, not to do unpaid labor," Nyah said.

"I can't help it. I like barista-ing." She called out the order and set it on the counter. The young new hire guy gave her a look like *Kindly get out of my workspace.* Maybe he was the one who'd picked the slightly more upbeat indie music.

Amit shooed her from behind the counter. "How's Joan?"

"Joan is great."

"Still treating you well?"

"Like a queen," Sadie said, smiling to herself.

"And the food truck?"

"It's going really well."

"If things go south, you can come back to work here," Amit said.

Crossing her arms, Sadie said, "You just miss being all up in my business."

"Never a dull moment in your love life."

"Well, thank you for the offer, but it won't be necessary."

A few seconds passed where she was pretty sure Amit was thinking *I highly doubt that.* "Have you talked to Greta lately?" he said.

"I don't really talk to her. She's Joan's friend." *And an active thief.* "I think she's in France."

"Maybe it's the time difference," Nyah said to Amit.

"Do you need her help to get out of the latest jam in whatever game you're playing?" Sadie said.

"Yes," they chorused.

She shook her head and went to straighten up the condiment counter. She didn't love that Greta hung out with them on occasion to talk gaming. That was probably all it was, and she was

Joan's best friend, so she probably wouldn't do anything to Joan's girlfriend's friends, but still…

Nyah joined her to check the small milk carafes. Leaning toward her, Sadie asked, "How's your aunt doing?"

"She's okay. Not better, but not worse. She still needs her regular dialysis."

"I'm sorry. But I'm glad to hear things are stable."

"Everything's so expensive, though. I've picked up some extra shifts to help her out."

"You're the best niece ever."

"She's worth it." Nyah smirked. "How's your mom handling the influx of Villains?"

Sadie rolled her eyes. "The daily texts are back." Her phone buzzed in her back pocket like she'd summoned her mother's check-in. Only it was Joan.

> Just wanted to make sure you got there okay.
> LMK when you want to be picked up.

> I'm here. I can walk to the truck when I'm done

"You weren't kidding," Nyah laughed.
"It's Joan. The other person constantly checking on me."

> Let me come and get you. It's raining.

Ugh, it was barely precipitating. Irritation prickled under her skin, but she understood. Joan didn't like these new Villains. She didn't trust them. Kind of like Sadie's mother.

Oh, no. Was she dating someone like her mother?

> If you insist. Come by in an hour

> Thank you sweetheart. Love you. 🤍

Nyah read the text chain over her shoulder. "Aww, that's sweet."

"It's...something." Sadie reacted to Joan's text with a heart.

"Joan's worried about you?"

"She's being overly cautious because of what happened the other night."

"Guess you can't blame her."

"I guess. But I was perfectly fine walking around by myself when we had Villains before."

Ny gave her a look. "You got abducted walking to work."

"That was different." Not that she could explain how.

"Yeah, that *was* different."

Glossing over more potential questions, Sadie said, "Trick was about using people, and these guys look like they want to break things. So I'll definitely not be hanging out by the front windows. But yeah, it's really nice to have a partner who cares enough about me to not want that to happen again. I'm just prickly about this stuff because my mom's so overbearing with her concern, y'know?"

"I get it." Nyah quirked a pierced eyebrow. "This must be tough for Joan."

You have no idea. "It is."

They moved over to let an older white man using a cane set his coffee down to grab some napkins. Nyah kept looking at Sadie with her usual amusement tinged with *This girl*.

Sadie slid her phone in her jeans pocket. "What sucks is that I was finally ready to take action on my café. But with the new Villains in town, I'm not sure."

"Insurance won't go down," Nyah said.

"Nothing will go down. If anything, rates will go up." Sadie gestured to the tables pushed away from the windows. "How soon did you move everything back after they showed up?"

"Before we left that night."

"See? I've always been worried that I'll open my café and it'll get destroyed."

"That's too bad. I was hoping you'd find the perfect spot."

"Me, too." She glanced over at Amit taking an order and

lowered her voice. "You know you'll be my first phone call. I want you to be the manager."

A wide smile spread across Nyah's face. "You do?"

"For sure. I'd trust you to run it efficiently and keep with the friendly vibe I'm going for. And to hire the best employees and train them right."

"Sure," Nyah said. "Just say the word. I could use a manager's salary to help my aunt more."

Sadie gave her friend a side hug. "I'd love to be able to do that for you. A belated birthday present."

"I'll take it. Thanks."

They side-squeezed before Ny went to assist behind the counter. She'd be a strong, upbeat manager for Sadie's Café.

Ugh, it really was old Vector City again, being unable to make future plans because of outside forces. Even with financial assistance and support, opening a new business right now was a massive hurdle to...hurdle.

Was she up for the challenge?

Joan's phone rang on the bedside table. Whoever was calling before nine a.m. could damn well wait. She rolled over into Sadie's warmth and wrapped an arm around her. Sadie lightly stirred and hummed sleepily.

They'd just drifted off when it rang again.

"Noooo," Sadie mumbled, tugging Joan closer.

"Sorry, honey," she whispered, then kissed Sadie on the temple. She rolled back to her side to see an unknown local number. "It might be the propane guy calling back."

She did her best to answer non-annoyedly.

"Joan," said a slightly familiar voice.

"Yes, this is Joan."

"It's Zee."

"Huh?"

"It's Zee."

"How did you get— Never mind. Why are you calling?"

"You need to come to Superhero headquarters," Zee said. "Now."

Her heart thwacked against her ribcage. Oh, shit. *Shit.* "Why? What happened?"

Sadie sat up and set a hand on Joan's shoulder.

"We need to see you and Mark and Perry," said Zee. "It's urgent."

Fucking shit hell. "What happened?"

"Nothing specific, other than the Villains who invaded our city."

"We have nothing to do with—"

"We know you have nothing to do with them. That's why we need to see you."

"I don't understand—"

"Get here within the hour. This is not a request to ignore," Zee stated. "I'm calling your brother and Perry, so just get here."

The call ended.

Sadie scooted closer. "What is it?"

Joan stared at her phone. "The Supers want us to report to their HQ. Zee wouldn't say why."

"Oh no."

"They said they know we aren't involved with the new Villains, so I don't know if we're in trouble, or…"

"I'll go with you," Sadie said, tossing back the covers.

"Stay here. Zee didn't say anything about you. I don't want you getting caught in the middle."

"But I want to be there for you."

Concern lines wrinkled Sadie's forehead. Joan cupped her cheek and said, "I'll feel better knowing you're safe at home."

She got out of bed before Sadie could debate her. Joan had no idea what she was walking into. A trap? A truce?

The Supers were probably fishing for intel. Not that the former

Villains could share much more than the unhelpful factoid that Oceanview Villains liked to party.

She pulled off her tank top and sleep shorts and threw on pants with some give in them and a red flannel. Looser clothes in case action was required.

After splashing water on her face and quickly brushing her teeth, she went to put on one of the pairs of sneakers at the door. "Wait," Sadie called, hurrying from the bedroom in her pink-and-white-striped pajamas.

She launched herself at Joan and hugged tight. "Be safe," Sadie said.

"I will."

"I love you so much."

"I love you more than anything."

"Let me know what's going on when you can."

"I'll try."

They kissed, and then Joan forced herself to pull away. She typed in the code to disarm the alarm. She hadn't even realized she'd stopped setting it before all this new activity began.

Sadie watched her from the doorway until they lost sight of each other.

Joan took the stairs to the parking garage to jog off nervous energy. Knowing Sadie was safe was the one thing easing her mind.

She spent the short drive trying not to freak out while texting with Mark. It had to be another push for information, like Zee and Kade grilling them after the Smash incident. That *had* to be it.

She drove up to the imposing concrete structure behind Mark's bright-blue sports car. Perry got out of the passenger seat before the car stopped moving.

A short young dude in glasses and a dark suit stepped out from under one of the soaring arches. The new-ish sidekick, right. He waved them around the side of the building. Perry made the angriest face he'd ever made and got back in Mark's car.

A garage door opened. Joan hastened to park and meet up with her brother and Per. Mark took one look at her and said, "Whoa there, Anxious Annie. Relax. Don't let them see you sweat."

Perry looked like he was quite literally going to rip someone's head off. Joan nodded at him. "Maybe you should tell that to Angry Andy."

He responded with a string of furious curses in Portuguese.

New Sidekick entered the garage. "Thank you for coming."

"Like we had a choice?" Joan said.

"Hey, New Sidekick," Mark said.

"Ward," the sidekick said.

"Ward. Right. You're still here? Good for you."

"Please follow me. The Supers are waiting for you."

They didn't go into the large lobby, but rather around to a back staircase. It felt kind of weird in here. Off, like there was something static in the air. Or maybe that was her heightened energy mixing with Perry's.

Ward led them into a brightly lit conference room with a long, oval black table, two large TV screens...

And all four Superheroes sitting and staring at them.

"Hi, guys," Kade said with a broad grin. "It's good to see you."

Darlene glared at Joan with her usual disdain. What was she wearing? Some kind of boxy striped turtleneck sweater with chunky square buttons.

They weren't in their Hero outfits. That was a good thing.

"It must be early for you," Ward said. "May I offer you some coffee or tea?"

"I'll take coffee with milk and sugar," Mark said conversationally. How the fuck was he so calm?

Ward looked to Joan and Perry. "And you?"

Joan stared at Otis. "What's this about?"

"Sit down," Otis said, specifically to Perry.

Per crossed his arms and planted his feet by the door. "I'll stand," he ground between his teeth.

An odd something passed between them. "Then have your minions sit," Otis said.

Perry didn't budge. "They're free to make their own decisions."

Ooh, there was some serious bad blood between those two. Joan tapped Mark's arm. Better to play along and get this over with.

They sat tentatively across from the Supers. It was like being in front of a jury or a parole hearing. Which was not entirely inaccurate.

Darlene cleared her throat. "We have another common enemy."

"Ene*mies*," said Kade.

"The arrival of Ether, Squawk and Prowl has been frustrating for the citizens of this fine city."

"And you," Mark added.

"And us." Joan gestured between them. "We're done with that life."

Otis and Darlene shared a look.

Ward delivered Mark's coffee in a commemorative Vector City Superheroes mug. "Thanks," Mark said. "Are your bosses being nice to you? Giving you days off and paid holidays?"

Ward chuckled. "Crime doesn't take a day off."

"Do they at least give you some of the free shit they're always getting?" Mark directed his focus across the table. "Or did they stop taking so much free shit because it's not cool and causes more hardship to the citizens of this fine city?"

Zee opened their mouth, then glanced at their cohorts and closed it.

Mark sipped his coffee, gagging when he swallowed. "Dude. What is this?"

"It's a Sumatran blend of organic fair-trade coffee," Ward said.

"It's dirt water. I think I've been spoiled by the things Sadie makes. It's not your fault, Ward. You have to work with the garbage your employers have for you to serve."

Perry continued to seethe by the doorway.

Joan set a fist on the tabletop. "So we have another common set of enemies."

"Yes." Otis stood, taking command of the room. "The last time we joined forces, the outcome was a success. We need to do it again."

"How?" Joan asked.

"We need you to pretend to still be Villains."

Mark tilted his head. "I'm sorry, what?"

Kade cupped his hands around his mouth. "*We need you to pretend—*"

"I'm operating under the assumption you know these Villains," Otis said.

"Hardly," Joan said.

"But you do know them," Darlene sneered.

"We know *of* them, the way Supers all somewhat know each other." *Like hooking up with one in Destine.*

"Then they know this was your city." Otis crossed his arms. "We need you to find them and tell them you tricked us into trusting you. That you're still operating on the down-low and have had no contact with us."

A flurry of thoughts raced through Joan's brain. "We don't have our suits anymore, and it's obvious we're operating a food truck, and we turned our backs on our own, which violates every code and unspoken rule, and..."

"That'll never work," Mark said. "Nobody will have anything to do with us, so no one can corroborate such a story."

Now Darlene stood. "We are not asking you to become Villains again. Tell them you worked with us to rid the city of Trick, Hide and Volt to get them out of the way. That is what many people believe. Then you went back to a life of crime but have kept it quiet so we wouldn't know about it."

"You can say the food truck is a cover for what you're really doing," Otis said.

Mark shook his head. "It still won't work."

"Why don't you get the Supers from Oceanview and Destine to deal with their Villains?" Joan said.

Zee leaned forward and said, "We tried. The Oceanview Supers said this was more of a…" They made air quotes. "'Vector City problem.'"

Kade leaned forward, his chair creaking under his weight. "They're still mad at us in Destine for not helping with the robotic sidekick disaster."

"They brought that on themselves," Otis muttered.

"So, wait," Joan said. "Supers from other cities won't help their fellow Supers? Even though it's Villains they're familiar with? What kind of crap is that?"

No one answered. Finally, Zee said, "Supers can be very territorial over their cities. It's almost like a competition."

"I think they're jealous," Kade said. "We got rid of all of our Villains. They're happy to let us have theirs."

Waving a hand, Mark said, "Why don't you just fight them the way you did with us?"

"We don't want to start new rivalries with endless battles," Otis said. "We'd rather send them away. It's easier to make them think Breeze, Ice and Spark are still in Vector City."

"It's the least disruptive option," Darlene said.

"More like the easiest-for-you option," Mark drawled.

Joan checked to make sure Perry hadn't spontaneously combusted before saying, "Our deal was helping you one time and getting out. We did that. We have too much at stake now to put that in jeopardy."

Her chest constricted from picturing Sadie anxiously pacing around their apartment.

Otis raised an eyebrow. "You don't really have a say in the matter."

"We can lock you up right now if you don't comply," Darlene stated, shifting her weight and raising her hands.

Zee started to say something, only Perry lunged forward. "I knew we never should have trusted you," he seethed.

"We're *not* going to lock you up," Zee said.

"But we do have that leverage," Otis said.

Darlene narrowed her gaze at Joan. "We always have that option."

She and Mark jumped up. "You're always gonna hold that over our heads," Joan growled, clenching her fists.

"Yes."

Mark swirled his hand to conjure a ball of ice. Nothing happened. He did it again. "The fuck?" he muttered.

Joan brought her hands together. A tiny spark flickered from one finger, but that was it. "What the hell?"

"A preventive measure," Otis said.

Perry blew out a wisp of a breath. He tried again, but his breezy ability didn't manifest.

Joan failed to get any of her fire going. It just wasn't there. "What did you do?"

Walking around the table, Otis said, "It's a low-grade frequency that operates on a molecular level. It disrupts our mutated cells and renders us powerless. We turned it on as a precaution."

"So you don't have your powers either?"

"We can disable it at any moment if need be."

"I can still kick your ass," Joan said to Darlene.

She snorted. "I'd like to see you try."

"Come on, Darlene," Kade said. "They're our friends now."

"They are *not* our friends. They will never be on our level."

"Cut it out," Zee said.

Well, wasn't that a cheap shot? *Never be on our level.* Like people who'd made a few missteps were subhuman.

Otis had been moving slowly toward them. It wasn't until he walked by that Joan saw the hard look he was exchanging with Perry.

"This is different," Otis said.

"It's always the same with you," Perry spat.

"This is for the common good."

"You want us to fight your battles for you. If we don't give you what you want, you'll betray us."

"Then give us what we want."

They stared at each other, a whirlwind of silent words floating between them.

"What's going on?" Kade whispered loudly.

"I don't know," Zee said. Their face said they really didn't.

"Perry's right," Joan said. "You want us to do your dirty work. Jesus, you're no better than Melvin."

"We want your help in exchange for our continued goodwill."

Mark turned to Zee at that. "A fancy way of saying we're on permanent probation?"

"You are," Darlene said.

Joan's internal fire should've been bouncing around her body. Not having it was like being slightly irritated instead of furious.

This fucking sucked. They didn't have a choice if they wanted freedom and…

Sadie.

She'd sworn to do whatever it took to be the partner Sadie deserved. If playing ball with the Supers meant keeping her safe and Joan out of jail, it was worth it.

She was still the girl who had to do what she had to do to survive.

"All right," she said. "We try to trick them into leaving town. If it works, you back off. Stop with the check-ins. Let us live our lives in peace."

Mark scrunched an eyebrow at her. Then he nodded in understanding. This was the only way forward.

"We need our suits," he said. "To make it more official."

"And to shield ourselves," Joan added.

"Yeah. We'll need protection in case this goes south, which I'm a hundred percent certain it will. These guys aren't fools. They won't fall for it."

Otis finally turned away from Perry. "Then brush up on your acting skills. Ward?"

The eager sidekick stepped forward, tablet in hand.

"Get the three containers from the—" Otis directed this at the former Villains "—*very secure* storage room with Breeze, Spark and Ice's confiscated gear."

"Confiscated," Mark snorted. "We handed them over voluntarily."

"Yes, sir," Ward said. He made a wide berth around a still smoldering Perry.

"I'll help," Zee said, getting up. "Darlene?"

She tore her gaze away from Joan. "What?"

"Can you help, too?"

"Get Lunk to do it."

"My strength is turned off," Kade said.

Darlene rolled her eyes and stomped toward the exit. Zee followed behind, mouthing, "*You're welcome*" to Joan and Mark.

Perry parked himself beside the door and stared into the distance.

"Are you ever gonna tell us what this is about?" Mark said to him.

"They use people for their own gains," Perry said.

"Hey," Kade said. "We're heroes. It's in our name."

"Ask Flight how heroic he was years ago. No, better yet, ask Atomic Man or Stretch Boy."

"Atomic Man died a few years ago. Stretch Boy is really old and has dementia."

Otis crossed back to his side of the table. "Do you really want to open that can of worms?"

Mark bounced on his toes. "Oh my god, yes please open that can."

An alert from SuperWatch popped onto one of the TV screens. The two Supers went to investigate.

"Damn it," Mark said. "Perry, I've never asked you for much."

Perry scoffed at that.

"Will you tell us why you hate the Supers so much? Pretty please with sugar on top?"

He figuratively lasered his eyes at Otis. "They're the ones who exposed me for having powers and turned me into Breeze."

"How?" Joan asked.

"One of them was sent to see if I had abilities. There had been an incident where I accidentally used them in public." Perry crossed his arms again. "They found out the truth and ruined my life, so I took the path they forced me to take."

"You hid your abilities," Joan said, never really connecting the dots before. "You had to when you were doing your MBA and art gallery stuff."

"What was the incident?" Mark looked like a kid about to open the biggest present under the Christmas tree.

"It was nothing."

Joan fully faced the man who'd raised her. "Then why are you so hard on us to not hide who we are? You're always saying I'm Spark, no matter what."

Perry stared at her. "Because I tried to hide it. The truth came out anyway."

A terrible memory from the moment Sadie realized Joan wasn't Catch poked at her from the depths of her mind. The horrified look on Sadie's face.

"It always does," Joan murmured.

She sent Sadie a quick text while Mark badgered Perry for more details.

Everything's fine. I'm okay.

Thank god I was so worried! Come home soon

Shit. What was Sadie going to think about Joan donning her Spark suit again?

Perry predictably clammed up. But that was more than they'd ever gotten out of him. The Supers had exposed him. They must not have liked someone running around with undetected abilities.

He sure was milking this old grudge. Flight was the only active Super from back then. Stretch Boy had retired right before

Joan and Mark's sixteenth birthday. Atomic Man had a few years before that. And Amazing Woman... It'd been so long, Joan wasn't even sure.

Was Amazing Woman still alive? She had to be a hundred years old, easy. Her indestructible body had aged so slowly, it'd been hard to tell by looking at her just how old she was.

Otis and Kade turned away from the screen. They'd rendered themselves powerless, too. They were that nervous about their visitors trying something. The trust was so not there.

Joan attempted to manifest a fireball, but it was still a no-go.

Kade grinned at her. "It's weird, huh? I don't like having that turned on. We usually just use it to keep Villains under control after we get them."

Ah-ha. "Is this how you keep them from using their powers in jail?"

"Uh-huh."

She'd always wondered how they did that. Melvin couldn't mind control his way out of prison. Ethel couldn't zap her cell open.

And Joan wouldn't be able to flame her way out.

"Don't ask me where the prison's located," Kade said. "I can't tell you."

"It's in some undisclosed location in the middle of nowhere," Joan said. "That much everyone knows." Which made sense, since they didn't want Supervillains to escape smack dab in the middle of a city.

Wrinkling his Roman nose, Kade said, "I really can't tell you. Nobody tells me where it is. I have a hard time keeping secrets."

"Good to know," Joan lightly teased, though that was an interesting bit of intel.

Ward, Zee and Darlene returned with three metal suitcases. A little thrill danced up Joan's spine. Maybe this wouldn't be the worst thing in the world. It could be atonement for not better protecting Vector City from future villainy. Send the message far and wide to stay away.

Doing this could prevent her from meeting the same fate as Trick, Hide and Volt. Maybe then the nightmares would stop.

Darlene set her case on the table. "This is temporary," she stated. "You will return them immediately after the assignment is completed."

"Assignment?" Mark said. "What is this, grade school?"

He exchanged a small but noticeable glance with Zee as they set a case in front of Mark. Maybe Zee had assured him he wasn't actually in danger of being arrested. That could explain why Mark wasn't freaking out. Then again, Mark was the chill one. Literally.

Joan opened the case, and there it was. The mask with that dark, annoying long wig. Her black boots. The black bodysuit with slashes of deep red. A part of her life for so many years, it was like reuniting with an old friend.

"Hello, gorgeous," she breathed. "I missed you."

CHAPTER 7

The riverfront warehouses proved to be a good secluded meeting spot that night. Joan didn't want anyone spying her and Mark as Spark and Ice. No need to create unnecessary panic by having them be seen with Ether and Prowl.

It hadn't been hard to contact them—Mark had Derek's phone number. They'd arranged a meetup while Perry followed a lead on Squawk from SuperWatch. Then they'd spent the day getting their stories straight at the warehouse, like the old days.

Joan shifted inside her bodysuit. A little too snug in spots from not exercising the way she used to. But it admittedly felt kind of nice to be wearing it again. To be Spark for the night, like playing dress-up.

"Dude, is yours as tight as mine is?" Mark muttered, tugging at the zipper down the front of his.

"We should get back to working out on our day off."

"That's probably a good idea."

The crisp air was rather pleasant. Stars winked in the clear night sky. Hopefully they could get Derek out of town so he would stop making things all weird and misty and green.

She flicked anxious sparks from her fingers. Her fire had

returned in full force after leaving the Supers' HQ, thank god. It was a part of her as much as her lungs or bones or brain.

Mark unzipped the pocket on his chest and checked his phone. "Why are they so late?"

"Villains aren't known for their punctuality," Joan reminded him. She pulled her phone out to make sure she hadn't missed anything from Sadie. After reassuring her with several phone calls that Joan was *not* going back to a life of crime, Sadie had agreed to stay at home today for her safety.

And because Joan didn't want her girlfriend to see her as Spark and dredge up the past.

The lock screen photo of Sadie laughing at the beach made her smile. Perry had treated them all to New Year's in the Caribbean— an abbreviated version of their usual few weeks around Christmastime. Joan had paid for Sadie's airfare and meals and souvenirs. Sadie never took vacations, and still didn't love the means with which everything had been paid for, but Joan was so happy to have given her a warm island getaway. The ends justified the means.

Sadie had been understanding but honest, as always. One of the very best things about her. She was sympathetic to the situation Joan now found herself in. Like it or not, the Supers still held her fate in their hands.

She'd agreed that this could be a good thing. They could send the interlopers back to their own cities and return to normal. So this bad idea had to work.

"Do you think it was smart to let Perry go by himself?" Joan asked as she put her phone away.

"Per's better with egotistical assholes. And you've exchanged bodily fluids with Prowl, so—"

"Don't remind me," she groaned.

Shuffling on a nearby rooftop snapped her to attention. Prowl's dark silhouette crouched low.

"I see you up there," said Joan.

Derek walked around the corner in his green Ether attire.

"Hey, buddy," Mark said. "Long time, no see. How's it going?"

Derek was normally a pretty carefree dude, only his mouth was set in a grim line. "We're not buddies anymore, traitor."

Mark held up his hands. "Whoa, hey, easy there."

"We shouldn't even be talking to you."

Ricki somersaulted off the roof, landing on her feet. "Curiosity got the better of me," she purred in her husky voice. "I wanted to watch you grovel your way into our good graces."

"We want nothing to do with you traitors," Derek said.

Playing it cool, Mark gave them a lazy smile. "Is this because of that thing with Trick a few months back? That was part of a much bigger plan."

"We got him out of the way so we could rule Vector City," Joan said.

"With the help of your Superheroes." Ricki shivered. "I've never heard anything more disturbing."

"It's not what it looked like."

"You heard we aligned with the Supers and turned in all our stuff." Mark gestured at his Ice getup. "Obviously, we did not."

Joan flexed her fingers. "We convinced them to work with us. Then we used them to snuff out our competition. They think we retired, but we—"

"Nobody liked Trick," Derek said. "But you still don't turn one of us in."

"And you *don't* work with Supers," Ricki reinforced.

"The press made it sound like we helped them." Joan chuckled. "If anything, they helped *us* gain a stronghold."

Mark held out a hand. "We want to extend you the courtesy that yes, okay, we didn't give to Trick, Hide and Volt. Vector City is still ours. It never stopped being ours. We're very much still in the game."

"No, you're not," Ricki scoffed.

"The Supers think we're done, but we just shifted how we're doing business."

"Didn't you open a restaurant or something?" Derek said.

"A food truck." Mark grinned. "It's the perfect cover. We're mobile, can go anywhere, can make deals that look like meals."

Ricki planted her hands on her hips. "What are you selling? It's not like you can stuff a painting through one of those windows."

"Information," Joan said.

"To who?" said Derek. "You're blacklisted."

"People always want information."

"We're selling secrets," Mark said. "Corporations will pay good money to get the skinny on their competition. And even more to stop them from getting leaked. Y'all know we love sticking it to big corporations."

Joan gave him a look like *Y'all? Really?* "We park our truck near Allegria Tower. It's so much easier than running around in spandex."

"And, y'know, if they don't pay…" Mark formed a long icicle, then shattered it against the ground.

This was a decent cover story. Maybe it would seal the deal.

Derek shook his head. "Nah. I heard you went totally legit."

"From who?" Mark said.

"Everyone."

"That's a reliable source."

Ricki slunk next to Joan, strong jasmine perfume wafting on the breeze. Her golden eyes shone bright against the deep purple of her facemask. "Everyone knows you're tight with the Supers now."

"They sometimes come by the food truck to check on us," Joan said. The best lies had a nugget of truth in them. "Like Mark said, it's the perfect cover. We appear to be legit."

Whoops, she'd used Mark's real name in public instead of Ice. Maybe they wouldn't notice that slip-up.

Mark took a step away from Derek. "So yeah, we're still here. We'd appreciate you going back to Oceanview, which let's face it, has better weather and gorgeous beaches. Ether, you still having those off-the-hook parties? Remember that one a few years ago when I made those ice slides into the ocean? Good times."

"Oh yeah," Derek said with a laugh, then sobered. "I mean, there's no way I trust a word you say. You'll turn on your own kind."

Joan shared a look with her brother. Might as well go with it. "This is a courtesy as much as a warning," she said. "Leave our city, or share a cell with our former friends."

Her breath hitched. If this went badly, she'd be the one locked up with Volt.

Ricki snorted a harsh laugh. "You're full of shit. You're not doing anything illegal. You wanted a way out of villainy and did whatever it took to get out."

Joan met her piercing gaze. Ricki knew exactly what she was doing in trying to provoke a reaction.

Keeping her voice steady, Joan forced out, "Then I guess we fooled you, too."

"No kidding," Mark said with false bravado. "You're making this way too easy for us."

Ricki curled into a half-crouch. Joan used to think it was sexy, but now knew it was the precursor to a verbal attack.

"The thing about you, *Spark*," she purred, "is that you've always thought you were too good for this life. You became a Villain out of necessity, not by choice. And now you're fighting to keep the peace in your city." She turned her smirk on Mark. "You do whatever she tells you to, so I'm not worried about your motivation."

"Hey," Mark said.

Fire rushed to Joan's fingertips. "I *will* fight for what I have."

"You shouldn't be fighting with your own kind," Ricki said. "We evolved past the norms. Stop giving them so much importance."

"Trick said the same thing. I didn't stand for it with him." Joan's glare said she wouldn't stand for it with anyone else either.

"You've never wanted to hurt people, even though norms are insignificant. I saw the news footage. You helped that hostage."

"She was really cute," she said calmly so she didn't blurt out *And the woman I love.*

"So what, you wanted her to think you're a hero? You're a coward."

True, she'd been a horrible coward before that day. But she'd finally done the right thing.

"Hellooo," Mark said. "Helping a hostage got us big brownie points. Who would suspect any more wrongdoing from us after that?"

"No, Prowl's right," Derek said, moving toward Mark. "You're bluffing. And you're cowards."

Twin flames flared from Joan's palms. "Call me a coward one more time."

Ricki blinked up at her. "Aw, did I hit a sore spot?"

"Joanie…" Mark muttered through his teeth.

"And here I thought you were miffed at me for not being into you." Ricki sneered. "Or women at all. Thanks for clearing that up for me."

Mark stood over her. "That's a homophobic low blow."

"I thought you liked low blows," she snickered.

Joan's flames crackled in irritation. Fucking Prowl. Taking her bait would draw too much attention, but damn it.

Derek puffed up like a proud rooster. "This is our city now. We're making bold moves you never dreamed of."

Ricki hopped onto the concrete barrier. "Keep doing corporate espionage or cooking or whatever. You're no match for us. Stay out of the way."

"Get out of our city." Joan enunciated every word.

"Or what?"

Ice shards tinkled from Mark's hands. "Or we stop playing nice."

A shrill cry rose in the distance, long and loud and angry.

Derek and Ricki looked up, then at each other. Then at Joan and Mark.

"Where's Breeze?" Derek said.

Mark opened his mouth, then hesitated.

"You really thought you could talk your way into getting us to leave?"

"I mean, not really," Mark said.

Joan gave him a look.

Another one of Squawk's piercing screams echoed through the air. Sounded like Perry wasn't faring any better in the convincing department.

"Why did you team up with him?" Joan wanted to know.

Ricki smirked at her. "All part of a bigger plan. You know about big, secret plans."

She leapt from the concrete barrier. The world spun around Joan. She landed on her ass and was being held in a chokehold. She blinked in surprise. Ricki kicked both legs and sent Mark flying back before kneeling.

"This is your only warning," she said against Joan's ear. "Next time, *we* stop playing nice."

"Go back to the shadows, cowards," Derek said.

Assholes. Joan shot a fireball that just missed him. Then she twisted and blasted Ricki off her. She didn't want to fight the Supers' battles for them, but she was no goddamn coward.

Ricki released an angry growl and lunged at her. Mark sprayed a shot of ice from his prone position that coated the blacktop. She jumped over it, taking Joan to the ground.

She swatted Joan's eyes, scraping her thick nails across the facemask. Joan raised her forearms to protect her exposed skin. She tried to sit up and push Ricki back but didn't have the core strength anymore. She flashed bright sparks from her fingers instead. They blinded Ricki enough so Joan could push her off.

The air thickened around them as Mark tussled with Derek. Containing Ricki was the—

Shit, she'd hopped onto a rooftop. Encasing her in a ring of fire wasn't an option. Joan shot several fireballs high in the hopes they'd knock her down and not make contact with the warehouse.

The clouds glowed green, and a buzz filled the air.

"Now I see whose side you're on," Ricki yelled.

"Go to hell," Joan yelled back, fire raging through her body.

Ricki slipped from view a second before the hard rain fell. Mark shot ice around to pelt the Villains, only the frozen raindrops hit him and Joan in the face.

Derek shouted something as he retreated that couldn't be heard over the hum of atmospheric intervention.

"Stop," Joan told her brother as she covered her head.

"Fuuuuuuuuuck," Mark ground out, throwing a ball of ice into the river.

The rain cooled Joan's heat. They hastened from behind the warehouses until they cleared the precipitation. Their suits were waterproof, but their wigs were a sopping wet mess.

"That went well," Mark said.

"What do you think they're planning?"

"I'm not sure."

"I know we didn't want to make a big deal out of this, but…"

"…we thought what Melvin was doing wasn't a big deal," Mark finished. "Unlike him, these guys *do* have something in the works."

Joan nodded in agreement. "We can't ignore this."

"No, because the damn Supers dragged us into it." He wiped at the water dripping off his dark wig.

Joan glanced down at her gloves. Her squeaky, wet Spark suit. "What are we supposed to do? We failed our mission. The Supers don't trust us. Now these guys hate us."

"We go back to the food truck. We told the Supers this was a bad idea. I don't want to get dragged into this."

"We're already in it."

Mark dropped another angry f-bomb and skittered an ice ball down the back alley. "I hate the power they hold over us."

"The Supers?"

"Supers, Villains, that whole frickin' world."

He was really and truly mad. Mark was always so blasé about everything, so this was clearly bugging him.

"I'm sorry, bud," Joan said.

"Eh, if it weren't for you, we wouldn't have gotten out at all."

Ricki's words rumbled around her head. That she'd do anything to protect the peace in Vector City. Which was a bit extreme. She'd fight for her new life, and sure, for the people she cared about. It was self-serving, not heroic. Not harming the norms was just basic human decency, which apparently Ricki and Derek did not possess.

"I'm not a hero," Joan murmured.

Mark's brow furrowed. "Huh?"

"We're entrepreneurs. Food truck restaurateurs. That's who we are now. I'm not letting your dream slip away, and I'm not putting Sadie in harm's way again."

"And Perry doesn't need any encouragement to backslide."

"So we'll return our suits after they dry." She pulled her gloves off. "This is the Supers' problem. We can at least give them the intel about the new guys having a real plan."

Mark unzipped his suit. "That's more than they had before."

"If they want to keep checking on us, fine. Let them. We've got nothing to hide."

They passed under a harsh floodlight. Mark did a double-take and squinted at Joan's face. "You've got a cut under your eye."

Joan touched the tender spot below her right eye. "Great."

"You think the Supers will reimburse us for medical treatment?"

"I'm sure."

"We can always overcharge them for fries."

"Done."

CHAPTER 8

The afternoon prep work vibe inside Hot and Cold was upbeat, only Sadie could tell Joan and Mark were tired and slightly forcing it. Their ordeal the other night had resulted in them working out in the warehouse this morning.

Joan yawned and stretched her back. The red scab under her eye was thanks to Prowl's assault. As if Sadie needed another reason to dislike that jerk.

She stirred the salted caramel hot chocolate, then studied her short, rounded and newly painted lavender nails. "I don't know if I like this color or not."

Joan glanced over. "It's okay, but I always prefer red."

"A dark crimson the same shade as on a former Supervillain's suit?"

"Exactly," she said with a cute wink.

The former Villains hadn't returned their suits to the Supers yet. The city's Heroes had been too busy with increased activity from the new Villains. Trying to get them to leave had made them more determined to stay and wreak havoc. They were doing things in broad daylight with Squawk breaking windows and Prowl hopping in and out of stores with armfuls of loot. The sky was frequently swirling and misty green and buzzy over specific areas.

At least Joan and Mark and Perry had tried to help. Fighting the new Villains showed they really did want them gone.

Joan stretched her arms forward, groaning from the effort.

"Sore from your workout?" Sadie guessed.

"Yeah." She leaned in, tilting her head to Sadie's ear. "Sorry we missed having morning sex."

"That's okay. We can always have good old-fashioned night-time sex."

One of Mark's eyebrows scrunched low. "Ew. Why would you do sex-type things when you're half asleep and have stinky breath?"

"We're usually too tired after work," Joan said. "This way, we know no matter what happens, we took care of that important business."

After a moment, Mark said, "That's actually a really good idea."

"I know, right?"

"Plus there's less chance of me dropping by and ruining the mood."

"You're not wrong about that."

Sadie just shook her head. "I would never in a million years discuss my sex life with my sister. Whenever Carrie has a baby, I'm going to assume it hatched, or one of those cartoon storks dropped it off."

"We don't have a normal sibling relationship," Joan said.

"Joanie's my best friend," Mark said. "I tell her everything."

"Aww," Sadie cooed as Joan drawled, "Yeah, he tells me *everything*."

"You love it."

Someone knocked on their rear entry. Sadie set her long metal spoon to the side and decreased the burner to a low simmer. Morris from Cajun Soul stood on the sidewalk in a puffy, bright-red jacket.

"Hi, friend," Sadie said.

"Hey, Sadie. Do you have any extra honey we could borrow?"

"I think so. Let me check."

"Thank you. I thought we had whole other bottle, but we can't find it."

"No problem." Sadie ducked back into the truck to investigate. "Morris and Tenia need to borrow some honey."

Mark chin-nodded at a high metal shelf. "There's some up there."

Sadie moved around containers of spices and condiments to find the bear-shaped plastic bottle. Joan followed her to the open doorway and said hello to Morris.

"You're a lifesaver." He accepted the bottle. "Can't make hot honey chicken without the honey."

"Happy to help," Sadie said.

Morris gazed at Joan. "Ouch. That's an angry scratch."

"It was from an angry creature," Joan said.

"A velociraptor?"

She grimaced. "No, a pissed-off cat."

Sadie rubbed Joanie's lower back.

"How's business been?" Morris asked. "We've noticed things slow down once the sun sets."

"We've noticed that, too," Joan said. "I don't think people want to be out after dark."

"The activity's not any worse. These Villains are just as bad in the daytime."

Joan's expression didn't change, but tiny flickers sparked in her amber eyes.

A few cars behind them, Wren and Beth-Ann stepped out of Powered by Plants. Sadie waved from the doorway, causing them to wave back. They walked over, Beth-Ann saying, "Hi, guys. What's new?"

"We were talking about how the streets clear out after dark," Morris said.

"Because of Prowl and Squawk?"

He nodded.

"You'd think people would be used to this," Wren said. "It's not like we haven't dealt with Supervillains before."

"Yeah, but we knew what to expect from Volt and Spark and the rest of them," said Morris. "The devil you know, y'know? I don't know about the new ones."

Mark joined them, wiping his hands on a towel. Sadie moved down to the long step flanked by the tall steel cabinet that housed the propane tank.

"Our old Supervillains were pretty tame compared to some of the other ones," Beth-Ann said.

"Tame?" Mark said.

Wren nodded. "They were more like ne'er-do-wells who broke stuff."

"They weren't tame," Mark insisted.

"Ice gave my sister three hundred bucks once," said Beth-Ann. "He saw her having trouble with an ATM, and he ran back from whatever he was doing to hand her a wad of cash. She always liked him after that."

Mark's body temperature dropped—the chill ran through Sadie's back. "Wait, she actually liked him?" he said.

"Well, I don't know if *like* is the right word, but she was grateful."

"Not all Villains are bad guys," Sadie said, careful not to look at either of the Malone twins.

"They're not good guys either," Morris said. "They busted up the bank we had our savings account at. It took a full extra year for us to get our funds squared away to open Cajun Soul."

Joan shifted her weight. Beth-Ann pointed to her face and said, "What happened to your eye?"

"Cat fight. The cat won." To Morris, Joan said, "Sorry about your money."

He shrugged. "Everyone's got a story like that."

Fiddling with his hand towel, Mark said, "I always thought Ice was a pretty good dude. He'd give money to small businesses that were affected by the Supers."

Joan raised an eyebrow at him. "*Ice* did that?"

"He did."

"I heard Spark was the most generous one," Sadie said.

"I heard that, too," Joan said, eyes brimming with amusement.

"It doesn't make up for everything else," Morris said. "There's been so much damage to the city. To every city."

"It's like none of the superpowered care about the little guys," said Beth-Ann.

"Some of them do," Joan said.

"It'd be nice if they all did."

Morris rolled the bottle of honey between his palms. "The Villains are villains, so I don't expect them to care. The Supers need to get their act together."

Nodding in agreement, Wren said, "And actually care about what happens to us when our reimbursement requests get denied by the city."

Joan and Mark went quiet. That was something that had bothered them forever.

"We don't even know what happened with our old Villains," Beth-Ann said. "Are they in jail? Did they bring in these new associates?"

"I think they're all out of the game," Sadie said. "Trick, Hide and Volt are locked up. I'd be willing to bet that Spark, Ice and Breeze got pardoned for helping rescue the person who had been kidnapped."

"That seems unlikely. Why would the Supers just let them go?"

"To show them kindness, or mercy?" Wren suggested.

"It was a diversion," Morris said. "They went underground. I doubt we've seen the last of them."

Pointing at him, Beth-Ann said, "It wouldn't surprise me if they're behind all this new activity."

"Which sucks." Wren rubbed at her buzzed dark hair. "Me and

my wife were looking at buying a condo. Now we're waiting to see about homeowners insurance rates."

"Yeah, my boyfriend's parents are trying to convince us to move back to his hometown."

Sadie rolled her eyes. "Believe me, I understand."

"I guess we'll get used to these Villains, too," Morris said. "Adjust to the new normal, like we always do."

Sadie nodded along with Wren and Beth-Ann. Joan and Mark copied the movement.

Beth-Ann noticed a couple of potential customers reading the menu board outside Powered By Plants. "Better get back to that new normal. Good sales tonight, everyone."

She and Wren walked back to their truck as Morris headed toward Cajun Soul. Sadie closed the Hot and Cold door, protecting them from outside opinions. She never told anyone she'd been the hostage that fateful day. It would invite too many questions. Nyah and Amit only knew because of her missing work.

"Tame," Mark grumbled, hacking his chef's knife into a red pepper.

"That's your takeaway from that conversation?" Sadie asked.

"No. Well, a little. I get why our old associates said we went soft. Apparently, we always were."

"Is it hard to stand there and listen to people talk about you?"

Both Joan and Mark shook their heads. "Nah," Joan said. "We're used to it."

True. Even Sadie had said some unkind things to her about Spark before knowing her real secret identity.

"I think I remember that woman at the ATM," Mark said. "It wasn't all thievery and mischief. We did do some good. I liked being able to help people out."

"Because Ice was the generous one," Joan teased. "But yeah, it felt like the right thing to do. God knows we understood not having enough money for essentials."

"That's the thing that separates us from the Supers. They

didn't have the struggles we did. They can't connect with the little guy."

"Yeah," Joan said again. She got that lost-in-a-memory look on her face. She never shied away from talking about her past when prompted, but there were a whole lot of buried emotions she didn't verbalize. She'd seen a lot in her thirty-five years.

Sadie rested her fingertips on Joan's arm. "Everything okay?"

"Yeah." She blinked and smiled. "I can't get over how the norms keep adjusting to Super activity. Our world was about holding grudges and bitter revenge."

"That's not very healthy," Sadie said.

"Not much we did was healthy. Except our random acts of altruism."

Mark diced his pepper strips. "Are we almost ready to open?"

"Just about," Joan said. She tapped the countertop. "This is our focus."

That wasn't the first time she'd said that recently. Reinforcing how the past was not going to encroach on their future.

"It's okay to acknowledge you did good things," Sadie said.

"We're doing better things now." Joan settled her Vultures ballcap on backwards.

"It's still okay to hear people appreciated what kindness you did as Spark and Ice."

"Most people don't know we did them."

"We didn't do it for the accolades the way the Supers do," Mark said.

"We did anonymous donations. Like the one I gave to Vector City Coffee that caused a lot of confusion between us."

"Maybe you should have taken the credit," Sadie said.

Joan snorted a wry laugh. "'Here's some money for your shattered windows. Warm regards from the Villains who broke them.' That doesn't make it better."

"At least it's an acknowledgment. The Supers just send you to a form on an app that probably never gets looked at."

Mark's bright blue eyes widened. "Did you just dis the Supers? I'm so proud of you."

"Well, no one can deny there are very few payouts to individuals or anything that's not a big corporation."

"Funny how Allegria Tower, the home of Allegria Insurance, got patched up in no time."

Sadie snagged her spoon to give the hot chocolate a stir. "Maybe we should get the word out about your past good deeds."

"It doesn't matter," Joan said. "We're not in that life anymore, so who cares what people think about some former Villains who disappeared?" She took a step toward the front of the truck, then rocked back and kissed Sadie's cheek. "But thank you for caring."

"It's more than caring," Sadie said. "It's not right that people are going around thinking the worst about you when there were glimmers of good."

Joan gave her a slight shrug and went to the side entry.

"It comes with the territory, Sades," Mark said. "Our misdeeds outweigh the rest. Which is fair."

"I just wish people knew about the rest."

The metal awning raised outside, bathing the interior of the truck in weak sunlight.

Mark scraped the diced peppers to one side. "The only way it would stick is if the Supers publicly said something. And as much as it's been civil with them, they won't admit they didn't bring us to justice. Letting us walk away means they'll let anyone off the hook."

"Which would send the wrong message to active Villains," Sadie murmured.

"Exactly."

Joanie rejoined them. Concern creased the skin between her eyebrows—a worry wrinkle that was more and more present every day.

Sadie rested the spoon in the pot and held her arms open. "Come here."

Joan didn't hesitate to accept the hug.

"You too, Markie. Get over here."

He rolled his eyes.

"You both need this."

Despite his nonchalance, he squeezed his arms tightly around them. His hug held the same weight as his sister's—the deep need for human connection.

"You two are amazing," Sadie said. "I've always known that, and I am historically an excellent judge of character."

They all laughed at that totally untrue fact.

Mark squeezed once more before letting go. "Let's have strong sales today, Team Hot and Cold."

Joan nestled into the hug, dislodging her ballcap. Her familiar scent of ginger and citrus wafted in the air.

Warmth flowed through Sadie's veins. Not just from Joan's natural heat, but from how much she loved giving Joanie reassurance. Her support meant everything. There had to be more Sadie could do to return the favor.

When they separated, she said, "I could tell people you rescued me. I mean, that Spark rescued me. I could come forward as the—"

"No. Don't put yourself through that. You'd be subjected to public scrutiny, which would draw attention to me, and Mark, and the food truck, and how we came out of nowhere with no traceable history or background."

"I could speak off the record. Say something like I'm hiding my identity 'cause I'm worried about other Villains retaliating. I want your story to be told."

Readjusting her hat, Joan said, "It's not a good idea. And again, it doesn't matter what people think."

"I just…"

"Thank you, and I love you, but no. Leave it be."

She slid the service window open, ready to start the day. Maybe it was an overstep to push her on this, but Joan deserved better. To not have the norms thinking she was in cahoots with Prowl. Prowl was awful.

Shoot. This was a complicated dance between support, respect, and not being Pushy Sadie. Part of her wanted everyone to know how great Joan was to prove Sadie had broken her streak of bad relationships and found a truly heroic partner. But that was putting too much focus on what other people wanted. Or at least what she thought they wanted. People-pleasing.

What mattered more was what Joan wanted and needed. And right now, that was backing off from what had happened and focusing on what was to come.

CHAPTER 9

That night, Sadie sipped her chamomile tea and caught up on things on her phone. She tucked her feet under the bottom rung of the tall barstool at the kitchen island. It was bedtime, and she still had to wash up and hopefully find the energy to fool around with Joanie.

Joan came out of the bedroom in a loose black cotton tank and tiny matching shorts, her short, dark waves of hair begging to be gripped in the heat of passion.

Sadie's mouth watered. A zing zipped through her belly and zoomed down, down, down. One look at her hot girlfriend was a better boost than any energy drink.

"Greta's back in town," Joan said. "She just texted to let me know."

"That's nice," Sadie said. "You have a lot to catch up on."

"She was like, 'I leave for a few weeks and everything goes to shit.'"

"Seriously."

A new text from Perry popped up.

This has your vibe.

He'd included a link to a listing for a storefront available for lease in Knollwood Village. It was in a charming vintage building that looked like it had most recently been a juice bar. Aged brown brick, big picture windows...

"Babe?" Joan said, setting her phone on the island.

"Hmm? Sorry, I was looking at something Perry sent me."

"What is it?"

"A Sadie's Café option."

Joan moved beside her to take a look. The scoop neck on her top gaped to reveal her perfect little breasts waiting for Sadie's attention. A deep throb pulsed in her lower abdomen.

"That's really cute," Joan said. "It reminds me of you."

"Perry said it has my vibe."

"It does. We should check it out."

"Mm-hmm."

"Where is it?"

"Knollwood Village."

Joan pressed a soft kiss to Sadie's temple. "You love shopping there, right?"

"I used to," Sadie said. "It's been a while, but I did get a lot of my clothes and décor from the little shops tucked along the side streets."

"We can make a day of it tomorrow."

"Monday funday." *But first, tonight fun-night.*

She glanced at the listing again. Her heart gave a tiny flutter. It was cute, but rent in the Village was notoriously high. It was probably way too out of reach. And anyway, her dream was on hold until everything going on in the city calmed down.

Joan sampled Sadie's tea. "I don't know how you make chamomile not taste like hot weeds."

"Fresh lemon and a pinch of grated ginger root," Sadie replied.

"You're a genius."

"You're..." She set her phone down and swiveled the barstool to face the full vision of Joanie's toned body in loose clothes. No word could describe the ache in Sadie's bones to touch her other than, "Mine."

A delicious chuckle rumbled in Joan's throat. "All yours, sweetheart."

Sadie leaned in and placed a slow kiss on Joan's warm and welcoming lips. Joanie wrapped her arms around her. Sadie slid her fingers over the stubble of the undercut above Joan's neck.

Their tongues met languidly, familiar and wonderful. Her favorite taste in the world was Joanie Maloney's mouth. Well, second favorite to another special place on Joanie's body.

Joan pulled back, tilting her head and taking in a deep breath. What she had to do to move all the fire roiling around her body to her heart. She looked at Sadie with so much love and tenderness, it almost melted her anyway.

"I really need this tonight," Joan murmured.

"Me, too."

They kissed deeply, sharing their mutual need.

"Wanna have some fun?" Sadie said.

"Always."

"We haven't used something from the toybox in a while."

Joan smiled against her mouth. "What do you want to play with?"

A rush of liquid heat filled Sadie's clit. The way Joan purred about playing with toys...

She nibbled on Joan's neck, cupping one of her breasts and kneading it. "Fuck, Joanie, I want you so bad."

Joan growled and snaked her hands under Sadie's pink blouse, undoing the clasp on her bra. "Nothing gets me hotter than when you say that."

Sadie licked at Joan's collarbone, using her teeth to pull the strap of the tank top down. This was exactly what they needed to yank the first orgasm out of them both. The second (and third and hopefully beyond) would be gentler.

She freed Joan's breast from her shirt and bent to savor it.

The front door opened. *Fuck!*

Joan jerked back with an angry "Damn it, Mark!"

Only Greta stood there, an amused smirk tugging at her lips.

"Damn it, Greta!" Joan amended, adjusting her shirt.

"Nice to see you, too," Greta said in her blunt voice.

Every cell in Sadie's body screamed at being denied the promise of release. Of course it was Greta deactivating the alarm and breaking in.

"When you said you wanted to get together," Joan said, "I didn't take that to mean right this minute."

"I texted you. Hi, Sadie."

"Hi, Greta. Welcome home." *Damn it!*

Joan grasped at the air, sparks flickering from her fingertips. "Boundaries, remember? I don't live alone anymore. You have to let me know if you're going to stop by."

She stalked to the alarm and pressed several buttons. Sadie pulled at her shirt, awkwardly tucking her boobs into the sagging cups on her unhooked bra. "How was France?"

"Great," Greta said. She looked rested and refreshed, her straight black hair cut a few inches shorter. Her army-style jacket and shiny black boots appeared to be new. Hopefully purchased and not pilfered.

She lounged against the island countertop. "Am I interrupting something?"

"*Yes,*" Joan said in the same tone as Sadie did in her head.

"You're gonna want to hear this." Greta glanced around, taking in the melded décor of Joan's modern tastes with Sadie's kitschy items. "You know I tune out what's going on when I'm out of town. But the news about what's happening here reached my little village."

"It's pretty bad," Sadie said.

"More than you know."

Joan joined her, resting her fingertips between Sadie's shoulder blades in what felt like a *To be continued* gesture.

"I spoke to some of our associates." Greta paused. "Well, my associates. You should hear what Ether and Prowl have promised them. Carte blanche on the city as soon as the last piece of the puzzle is in place."

"What about Squawk?" Joan asked.

"No one gets that close to him."

"The screeching?" Sadie guessed.

"Yeah. But also, he's a dickwad."

Joan leaned against Sadie's barstool. "What's the last piece of the puzzle?"

Greta shifted her weight. "Did you hear about the gas line explosion yesterday?"

Sadie nodded. Her mother had called about the accident at a construction site on the south end of the business district. It'd almost leveled the building. Thank god no one had been injured since it was a Saturday and the crew hadn't been working.

"It wasn't a gas line."

Joan stiffened.

Greta shifted again, uncharacteristically uncomfortable. "It was Big Quake."

"What?" Sadie and Joan said together.

"Big Quake is back in Vector City."

"He's still alive?" Joan said.

"I thought he died after that last battle," Sadie said.

"No one ever confirmed that," said Greta. "I heard rumblings for years that he was doing illegal diamond mining in South Africa. Turns out, that's true. He's come back for vengeance. And I guess he's just Quake now."

"Why is no one reporting this?" Sadie grabbed her phone to check SuperWatch.

"The Supers and Mayor Thorpe are trying to suppress it. They don't want to cause a panic."

Joan hesitated, then said, "This is serious."

"Very," Greta said.

There was nothing important on SuperWatch. Big Quake was in Vector City? *Big Quake?* The idea chilled Sadie to the bone.

"No one says his name," Joan said. "No one in villainy. Perry told me never to mention him because we never wanted to be associated with him in any way, shape or form."

"Well, this new world order wants to be." Greta crossed her arms, silver rings glinting. "Quake is going to disrupt our infrastructure, and the others are going to create chaos. There'll be too much mayhem for the Supers to handle."

Joan began to pace. "How is this staying quiet? People need to know about it."

"This was a test run. They're doing a big reveal soon."

"We need to te—" Joan met Sadie's eyes. "Someone should tell the Supers."

"They already know," Greta said.

"Then they should be warning people. The civilians they claim to be protecting."

Sadie stood, too keyed up to sit anymore. "They don't want people freaking out."

"What's worse, though?" Joan paced back and forth. "Finding out because of a warning, or because he brings down a building with people in it next time?"

"I'm just the harbinger of information." Greta raised one thin eyebrow. "Hope it was worth interrupting your private time."

Joan's phone chimed with an incoming text. "Probably Mark," she said, reaching for it. "He needs to know about this."

Sadie caught Z as the contact. Definitely not Mark.

Emergency meeting at HQ. Ward will let you in.

Zee had sent it to Mark and Perry, too. Oh, no. Now what? Joan typed a quick reply:

Should we bring our suits?

Three dots appeared, then disappeared. Then reappeared.

Leave them for now.

Greta walked toward them. "What's he want?"

Joan quickly clicked her phone off. "He wants me to come over."

"Want me to go with?"

"Nah," she said. "It's about this week's menus."

Ooh, Joan just lied to her best friend. Though she had to, right? She couldn't tell Greta she was meeting with the Supers, both to protect her thieving pal and from letting Greta know they'd worked together again. Greta had not reacted well to that happening before.

Greta turned her sharp gaze onto Sadie. "We could hang out."

"Oh, thanks, but…"

"Good idea," Joan said.

Sadie raised her eyebrows.

"I'd feel better knowing you're together now that fucking Big Quake is back."

Sadie scrunched her brows like *Are you sure?*

Joan gave her a look that said *I trust both of you.*

She did trust Greta. Sadie supposed she had to trust her, too.

"Thanks for telling me, Grets," Joan said. "I'll tell Mark and Per."

"Keep your head on a swivel," Greta said. "I don't know what this means for you."

Heading for the bedroom, Joan said, "Yeah, we'll have to talk more later."

Sadie followed her, muttering, "Oh boy, do you have to tell her some things."

"Not now," Joan muttered back.

In the safety of their cozy bedroom, Sadie opened her mouth to ask if Joan thought this emergency meeting was about Big

Quake. Only Joan pulled off her tank top and revealed the breasts that Sadie was now being denied. Her clit throbbed in agony.

"Please find a speedy resolution so we can pick up where we left off," she said.

"Nothing I want more, sweetheart."

Joan dressed in the same violet-and-navy plaid flannel and black pants she'd worn that day. They probably still smelled like Hot and Cold and its oils and proteins and general cookery. Wearing the clothes from one identity to deal with the other.

Poor Joanie. She was never going to get away from being Spark.

But what if Spark could be something more? Something better?

"I know it's hard to work with the Supers," Sadie said. "But I'm proud of you. You're doing the right thing."

"I'm doing the only thing I can. They own my ass."

"Better them than these new Villains. And Big Quake." Sadie hugged her arms. "Now I definitely don't want people thinking you're working with them. I'm pretty sure Big Quake is the reason my mom's so afraid of the city."

Joan pulled her hair back, grimacing when a chunk fell over one eye. She grabbed a dark hair tie from the small garnet-red ceramic bowl Sadie had given her as a Christmas present. "Greta loves tea. She'd like your chamomile concoction."

"You don't want her out and about gathering more intel?"

"She'll look after you."

Slight irritation needled at her neck. "I don't need anyone to look after me."

"You know what I mean. You'll be together. I can account for everyone I care about."

That wasn't what she meant. Not entirely. Greta could kick anyone's ass, so she'd be able to defend Sadie.

Why didn't anyone think she could defend herself? Joan trusted Greta, but sometimes she didn't trust Sadie in the same way.

Joan started for the doorway. Sadie held out a hand. "Can you redo my bra really quick?"

"Of course." Joan moved her hands under Sadie's blouse. Ooh, wow, they were hot. She was a lot more worried than she was letting on.

"Text me if you need anything," Sadie said. "Be safe. I love you."

"Love you, too." Joan kissed her cheek before striding out of the bedroom.

Greta watched her old friend disarm the alarm. Then she looked between Joan and Sadie. "The domestic life suits you."

That would've made Sadie happy any other time. This was supposed to be their sanctuary, only it was getting more and more intruded upon.

"Have fun," Joan said, although her faraway look told them she was focused on something un-fun.

Once the door closed, Sadie locked it. "Do you like chamomile tea?"

"Where's she really going?" Greta asked.

Crap. "Trust me, you do not want to be around her and Mark when they're—"

"That wasn't Mark who texted. Don't make me hack her phone. Where's she going?"

"Uhh…"

"If she didn't tell me, it was someone she doesn't want me to know about. The only people I don't want to know about are our city's Superheroes. So that must mean—"

"It was Race," Sadie blurted out. "They're kind of friends now. Mark has a crush on them he's totally denying. Race wanted to hang out with them both. Joanie doesn't want you worrying."

"You mean Zee," Greta said. "I know their names."

Her impassive face gave nothing away. Did she believe that story? It was mostly the truth.

"Why didn't you go?"

"Uh, have you ever hung out with a bunch of superpowered

people trying to out-power each other? It's really boring. And I'm tired. I was just telling Joanie right before you got here I wanted to go to bed." *And do marvelously sexy things, damn it.*

"You can stop." Greta wandered over to Sadie's mug of tea. "Word of advice. A lie works best when you don't overexplain."

"It's mostly not a lie," Sadie admitted.

"Then she is going to see Zee."

"Well yeah, but…"

"About this Quake situation."

"Probably."

Greta pinned her with a steely glare. "She's still working with the Supers?"

"Not *still*. There was a situation the other day. The Supers forced Joan and Mark and Perry to—"

"Oh, I heard about that. They're claiming to still be in the game. Absolutely no one believes that."

"It wasn't their idea," Sadie said. "You know the Supers could arrest Joanie at any moment. She has to do what they want, even though she doesn't want to."

"She chose her side," Greta said so quietly, Sadie almost missed it. She straightened and turned on her heel. "On second thought, I don't feel safe here. If you'll excuse me…"

"Joanie would never turn you in," Sadie said.

"But her new friends would."

"They're not *friend* friends."

"Semantics. If they're watching her, they're watching everyone around her."

"I think you'd be safe here."

Gesturing to herself, Greta said, "I don't have a secret identity. I've never worn a mask, and I own my work. Proudly. If the Supers are anywhere around Joan, then I can't be."

Sadie started to ask why that was a problem now—Greta and Joan had been in scrapes with the Supers countless times. But that was before Joan stood beside the good guys. Still…

"Joanie would protect you," Sadie said. "She's beyond loyal and can fight fire with fire. Literally."

"I know she'd try."

"I hope you're also protecting her."

Greta snorted. "You have no idea how much I've protected her."

Fidgeting with her shirttails, Sadie said, "She was really hurt when you disappeared after she saved me."

"After she made a deal with the Supers to get rid of her own kind, you mean."

"No, after she *saved me*. Everyone keeps focusing on that other part, which yes, was a big deal. But nobody remembers her rescuing me. She became a hero in my eyes that day." Sadie stared at the floor and murmured, "I wish she was a hero in other people's eyes."

Greta walked to the front door, then paused. She glanced over her shoulder. "I like you, Sadie. And I like you for Joan. So I don't mean this with malice, but you need to stay out of things you can't possibly understand."

Sadie crossed her arms. "What's that supposed to mean?" she said with more confidence than she felt.

"Loyalty is not turning on your found family. Joan got what she wanted at a cost."

"Yeah, she lost almost everyone from that time in her life. I was hoping that wouldn't include you, too. You mean a lot to her."

"Let's hope it doesn't come to that," Greta said, and slipped out of the apartment.

Well, this sucked. Greta didn't trust Joan anymore. And Joanie put so much trust into so very few people. It would crush her to learn Greta might choose self-protection over friendship.

"What do you know about loyalty, Greta?" Sadie grumbled. "You're a thief. A norm who does it because you enjoy it. Maybe Joanie would be better off without you. She has new friends. Better friends. Sure, she feels a little weird hanging out with my friends, but that's just because she has a hard time relating to them after all she's been thr—"

And that was exactly why Joanie needed her best friend. Greta did understand her. She'd been around for a long time, through good and bad.

It wasn't that Sadie disliked Greta. She didn't like that Greta was a tie to Joanie's old life. But it was an essential tie for Joan to maintain. Because she *was* loyal—to the right people. To those who deserved it. No matter the cost.

CHAPTER 10

Joan studied the Supers on the opposite side of the oval conference table, feigning surprise at their revealing Big Quake was back. She'd arrived first and hadn't gotten the chance to warn Mark and Perry beyond a few quick texts.

"What the actual fuck?" Mark said.

Otis gripped the back of the office chair in front of him. He looked exhausted. They all did. "We received a video message from him and the other Villains claiming responsibility for yesterday's building collapse. They said it was a gift for us before their plan is put in action."

"How do you know it was Big Quake?" Mark said. "I thought that dude was mortally wounded decades ago."

"He's just going by Quake now," Kade said.

Otis shared an uncomfortable look with his other cohorts. "He survived that last battle in Vector City."

Mark scrunched his face. "Okay, but he's gotta be, like, sixty? Seventy? Are you sure that was him in the video?"

"Yes," said Otis. "It's him."

"Did you know he survived?" Joan asked.

"They've always known," Perry stated.

"Then where's he been all these years?" Mark said.

Crossing her arms, Darlene said, "He's been involved with various illicit operations throughout the world. Mining for rare metals for high profits. Nothing that would raise suspicion that it was being done with superpowers."

Zee cut Joan off from asking the obvious question of why they didn't go after him. "There were a lot of rumors and unsubstantiated claims. And it was out of our jurisdiction."

"You wanted to pretend like you defeated him," Perry fumed. "Better to let him go than admit you failed."

"That's not what happened," Otis said.

"Bullshit."

"So is he their ringleader?" Mark said. "The one who's calling the shots?"

"It appears they have a common goal," said Darlene. "Destruction and chaos."

Kade frowned, a sad palomino. "He said he's gonna finish what he started. I don't like the sound of that."

"Nobody does, buddy," Mark said.

"We called you here to get your input as former Villains," Otis said. "Do you have any ideas on what we can do to get rid of them?"

Whoa, they were getting desperate. Joan leaned her forearms on the table. "How did you defeat Big Quake last time?"

"He was injured," Otis said. "Badly. We figured he bled out when he got into a helicopter and out-maneuvered us in bad weather."

"Bad weather," Joan murmured to herself. *A cover.* That could explain him wanting to work with Ether.

"Atomic Man blasted him really good." Kade grinned. "He told me more than once he'd taken Big Quake out of commission."

Perry snorted in disgust. "Fucking liar."

Ooh, two curses in under a minute. He was pissed.

Otis pushed his chair in and stood tall. "No, actually, that is the truth. And Amazing Woman is the reason he got away."

"Don't you…" Perry hefted out a breath like he was trying not to lunge across the table and strangle Otis. "Don't you pin that on her."

"She failed to stop him from getting into that helicopter."

He stared at Otis like his thoughts could incinerate. The weird feeling in the air meant they'd turned on that power-blocking device again. Maybe that was a good thing. Why was Per so riled up about Amazing Woman?

Darlene cleared her throat. "Regardless of what happened before, this is different. There are Villains aligning with him. This is a much more dangerous situation."

"We're looking for anything that can take them down," Zee said. "Any weakness to exploit. Anything you can give us. Lives are at stake. We don't want people to get hurt."

They were right—and more importantly, Zee was sincere. This wasn't about glory or photo ops. Big Quake, regular Quake, whatever he was calling himself, was no joke. Neither were Prowl, Ether or Squawk.

The knot festering in Joan's gut churned and pulsed. She couldn't shake the guilt from Morris and Tenia having their food truck dream pushed back. Or how Wren couldn't buy a home. Mark had focused on the *People liked Ice because he was generous* angle, but that was such a tiny amount compared to all the bad.

She'd been looking forward to burying the pain tonight with hot sex and Sadie snuggles, but that went to shit. Everything was going to shit. That's what she got for being a shit as Spark.

Maybe Sadie was right about seeing more of the good stuff Spark had done. And could still do.

"I heard that destruction and chaos is exactly what they want," Joan said. "The rest of the criminal element will thrive because you'll be too busy to stop all of it."

"Who told you that?" Darlene said, eyes narrowed in suspicion.

"Someone looking out for my best interests."

Ward pushed through the conference room door carrying a

tray loaded with bottles of iced coffee and tea, mineral water, and energy drinks. He dropped it on the side table beside a basket of fancy prepackaged snacks.

Darlene planted her hands on the table and stood. "I want the name of your criminal contact."

"Your mom," Mark said.

Zee gave him their usual smirk. "Are you still doing *your mom* jokes?"

Joan wasn't about to put Greta on their radar, so she said, "Don't get your panties in a bunch. It's just the rumor floating around."

Ward approached with two bottles of iced coffee. "I took the liberty of getting things I thought you might like. It'll probably be a late night."

"You read my mind," Mark said, accepting one of them.

Joan took the other, though she didn't need the caffeine just yet. Darlene was over there muttering to Otis about wanting the name of "Spark's secret informant." Ugh, what she wouldn't give to have her fire active.

She flicked her fingers, just in case. Nothing.

Ward turned to Perry. "Mr. Breeze, may I offer you a drink?"

"No."

"Come on, Per." Mark gestured with his bottle. "Take their free shit."

Perry glanced at the beverage options. "Water." He flexed his fingers like he was also trying to wake up his superpowers.

"I might regret asking this," Joan said, "but why haven't you used this power-blocking tech to take out Villains?"

"A few reasons," Otis said. "Mainly because it disrupts our powers, too."

"Yeah, but you all can fight. Darlene can really throw a punch."

Darlene's eyes went wide. Wait, was that an unintentional compliment?

"But I throw them better," Joan added.

"No you don't," Darlene shot back.

"The tech doesn't fully solve the problem," Otis said. "Ward, where's my peach iced tea?"

"Coming right up, Mr. Flight." Ward tucked Perry's mineral water under one arm and grabbed three different types of bottled tea.

Surveying the visitors across the table, Darlene said, "Do you have any other intelligence to provide us?"

"Perry, did you ever work with him?" Zee asked.

Perry shot him a murder face. "I wasn't in the life back then."

"You seem to know a lot about—"

"Not about Big Quake."

"It's just Quake now," Kade said, irritation wrinkling his broad forehead.

Ward held out Otis's tea. "Here you are, sir. Ms. Catch, your no sugar mint tea. Mx. Race, your green tea."

They took the bottles without acknowledging their sidekick. Joan made a mental note to thank him next time. Ward got the norm treatment big time from his bosses.

"My only advice is to not let them separate," she said. "It's harder for you to track us—er, them—when they scatter."

"Yeah, we know," Kade said, rolling his eyes.

"Setting a trap to get them in the same place is the best course of action. But it has to be something they won't expect. Like what we did with Trick."

Her heart squeezed. These Villains would be beyond pissed at such a betrayal. The consequences of any failed attempts would be disastrous.

"It needs to be a really good plan," Mark said, reading her mind. Or possibly her hand death-gripping her iced coffee. "If they see you coming, their retaliation will be *bad*."

Zee gave a thin smile. "Good thing we have three worldclass masterminds at deception to help formulate that plan."

"Who, us?" Mark grinned. "I'm flattered. I think I'll get 'worldclass mastermind' printed on my business cards."

"You're going to help us come up with a plan," Darlene stated.

"It'll be fun," Kade said. "Teaming up again."

No one reacted in any way that telegraphed fun. Ward scuttled over to him with a jumbo energy drink and bag of gourmet pretzels.

This really was the Melvin situation all over again. He'd wanted Joan and Mark to come up with his grand plan of world domination. When they didn't, he kidnapped Sadie. What would the Supers do if…

Prison. Losing my powers forever.

Fuck.

An incoming video call popped up on one of the large TVs.

"Finally," Darlene huffed.

Otis reached for a button on the center console. "We've been trying to consult with Aura."

A middle-aged Black woman with shoulder-length locs appeared onscreen. Aura, the Destine Super who could influence your mood.

"Thank you for returning my call," Otis said.

"At least one of us knows how to return a phone call," Aura drawled.

Laughing uneasily, Otis peered down the length of the conference table. "Let's keep this professional, Sherrelle."

"Oh, I'll keep it professional. Lord knows all you want to do is keep things professional. Unless it's at a hotel twenty miles outside of Destine. Then it can be all kinds of nasty."

Mark nearly did a spit-take with his coffee.

"*Sherrelle.*" Otis gave another painfully fake laugh. "We're dealing with one of your Villains. Let's talk about Squawk."

Aura grumbled to herself, then noticed the newcomers. "Is that Breeze there with Spark and Ice?"

"Yes. They're—"

"Well, bang my ass sideways. You really did form an alliance with your former Villains."

"Not exactly," Otis said as Darlene vehemently stated, "No."

Aura waved a hand tipped with pale pink nails. "It wouldn't be the first time. There's that dude up in Canada who went from Villain to Hero. What's his name? Bleep?"

"Blip," Kade supplied.

"Yeah. The one who runs through walls and shit."

"It's a means to an end," Otis said. "What can you tell us about Squawk?"

"Rude. Loud. His facemask has built-in sound dampening 'cause even he can't handle his screams."

"Seriously?" Mark laughed.

"Yup. Don't try to fight noise with noise with him. He blocks it out."

Darlene crossed her arms. "Does he usually work alone or with others?"

"Alone." Aura pointed to her ear. "The screaming."

"Why is he aligning with other Villains in Vector City?"

"My guess is ego. He likes money a lot, but he really loves having people afraid of him. This new faction is the perfect storm of assholes."

"More than you know," Otis said. "We've gotten word Big Quake has returned."

"Big—oh, shit. That's no joke. You get Squawk's soundwaves with Big Quake's ability to move earth, and that's..."

"Oh, shit," Zee finished.

Now the puzzle pieces were fitting together. "So Squawk can amplify Quake's powers," Joan said. "And Ether can cover what they're doing. Why is Prowl in on this? What's she contributing?"

"Prowl can go toe-to-toe with people up close," Mark said. "The others aren't known to be fighters."

Joan nodded. "Good point."

Otis glanced at their sidekick organizing the snacks. "Ward, why aren't you taking notes?"

Ward fumbled with a small bag of popcorn and hastened to the table. "I'm sorry, sir." He grabbed a laptop and flipped the cover up.

"You still only use one sidekick?" said Aura.

"Do you know how hard it is to find qualified applicants who can pass our background checks?" Otis said.

"No wonder they don't last long."

Kade coughed behind his meaty hand. "Our humans are better than your robotic sidekicks."

Zee stifled a grin.

"They were android assistants," Aura said half-heartedly.

"Robots," Kade muttered.

"And I was against them from the start. Otis should've told you that. If he ever talks about me."

Mark leaned close to Joan and whispered, "This is amazing."

"When you lose that human connection, you lose control." Aura waved her hands. A shimmering golden glow surrounded her. "And I know human connection."

"So we have an expert on Squawk." Darlene ticked that off on one finger. "And experts on Prowl and Ether, who I am convinced know more than they're letting on." She ticked that off. Joan gave her a one-finger salute. "Flight, you are our expert on Quake."

"The only active one," Otis said.

Darlene started to speak, then hesitated. Then said, "There is another option."

"Not that again."

Kade raised his hand like an obedient student. "Stretch Boy has dementia. I don't think he'll be a lot of help."

Darlene turned to fully face Otis. "We should contact her."

Perry sucked in a sudden breath. "Don't," he said, quiet but weighted.

"She's made it very clear never to bother her," Otis said.

"Who?" Mark said.

"This is urgent," Darlene pressed. "She has the most intel on Big Quake."

"Guys, it's just Quake now," Kade insisted.

Mark bounced in his seat. "*Who?*"

Darlene glanced at him. "Amazing Woman."

"Amazing Woman?" he scoffed. "She's still alive?"

"Yes," Otis said.

"Don't get her involved in this," Perry said.

"What is she, a hundred years old?" Mark said.

"Ninety-three."

Otis shook his head. "The last time I tried reaching out, she said in no uncertain terms am I allowed to contact her again. She lives off the grid for a reason."

"This is her archnemesis," Darlene said. "Wouldn't she finally want justice?"

"She's out of this life," Perry said.

Mark leaned forward. "How do you know so much about Amazing Woman?"

Everyone in the room—including Aura—stared at him. Perry scowled. "History."

Oh. *Oh.* "She was the Super who betrayed you," Joan realized.

"She was forced to by the others."

"Aw man, you must hate her guts," Mark said.

Perry said nothing, but in that moment, Joan got everything she needed. The woman who had betrayed him, who'd turned him into Breeze, was a Superhero.

Only he wasn't ranting and raving about her. He'd cared for her.

Darlene broke the silence. "A Superhero pledges to protect the people. She'll want justice and to defend Vector City."

"I'd leave her alone," Aura said. "She put in her time. She's been through enough."

"Flight also battled Big Quake—"

"No, I mean she went *through it*. You sent her in first, every time, to take the brunt of an assault. She was indestructible, but that doesn't mean it didn't hurt. She was treated like crap. Being a woman Super in the old days was hard. Not that it's all that better today."

"I'm not suggesting she join the fight," Darlene said. "It would be to help us with a plan of attack."

Per had the weirdest look on his face. Like he wanted to shout about something, but also troubled in a way Joan had never seen.

Zee held up a hand. "Can we go back to age? Is Quake able to do what he used to? Powers diminish with age."

"That's why he's teamed up with the others," Joan said.

"Then shouldn't we want to separate them?"

Huh. Another good point.

Aura tilted her head to see above her screen. "I've got to go. Crime never sleeps in Destine. Let me know if you need something. Or, y'know, if you just want to talk."

She sent Otis a pointed glare before the call ended.

Darlene began to walk around the table. "I'll reach out to her."

"She'll say no," Perry said. "After what happened with Big Quake, she vowed to never get involved again."

"She told you that?" Otis said.

"She told *you* that. In no uncertain terms, as you said."

"Can we take five?" Mark shook his index finger at Perry. "I have a few questions for my associate that he won't answer in a room full of people."

"You can go in the hallway," Otis said. "While I review notes with Ward."

"Keep the door open," Darlene said. "I'll be watching. We have cameras everywhere."

Joan ignored her because damn it, she was finally about to get Perry's origin story. He looked resigned enough to open up.

The trio went to the opposite side of the wood-paneled hall. "So Amazing Woman, huh?" she said.

Perry released a deep breath. "Her name is Augusta Abernathy. She goes by Gus. She came into the art gallery where I was working. We struck up a friendship."

"A friendship, or a *friendship*?" Mark asked. "She's like, *so* much older than you."

"Colleagues. I appreciated her intelligence and wit. She's a talented artist in her own right. I didn't know she'd been sent by the other Supers to see if I had powers. Eventually Gus told me the truth. The other Supers ambushed me before my first big show opened. They caught me off guard, and I reacted with my powers. The gallery was destroyed. I had to leave my dream job. Gus retired shortly afterward."

"She retired after that Big Quake battle," Joan said. "Did you have anything to do with—"

"No. Though people's fear of him was a lot of why I hid my powers. Gus later told me she was distracted and disillusioned by what her cohorts made her do. It affected her performance."

"Hang on. She told you later?" Mark's eyebrows met in the middle. "Have you spoken to her since then?"

"I didn't for a long time. Not when I became Breeze. One day, she reached out to apologize. We talked, and slowly became friends again. We..." Perry avoided eye contact. "We see each other now and again."

"*What?*" Joan said, and Mark echoed her.

"We've been friends for a while."

"Friends with benefits, or..." He cringed. "Oh Jesus, she's a hundred years old. That's like *age gap*."

"She still looks like she's my age."

"Yeah, but..."

Joan shook her head at whatever inappropriate thing Mark was about to say about Amazing Woman's "antique plumbing." "Do you know where she lives?"

"I've been to her house many times," Perry said.

Mark smacked Joan's arm. "Is that where you're going when you duck out of town?"

"Sometimes."

Joan smacked her brother back. "Do you talk about us? Does she know about us?"

"We talk about you often."

"For real?"

"She's given me a lot of advice on what to do with you two."

"But she was a Superhero," Mark said. "You just gloss over the fact that you were a Villain who raised two young Villains? That wasn't... How did that work?"

Perry shrugged one shoulder. "We made peace with our past and don't talk about that part of our lives."

"What the actual, *actual* fuck?" Mark giggled.

"Have we ever met her?" Joan wondered. "Like has she come back to Vector City?"

"No," Perry said. "She lives off the grid in the middle of nowhere."

"Now we know why you hate the Supers," Joan said. "Well, all of them but Amazing Woman." *What the actual fuck indeed.*

"They outed you," Mark said. Sympathetic pain flashed in his blue eyes. "I know what that feels like."

"It's why I took you in." Perry shook his head slightly. "I didn't know you two were gay. I just knew you had powers and were scared. I didn't want what happened to me to happen to you."

"Thanks, Per." Joan lightly punched his bicep.

"Dude, I told you I was gay," Mark said. "Remember how I was all, 'You better not try anything, you old creep.'"

"Old." Perry snorted. "I was thirty."

"And how old was Amazing Woman? I mean how old was she when—"

A thump against the wall inside the conference room was followed by someone going, "Shh." Ah, leave it to the Supers to spy on them.

Perry glared at the open doorway, but his face said he wasn't surprised.

For everyone's benefit, Joan asked, "Do you think you could talk her into coming back to help with this Quake situation?"

"I doubt it," said Perry. "If you think I'm stubborn and unco-operative..."

"We should get him to ask her," Kade's deep voice said through the wall.

"Shh," someone hissed. Probably Darlene.

Perry stared at the wall. "She'd want to be involved less than we do," he said loudly enough for all to hear.

Joan flicked her fingers by habit. Four clueless Superheroes, three reluctant former Villains, and one really old Hero who wanted nothing to do with any of this.

Vector City was kind of fucked.

CHAPTER 11

Having their monthly meeting early the next afternoon felt odd. Joan shifted in her usual seat at the warehouse table, antsy and restless.

They used to meet here to review villainous exploits, then to go over things for Hot and Cold. Today was supposed to be about the food truck, but all she could think about was what had transpired the night before.

The Supers really sucked at working together. No wonder it'd been easy to fool them for so many years. It was about individual success to them. Things had ended last night with them going around in circles with what to do.

The only thing they did agree on was that Perry needed to convince Amazing Woman to help out. Or at least agree to a video call from wherever she was hiding. Per seemed intent on protecting her. There was a whole lot more to his *We're just friends* story.

Sadie winked from across the table. She too was fascinated by Perry's secret.

Speaking of secrets… Mark had been furiously texting since he'd arrived.

"Hot date?" Joan asked him.

"Hardly."

"It's Zee," Sadie said.

Mark's fingers stilled for a perceptible second.

"I see," Joan drawled.

"They keep bugging me about annoying crap," Mark muttered.

Sadie met Joan's eyes and mouthed, *"Meeting up."*

"I saw that, Sades. It's about talking about a plan."

"Is that what it's about?" Sadie teased.

Joan checked her phone. "I haven't gotten anything about a meeting."

"Y'know what's strange? Mark never gets defensive when we talk about his other romantic escapades."

"Because it's not a romantic escapade," he said.

"That *is* strange," Joan said.

Glancing up with a sneer, Mark said, "Go back to making googly eyes at each other."

Sadie blew Joan an exaggerated kiss that she caught like an outfielder at Vulture Stadium. They still hadn't had sex because of sleeping late and needing to get to this meeting. And she'd been a little off last night from Greta needing to leave in a hurry for some obscure Greta-y reason. Both their phones were getting turned off the second they got home. Maybe they should stick a chair under the front doorknob for insurance.

Not that anyone Joan knew wouldn't just find some other way in.

The garage door opened to Perry's shimmering gray luxury import. "He's never late," Sadie said. "Do you think he was on the phone with Amazing Woman?"

"Hopefully," Joan said.

She and Sadie had looked up photos of the Superhero. It was wild how slowly she'd aged in her decades of service. She'd started so young—a teenager. The perky blonde in a miniskirt and go-go boots had a bone-weary air about her in her later years. And a full bodysuit to go with her simple eye mask.

They'd done the math to figure out she'd been in her late sixties when she'd met a twentysomething Perry. Something about her skeptical blue eyes said she'd be the perfect companion for Per, no matter how many years were between them.

He stepped out in an impeccable navy-blue suit and striped shirt.

"You look nice today," Sadie said.

"Any special occasion?" Mark said, sending a text.

"Sorry I'm late," Perry said. "Let's get to the agenda. I have last month's sales numbers."

He placed his briefcase on the table. The other three looked at each other like *Not so fast*.

"Should we talk about the Superhero-sized elephant in the room?" Mark said, setting his phone down.

"Did you reach out to her?" Joan asked.

"I told you Gus is done with all of that." Perry took out several stapled groupings of paper.

"But I guess Quake was her archnemesis. Wouldn't she want to—"

"This isn't our fight," he said, and handed Joan a sales report. "The Supers want us to do their job for them. You said it yourself, Joanie. They're no better than Melvin."

"You're not wrong," Mark said. "But this situation is serious enough for them to turn to us."

"They should get more than one Superhero from another city to help them." Perry set a report in front of Mark, then another in front of Sadie.

Joan held hers up. "What's the point of this when there's a literal disaster waiting to happen?"

"Because you wanted to be normal. This is what it's like to be normal."

She opened her mouth, but the rebuttal died. If they weren't going to be the bad guys or fight the bad guys, they had to be the regular clueless guys.

Perry flipped through his pages. "As you can see in the

comparison between December and January, we did a better job anticipating costs this month."

"Regardless of what you do," Joan said, "can we meet Gus? She's an important person in your life we just found out about."

"I want to meet her," Mark said.

Perry sent Sadie an exasperated look. "You see why I never told those two."

"Oh, one hundred percent. They're relentless." She glanced at Joan mischievously. "But I want to meet her, too. I mean, Amazing Woman? She's a legend. The stories she must have…"

Sadie's phone jingled. She made the cringey face that said it was her mother.

"Shoot, I forgot to call my mom back. Give me two minutes." She walked to the hidden side entrance, answering as she went outdoors.

Mark checked an incoming text on his phone. "I can't get over how Per kept this huge secret from us for, like, ever."

"If there's one person who could, it's Per." Joan raised her eyebrows at Perry. "I can't get over how his secret best friend is a former Superhero."

"She's far removed from that life," Perry said.

"But you're not. She really just looked the other way?"

"We have an unspoken rule not to talk about it." He hesitated for a moment. "Obviously I didn't tell you while we were active in the life. Now you might understand, being on the other side."

"Not really," Joan said.

"She wants a normal life, too."

Joan and Mark shook their heads at each other. "Still so weird," Mark said.

Another text popped up on his phone—a cartoon GIF of thin noodles dangling from chopsticks. Hmm. Mark's favorite comfort food was beef lo mein.

"Is Zee offering to buy you dinner?" Joan asked.

He shoved his phone out of her sightline. "It's nothing."

To Perry, she said, "I guess we can't give you guff, considering Mark's flirting with an actual—"

"Shut up, you're the worst."

"—currently active Super."

"What if it's Kade?" Mark said.

"It's not Kade."

"It could be. He texts me about food. He loves to eat."

Perry planted a hand on his hip. "Texting with *two* Supers? That's double my record."

Joan cackled at his rare participation in teasing. She rubbed at the itchy scab under her eye. Then her phone dinged with a SuperWatch emergency alert.

A live video notification. Another one. Several more. They flooded her lock screen.

QUAKE!

Holy @*$&% Big Quake

Big quake and villains!!!

"Shit." She clicked on one, waving Mark and Perry over.

The live feed showed the trio of new Villains behind a person completely covered in an updated version of Big Quake's brown-and-black getup. His head was obscured by a full mask.

"...came back to Vector City to finish what I started," he was saying. "But then I realized there's a lot more I can do."

He turned and flexed his hands toward the grass at the foot of a hill. The earth rumbled and shook and broke apart in large pieces. Whoever was videoing raised their phone to show the tall cell tower at the top.

People screamed and ran in the opposite direction. The hill gyrated, making the tall metal structure sway precariously.

Quake peered over one shoulder to say, "Let's see how you do without your precious internet."

He swung his arms and tensed his hands. A terrible groaning

metallic sound melded with the crumbling of the concrete base. Mark and Perry swore, and—

"Sadie!" Joan shoved her phone at her brother and ran to the side entrance.

She slammed the door open and frantically searched the gangway between warehouses. Her heart leaped spying Sadie huddled against the cement wall, mouth open as she stared at her phone.

Joan raced over and grabbed her arm. "Get inside!"

Sadie stumbled but found her footing. "That looks like somewhere north of here."

"Sadie!" her mom shouted through the phone. "Are you still there?"

"I'm here. I'm okay." She followed Joan into the warehouse.

"What is going on in that awful city?"

Sadie mumbled something to her mother. Possibly said it loudly, but Joan couldn't hear anything over the roar of fire and fear in her ears. She wrapped Sadie in her arms and held tight.

Sadie slipped her phone from between them so they could watch the cell tower keel over onto a series of power lines. Booming crashes and pops sounded in the distance.

The live feed went dead.

So did Sadie's phone call.

"Damn it." She pushed away from Joan and tried to call her mother back. "She's gonna have a coronary."

Joan held her by the shoulders, inspecting for any hint of harm. "Are you okay?"

"I'm fine. Ow, you're burning up."

She quickly removed her hands. Her fire was at the surface, ready to go.

Mark held his phone high, trying to get reception. "Looks like the destruction and chaos has begun."

"The Supers wasted too much time." Perry set his mouth in a grim line.

Joan checked Sadie one more time—she was fine, but fuck, not being with her during an attack had been terrifying. "The other Villains didn't help him," Joan noted. "It doesn't look like he needs their help to destroy shit."

"He might need it for larger-scale things," Mark said.

She sucked in an unsteady breath, willing the fire to subside. She shook out her hands and wandered back and forth. The monthly reports sat on the table. How were they supposed to focus on the price of potatoes when the city was in serious trouble?

What were her food truck friends thinking right now? They had to be scared for their families, for their businesses... Or was this just another adjustment they had to get used to? It must be so weird being a norm. She had one foot in that world and hated all the uncertainty.

Mark wiggled his phone. "I'm getting an extremely weak signal."

Sadie attempted to get back on SuperWatch, gave up, then called her mom back. "I'm okay," she said. "Don't worry. I'm with Joanie. She doesn't let anything bad happen to me."

Joan took Sadie's free hand and kissed it. Sadie smiled, but it didn't reach her eyes. She drew her hand back and whispered, "Still too hot" away from the phone.

"Sorry," Joan whispered back.

She left Sadie to fruitlessly assure her mother of her safety and went to pester Perry. He leaned his ass against the table, hands braced on either side.

She glanced at his agenda. The last item on the list was—ugh. *Consult with Sadie about Knollwood Village property.*

They had to get this under control so they could go back to food trucks and cafés and all the good things they were building for themselves.

"We need to do something," Joan said. "You have to call her, Per."

He sighed, his wind energy ruffling his suit jacket. "I know."

CHAPTER 12

Sadie tried not to spin in a circle to take in the large lobby at Superhero headquarters. She'd always wondered what it looked like behind the concrete arches. She never thought she'd be allowed inside with her ex-Villain girlfriend, but here they were, waiting for the arrival of Amazing Woman.

The design was Art Deco meets fortress: bold rectangular shapes, a large crystal chandelier, pale blue walls, high windows to let in light but not prying eyes. Even the broad marble staircase said both opulence and fortification. It smelled cold, like when Mark used his icy abilities.

Joan reached for her hand so they could follow Ward upstairs. Sadie had never actually met him before he'd let them into the garage. He was polite but clearly frazzled and distracted.

"Are your powers being suppressed?" she murmured to Joan.

"Yup." She was also distracted by all the things.

For the past twenty-four hours, Joan had stuck to her like glue. Industrial strength, could adhere a bumper to a car glue. Last night, Sadie had not-so-jokingly asked permission to use the bathroom alone in their own home. It didn't help that Joan had a terrible nightmare about Sadie being in danger and not being able to get to her.

She adjusted the handles of the rainbow-striped tote hanging on her shoulder. Joan had said she wanted Sadie there to provide better coffee, but everyone knew it was to keep her safe. Which was thoughtful, and she wouldn't have gotten the opportunity to observe a Superhero meeting otherwise—another dream come true. Still, it'd be nice to have a say in it rather than someone else deciding what was best for her.

At the top of the staircase, Ward held out a hand at a huge painting of Flight with his fists on his waist, red cape flapping. "This is our Gallery of Heroes."

Opulent portraits ran the full length of the second floor. The current Supers were in the middle. As they headed to the left, they passed a painting of Atomic Man looking off in the distance in his blue-and-red ensemble. Stretch Boy's noodle-y arms were extended like he was protecting Vector City. The were all classic oil on canvas, like something in an old manor home.

"I think we finally found art Perry won't want to steal," Sadie said.

Joan cracked a small smile. Her fingers tightened around Sadie's as Ward led them into a pretty nondescript conference room. Mark and Perry were already there, standing by a credenza with a coffeemaker, a selection of bottled drinks, and trays of Mexican food. Kade was busy taking a huge bite out of a burrito. Darlene and Otis toyed with a touchscreen TV.

Wow. This was surreal. She'd seen all of them at the food truck, but this was different. This was Lunk, Catch and Flight. Even in their civilian clothes, they were Superheroes.

Otis tapped the red-and-yellow SuperWatch icon to no avail. Shortly after the cell tower went down yesterday, Squawk took a chunk out of the building that housed SuperWatch's servers at their corporate campus. The app was down not just in Vector City, but all across the country.

"Now we're being blamed for this," Otis grumbled, waving at the screen.

Kade noticed the newcomers and grinned. "Hi, Sadie."

"Hi, Kade. Er, Lunk? I'm not sure what I'm supposed to call you here."

"Whatever you want. Just don't call me late for dinner."

She laughed at how goofy he was. The huge Hero with the friendly baritone was a golden retriever in human form.

Darlene narrowed her eyes at Sadie and Joan. She didn't think she'd ever seen Darlene smile. Catch did when justice prevailed or she was dealing with children, but Darlene…did not.

On the flip side, Mark was jazzed about this meeting. "It's a big day," he said, doing a little butt-wiggling dance.

Sadie untangled her hand from Joan's and went to Perry. He looked his usual calm, cool and collected, but she asked anyway, "Are you nervous or excited for this?"

"This isn't going to give anyone what they want," Perry said.

She didn't know what he'd said to make Amazing Gus agree to come (she was thinking of her as Amazing Gus). He kept insisting it wasn't a magic solution.

Ward shoved his tablet under his arm and struggled to organize the plates and silverware. "Mr. Flight, are you sure you don't want me to wait downstairs to escort Ms. Amazing Woman?"

"She still has access," Otis said. "Get your laptop and take good notes. Every suggestion."

The sidekick glanced between his handful of spoons and the open laptop on the table.

"Can I lend you a hand?" Sadie said. "I brought freshly ground coffee. Food and beverage is what I do best."

"Oh thank god," Ward breathed with heavy relief. "I mean, thank you. That would be a big help." He leaned in and added, "There are so many people in these meetings now."

"I'm a temporary sidekick," she joked. Her heart fluttered. *Sidekick Sadie.*

She set her tote bag on the floor and pulled out the Brazilian blend Perry had turned her onto. Grinding the coffee beans that morning had been a calming ritual during all this upheaval.

The door opened fully, and everyone turned. It was Zee in their cream-colored Race bodysuit minus the facemask.

They limped into the room with a grimace. "Tell me you're turning power blocking on next time. I got halfway inside and my speed cut out. I almost fell on my head."

Mark snorted, though his eyes darkened to a warm aquamarine. Like his sister, his eyes always gave him away. He was into Zee.

Otis moved over to the table. "Did you find any evidence of where they could be hiding out?"

"No." Zee rubbed their shin.

"Wow," Mark said to the other Supers. "You have one whole Superhero out there while the rest of you are huddled inside."

Oh yeah, he was definitely into Zee.

Crossing her arms, Darlene said, "We are formulating a proper plan."

Mark dipped a tortilla chip in salsa. "Jesus, I thought Perry liked meetings. You lot take the cake."

"We need to be prepared. Each one of us has our role to execute."

"Use your superpowers," Joan said. "Stop the bad guys. It's not that hard."

"I couldn't agree more," came from the doorway.

There stood Amazing Woman—*the* Amazing Woman! Well, an older white woman with ash-blonde hair falling past her shoulders. Her loose jeans and fisherman's sweater said *comfort*.

"Hello, Gus," Otis said. "Been a long time."

Amazing Gus's gaze swept over the room, pausing for a second on Perry.

Darlene squared her shoulders and marched over with a nervous smile (so she did actually smile). "Thank you for coming. I'm Catch. You may recall we met once many years ago."

"I remember you." Gus stared down at the hand Darlene had thrust out but didn't take it.

Kade leaned forward, mouth slightly agape. "You look exactly the same. That's…"

"Amazing?" Gus raised one sandy eyebrow. "Not having to use my energy to block bullets and laser eyes has resulted in me aging rather slowly these days."

Her weary voice somewhat gave away her age, but wow. She really did look a solid thirty years younger.

Zee and Kade introduced themselves. Amazing Gus was similarly disinterested.

Mark grinned and pointed at himself and Joanie. "We're Mark and Joan. It's so weird to meet you. Perry never mentioned your *long friendship.*"

The way he drew out those last words made Perry scowl at him.

Gus arched her eyebrows, and her lips quirked. "So you're the twins."

"Hi," Joan said. "It's nice to finally—"

"I thought you'd be taller."

"Uh, no, we're pretty average."

Her gaze brushed past Ward, then Sadie. Then she turned to Otis and said, "Is this it?"

"Aura is also assisting us from Destine," Otis said.

"Destine? The city that broke itself with robots?"

"The other cities are, uh, dealing with their own issues."

Gus pursed her lips. "Nice to see things haven't changed. If you want the glory, you let someone else take the brunt of the assault."

Ward inched his way toward her. "Ms. Amazing Woman, I'm such a big fan. I'm Ward. May I offer you—"

"Are you the sidekick?"

"I am, ma'am."

"Then I'm sorry for you. I'm sure your life is taxing, always being at their beck and call. We went through dozens of you in my time."

Ward's eyes widened behind his glasses. "Dozens?"

Gus focused her attention on Sadie. "Who are you?"

Her heart skipped a beat. Gus was fairly petite, but her commanding presence was a little intimidating. "I'm Sadie."

"What do you do?"

She held up the Brazilian blend. "I brought the coffee."

"Sadie's here with me," Joan said.

Gus snorted. "You're the girlfriend." To Otis, she said, "You'll let anyone in here these days."

Uhh… Sadie just stood there. She lowered the coffee, looking to Perry. This was the woman he was protecting? She didn't need protection from anyone or anything.

Joan stepped closer. "Sadie's been involved since some Villains kidnapped her."

"Oh, yes. I heard about that." Gus walked to the conference table. "Sidekick?"

"Ward," Ward prompted.

"I need a Diet Zap Cola and a large pad of paper."

Ward exchanged a horrified glance with Otis. "I told you to get Diet Zap," Otis gritted through his teeth.

"They don't make it anymore," Ward said. "I'm so sorry, ma'am. They stopped manufacturing all Zap Cola some time ago."

Sitting in one of the rolling chairs, Gus said, "Is that so? Well then, iced tea will do."

Perry sent the twins an *I told you so* look and deliberately took a seat several away from Gus. She was, uh, definitely opinionated. Like Sadie's grandma, finding fault in nitpicky ways.

"When did they stop making Diet Zap?" Gus asked no one in particular.

"About ten years ago, ma'am," Ward said, snagging a bottle of black tea. "It caused several young people to have seizures."

"Ah. Caffeine has no effect on me. Nor alcohol. Nor anything."

Sadie smiled and offered, "I'm about to make a fresh pot of coffee. It's a Brazilian blend."

"I didn't come here for teatime," Gus said. "Tell me what's been happening."

Apparently, she only likes Brazilian men.

Otis filled her in on the situation while everyone else sat and Sadie started to—

Oops, she needed water for the coffeemaker. There was a pitcher of cucumber water, but that would be gross to use. Ward had taken up post at his laptop after getting Gus a legal pad and pen, so she couldn't ask him for help.

She subtly caught Joan's eye, wiggled the bag of coffee, pointed to the pot and mouthed, "*Water?*"

Joan shrugged, then waved like *Just leave it.* Then beckoned Sadie over to the table. Wait, she could actually partake? Sit in on a meeting of superpowered minds?

Hell yes!

She discreetly slid into the chair next to Joan's.

Gus crossed her arms and leaned back. "What have you done to stop them?" she asked.

"We've fought several times with Ether, Squawk and Prowl," Darlene said.

"Prowl gets off on that," Joan said.

"But what have you *done*? Set a trap? Shaken down their associates?"

"I was hoping they would be of help." Darlene nodded at the former Villains. "They conveniently know very little."

"Is Otis tossing you into the frontlines? There was a time I was you, the woman with the most power. They liked to send me in first to get shot at, run over, fight whoever came my way. Then they would swoop in and take the credit."

Darlene gave a decisive headshake. "I'm treated as an equal."

Gus looked at Zee. "I hope you all are."

Zee seemed kind of surprised but pleased at her acknowledgment.

"Times have changed, Gus," Otis said.

"But threats remain a constant." Gus wrote something on

her legal pad. "Big Quake thrives on power. No better way for him to exert his control than by taking down the city that got rid of all its Villains. Have people see who's *really* in charge."

"Where do you think he'll strike next?" Zee said. "He's taken out one of the main cell towers in the city. That's caused considerable service disruptions. And SuperWatch isn't up and running yet."

"Super—what? What are you talking about?"

"SuperWatch. The app. Where we do everything?"

Gus blinked at them. "Is this one of those computer things?"

"It's on your phone," Kade helpfully supplied.

"I don't use those. Nothing wrong with writing a letter."

Definite Grandma Energy coming from Gus. Sadie gave her a polite smile—she loved handwritten notes.

Darlene clasped her hands on the table. "The internet is how everything is done today. These Villains are strategically interfering with all forms of commerce, communications, medical records…"

"Hitting people where it hurts the most," Otis said.

"I imagine it's causing you a headache," said Gus.

"We rely heavily on SuperWatch."

She skewered him with a sharp glare. "You rely on a computer instead of your instincts?"

"It gives us the word on the street in real time," Kade said.

"What are your citizens saying?"

"I dunno. That's what we need SuperWatch for."

"When you talk to them," Gus said. "What do they want?"

The Heroes looked at each other, unsure. The clacking of Ward's typing stilled.

Gus exhaled a huff of air. "On your daily patrols. When you stop and talk to the people, see what they need, what their concerns are."

"They haven't done that in a long time," Perry said.

Mark laughed and said, "They never did that with us."

Darlene sneered. "What were your concerns? How many banks you could rob in one week?"

"I meant when we were living on the streets, Darlene. Because they couldn't be bothered to help us."

She didn't respond to that. Sadie set a reassuring hand on Joan's thigh and squeezed.

"If you talked to your citizens, you'd have a better idea of where to focus your energy," said Gus. "Flapping your gums at one another in here does nothing to help out there."

The smug look on Perry's face… Sadie had to cover her mouth so she didn't laugh out loud. He was very much enjoying this.

Ward held up a finger as he typed with his other hand. "Sorry, should I add that to the meeting notes?"

"No." Otis crossed his arms. "I'm sure our citizens' primary concern right now is safety."

The other Supers gave similar assessments that Ward dutifully recorded. Sadie shifted in her seat. *I'm a norm. Ask me how much the claim filing system on SuperWatch sucks.*

The meeting languished on with more of the same: Gus telling the Supers everything they were doing wrong, the Supers bumbling to explain, Mark making snide comments. How could anything get done when no one really listened?

Sadie glanced at Perry. This was probably his ultimate revenge fantasy: a former Superhero he was friends with ripping into the current ones.

Gus looked over at the Malone twins from whatever she was writing. "What are you even doing here if you're not going to contribute?"

"Free tacos," Mark said, jutting his thumb at the spread of food. "And to meet you."

"I agree with you, Gus," Joan said. "They should be out there gathering intel."

"You're not going to help?" Gus said.

"I'm not a Superhero."

"Then you're happy to let more harm come to the city?"

Joan blinked. "No, I'm just…ah…"

"We run a food truck," Mark said. "One we'd like to get back to so everything doesn't spoil while we're sitting around."

Indicating the door, Darlene said, "You can leave anytime."

Perry pushed his chair back like he was about to do just that. Good lord, this meeting was less productive and more snarky than the ones he presided over. How were the Supers so inefficient?

"I need to use the restroom," Gus said. "Sidekick, don't put that in your notes."

Ward raised his hands off the keyboard.

"Ward's all right." Mark nodded at him. "Put that in your notes. Along with you need a raise."

The sidekick stifled a smile.

Otis stood. "Why don't we take five and regroup?"

"Yes, yes." Gus eased her way out of her chair. "Enjoy the spoils of your profession. The free goods you insist upon. What local business did you rip off to get all that food?"

"We paid for it," Zee said in an irritated tone they rarely used.

"The city paid for it. Which means taxpayers bought it."

"Damn it," Mark muttered. "I knew my tax dollars were being misappropriated."

Flexing their long fingers, Zee said, "We get offered free stuff all the time. It's just given to us, even when we try to turn it down. I turn things down all the time."

They glowered at Mark as if telling him directly. Mark pretended to be all eyeroll-y.

Gus regarded Zee for a moment. "If that's the case, then maybe things have changed for the better."

Darlene stared at her lap. Kade looked confused—no, wait, upset. Well, Sadie had witnessed Lunk and Flight demanding sandwiches from the owners of a convenience store who'd just had their shop damaged—by Lunk and Flight. Maybe Zee turned things down, but the others sure didn't.

The second Gus stepped out of the room, Joan and Mark turned to Perry. "I have questions," Mark said.

"I have none at all," Joan said. "I totally get it."

"Joanie, it's like Perry's hanging out with our nana."

"A crabby, honest person who clearly has a bone to pick with..." Joan made a subtle head gesture at the Supers.

"I see it," Sadie admitted.

Perry sipped his mineral water and ignored them.

The Supers headed for the food. Mark leaned toward Perry and said, "Is she staying at your place?"

"She's going home tonight."

"Really? Just one day?"

Nodding toward the Supers, Perry said, "They're lucky they got one day."

"Can we invite her over for dinner?" Joan asked. "Mark and I can cook, we can get to know her..."

Perry swiveled his chair to look at them. "She won't want to."

"What do you want?" Sadie wondered. Surely, Perry would like to—

"You've met. That's good. Maybe when things calm down, we can revisit dinner."

"I'm gonna ask her." Joan touched Sadie's arm. "That's okay, right, if we have her over tonight?"

"Of course," Sadie said.

She got up to grab some lunch—she'd paid for it, after all. Oh, wait—the coffee.

As she worked on detaching the water reservoir, Mark not so subtly reached behind Zee to grab a plate.

"I'm serious about the freebies," Zee muttered. "It's hard to turn stuff down when someone's shoving it into your hands as a thank-you."

"Yet you seem to find a way to take it," Mark returned.

"Stop with all the digs."

"I will when your cohorts subscribe to the same theory."

Hmm. This was an area of contention between them. But

really, how could it not be? Zee was part of a group with access to limitless funds while Mark had had to live by any means necessary.

Joan sidled up beside her. "So Gus, huh?"

Sadie scrunched her eyebrows together. "I'm all for unconventional relationships, but one thing's confusing me. I see why they like each other, but why not want us to get to know her?"

"I guess it's a way for them to compartmentalize their lives."

"Perry is good at that," Sadie murmured. Like how he frequented the art museum and took his secret vacations.

Mark and Zee continued whisper-sniping at each other. The other three muttered amongst themselves. Ward looked like he wasn't sure whether to type or serve.

"Are these meetings usually this unproductive?" Sadie asked.

"Usually."

"Gus does have a point. They should listen to the people more."

"You can speak up," Joan said.

"What am I going to say that you probably haven't? Filing a claim is useless. People just want a sense of security. We want Heroes with our best interests at heart."

"Good luck with that."

It wasn't that the Supers didn't care. It just felt like Joan cared a little more. She'd spent time getting to know everyday people. She understood their struggles, their dreams and desires. She'd be a real asset if the Supers would listen to her instead of using her for her criminal background.

Joanie was the one who could turn this around.

———

Joan waited for Sadie and Ward in the doorway of a kitchen so nice, she wanted to cry. It was not a shit-tastic warehouse kitchenette, oh no. This was something that belonged in a fancy house with top-of-the-line appliances, gleaming white subway tiles, pale-gray granite countertops. She couldn't even step foot in it, she was so jealous. Mark would probably throw himself on the white-tiled floor in ecstasy and declare he lived here now.

Sadie was being her adorable, charming self, thanking Ward for his help in getting filtered water from the fridge. He was supposed to be babysitting Joan, but whatever. She wanted to catch Gus alone to invite her to dinner. Maybe away from prying eyes, she'd be more receptive.

The kitchen was on the ground floor, so she made her way up the back staircase. Near the top, she heard Darlene saying, "I've carried the advice you gave me about fighting for justice no matter the personal cost."

"Did I say that?" Gus replied.

"Yes. I assure you, I've lived my life to serve the citizens of Vector City."

"You were a child."

"It was my fifth birthday. The only thing I wanted was to meet you at the children's museum. I told you I thought I had powers the way you did." A pause, then Darlene continued, "You were the first person I shared that with."

Joan peered around the corner to see that Darlene had waylaid Gus outside the bathroom.

Gus pursed her lips. "When you came on the scene, they said you were the next Amazing Woman. A young prodigy, like I had been."

"Yes." Darlene's face lit up in a way Joan didn't think was physically possible for her. "When I was introduced to the city as the newest Hero, I thanked you for that advice and said I would carry on your legacy."

"You misunderstood me. It was a warning."

"No, it was—"

"It's a losing battle," Gus said. "The fact is, it doesn't matter what you do. There will always be bad guys to fight. The hits keep coming."

"We're here to provide justice when they do," Darlene said.

"Justice." Gus snorted. "Let me tell you something. There is no real justice. What you do will never be enough."

Darlene's jaw hung loose.

"I'm not saying it isn't important. I dedicated my life to the cause. I ended up getting blamed for everything that went wrong. The others made me the scapegoat for why Big Quake got away. The mayor forced my retirement. That was the thanks I got for the sacrifice."

That explains a few things.

"I... I'm sorry that happened to you." Darlene awkwardly patted Gus's shoulder. "It shouldn't have. You were a true hero. You sacrificed for the greater good."

"That's what a hero does."

"That's what I will continue to do."

"Just be ready for the backlash when it comes. Because it will come."

Gus brushed past Darlene. Darlene's body deflated. Now it made sense why she was so hell-bent on justice. And why Gus's approval meant so much to her.

Hurried footsteps echoed from downstairs. Ward must've realized Joan was gone.

She stepped into the hallway. Darlene met her eyes, and for a split second, there was raw humanity in them. Then she looked embarrassed.

"It sucks when your heroes let you down, doesn't it?" Joan said.

The Super's face hardened. She stood up straight and tall once more. "What would you know about that?" she said, crossing her arms.

"There was a time I thought the good guys might be able to help me."

Darlene spluttered a few times. "You're the reason we need to protect the city. You and your kind, Villain."

She turned on her heel and marched toward the conference room.

Joan wanted to be mad, but honestly, she kind of got Darlene. And Gus. A lot of weight had been put on their shoulders to live up to unreasonable expectations. Extraordinary Supers who were supposed to save the city, time and time again. Catch had been touted as "the next Amazing Woman." At the rate she was going, that'd be a sadly fulfilled prophecy of burnout.

Darlene had taken the path of doing what she thought was right, pursuing justice at all costs. Joan had rebelled against that for a long time. But now…

As gross as it sounded, maybe a little bit of justice needed to prevail in Vector City.

CHAPTER 13

The sun tried peeking through the gray clouds over Knollwood Village. Sadie squinted up at the sky, sending positive vibes for a few rays to break through.

After yesterday's meeting, Joanie and Mark had decided to work out this morning and open the truck a bit late. They probably had some pent-up fire and ice to get rid of, considering not much got accomplished other than Gus convincing the Supers to patrol more "boots on the ground" before declaring she wanted to head home before it got too late. She did give them some of Quake's old hangout spots and contacts, so that was something.

The lunchtime crowd was starting to mill about Hampton Street, the main drag of the mostly residential area. Sadie hadn't gotten her eyebrows tinted in forever, so she'd convinced Joan to let her go it alone for a little self-care. What else was she gonna do with unexpected time off but visit the brow bar that could match her dyed hair perfectly? Even if it meant trekking across the river.

She rubbed the nape of her neck under Joanie's red-and-black flannel. Usually she couldn't borrow anything because, hello, she had boobs and hips Joanie did not. But this was a looser fit shirt, and it was snuggly and had a hint of citrusy ginger on it.

There hadn't been any reported Villain activity, which in itself was Villain activity. Keeping everyone on edge about when and where the next strike would occur. SuperWatch was up and running again, though internet access continued to be spotty.

Sadie smiled at a woman in a forest-green hijab pushing a stroller with a snoozing young kid tucked inside. She stepped around two men each holding a longhaired dachshund and cooing about how cute their babies looked after getting groomed. Knollwood Village was where queer folks settled down to start a family—especially if it was of the four-legged variety.

The Supers should've been in places like this, seeing how people really lived. You couldn't argue with Gus's old-school thoughts on that.

Amazing Gus was officially weird. But weird like Perry in that *I refuse to talk about things I don't want to talk about* way. Maybe Joanie was right that it was a coping mechanism to compartmentalize their lives. A trauma response to all they'd been through.

Sadie crossed a side street to get to the bus stop. She passed the florist that had been there forever. As long as she was here, might as well check out that retail space Perry had recommended. Scratch it off the list.

The brown-brick building had a bright-blue For Lease sign in one of the wide windows. Hadn't this been an ice cream parlor when she'd lived here? Or a tearoom?

She peeked through the glass door at the empty unit. A long counter along the wall to the right, ample space for tables and chairs, a place for a nook in the back that'd be perfect for a couch...

Her heartbeat quickened. The too-white color scheme didn't work with the exposed brick walls. With warm earth tones and pops of color, this could be really cozy.

She shielded her eyes to stare at the counter. An image flashed in her mind of herself standing behind it, handing a to-go cup to a customer. And there was a case of fresh bakery goods. And she was smiling—grinning and happy because this was *hers*.

She stepped back and studied the outdoor space. Two small

tables could easily fit on both sides of the door. And a doggie station with a little container of treats and a large water bowl for hot summer days. She could make a super-cute open/closed sign to hang in the door. And oh, the kitschy sayings she could write on a sandwich board to draw customers in.

And this street! Decent foot traffic. Car traffic that was busy but not hectic. Joanie and Mark could park Hot and Cold in front and easily make a killing. Perry could open an art gallery nearby.

Tears pooled in her eyes. This was Sadie's Café.

Elation surged through her chest, followed by reality squashing it down. This was too perfect a location. The rent had to be ridiculous. What was the cost of everything now that Quake was back?

She shook her head, wiping at her eyes, and forced her feet to move. Then stopped and turned.

Sunlight burst through the clouds, brightening the whole street. Highlighting the perfect place she'd been dreaming of for years and years.

Don't discount it, Sadie.

She had financial backers ready to invest. Maybe nobody would want to start a new business during heightened Villain activity. Maybe she could get a good deal. Perry could negotiate for her—he'd probably really enjoy that. And Joanie would support her every step of the way. Give her reassuring hugs when things got hard, the way Sadie did with Hot and Cold.

Do it. Call to get more information.

Just a phone call. Gather data. Laugh when the landlord or realtor or whoever told her the exorbitant cost.

She walked back to the—well, to Sadie's Café. Dialed the number on the sign before she lost her nerve.

Voicemail kicked in for a woman named Lorraine at the management company. "Uh, hi. Hello. My name is Sadie Eagan. I'm calling to inquire about the retail space available in Knollwood Village. The—" *Don't say super cute, that sounds unprofes-*

sional. "—space at 1007 North Hampton. It looks like it would meet the needs for my current project."

There, that was profesh.

Then she grinned and couldn't help gushing, "Okay, I know this sounds some kind of way, but this is exactly what I've been looking for. I think it would fit my needs for a coffeehouse I've been wanting to open for years. I'd love to get more information from you, and possibly schedule a tour."

She left her phone number, then said, "I look forward to hearing from you."

She ended the call and squealed, dancing in a little circle. *You did it! Way to go!*

It probably wouldn't amount to anything, but...

No, she had to stay positive on this one. This was it. This was Sadie's Café, and she had to push past her fear. She had the support to get through it.

Joan had been brave enough to start a whole new life, and was brave every time she interacted with the Supers.

Time for Sadie to be brave, too.

Joan didn't think she'd ever been to Vector City Coffee without Sadie there. But Sadie was working with Mark that afternoon to keep their food truck going. Trying to connect with Greta had been hit and miss. Grets had picked this day and time and place because it was—as she put it—neutral ground.

She paused outside the entrance to make sure her phone was silenced. Zee had been texting about helping them gain access to some of the seedier spots of the city. There had been a flurry of Villain activity last night. Squawk had shattered almost every window at City Hall, and Ether basically shut down the airport with funky skies.

Mark was most likely going to help Zee out, even though Joan had told him it was a bad idea. Anyone recognizing him would be no bueno.

No one was listening to her lately. The Supers just wanted Villain intel. Perry was still being weird and cagey about why Gus wouldn't stay for dinner. That was something to dig into another day.

Sadie had gone all the way to the Village without her yesterday. It was great that she was excited about finding a perfect location for her café, so Joan had to bite her tongue and not freak out. And then bite her tongue again when Sadie mentioned this morning that Greta actually left the other night because she was on to Joan's Super meeting.

She knew why Sadie hadn't told her, even before Sadie explained. The ex-Villain and thief needed one another.

Joan entered to the familiar scent of coffee grounds and quiet indie music. She reached to pull off sunglasses she wasn't wearing, ever the creature of habit.

Greta was chatting with Nyah and Amit at a small table against the wall. "Well, well, well," Amit said. "Look what the cat dragged in."

More like the cat burglar. "Hey, Amit. Hi, Nyah."

"Hey, stranger," Nyah teased. "What, your girlfriend stops working here and you don't come by anymore?"

"Terrible, I know." Joan gave Greta a small smile. "Hey."

"I ordered for you," Greta said. That meant she wasn't planning on staying long.

"Thanks." Joan slid into the metal chair across from her friend. "What's new at VCC?"

Amit nodded toward the front. "We still have all our windows."

"That is novel," Joan joked. She snagged the paper cup with *Kick Me Up* written on it. "Ah, my favorite."

She took a sip. Not as good as when Sadie made them, but still a banger with the cayenne pepper kick.

They chitchatted for a few minutes until Amit and Nyah went

back to work. "Nice scar," Greta said, gesturing at Joan's right eye.

"Gift from Ricki."

Greta's upper lip curled. "You shouldn't have messed with her."

"I tried not to."

"You have to get to the truck soon."

"I have time. We haven't hung out in forever."

"You haven't been around. What with spending so much time with your new pals."

Joan conceded that with a slow nod. "I owe you an explanation."

"Not really. Sadie explained it just fine."

"We don't have a choice. We're basically on permanent probation."

Greta tapped her fingertips on her coffee cup. "At what point will it go from a necessity to something you want to do?"

"Hopefully never."

"You don't hope that."

After glancing over both shoulders, Joan leaned in and said, "It sucks. I just want to be at Hot and Cold. This crap keeps dragging me away from it."

"And keeping you from me."

"I won't let that happen."

Her oldest friend looked at her with rare sadness in her dark eyes. "If you work with them, I can't be around you anymore."

"Grets—"

"It's not safe. I met you here because I also come here to see Nyah and Amit. It shouldn't raise suspicion."

"They're not watching every move I make," Joan said.

"They're at your food truck. If Mark's hanging out with Zee, it's only a matter of time before they turn up at your place."

"Maybe if either one of you let me know before you drop by unannounced…"

"I have to look out for my own ass," Greta said.

Joan nodded in understanding. Greta was a lone wolf—always had been, probably always would be. While they'd both been kicked out as teenagers, Joan had joined Team Villain. Even when things weren't great with Melvin or Ethel or Irving, she'd always had Mark and Perry.

"I get it," she said. "But this is temporary. Once we get rid of these new Villains—"

"Did you just hear yourself?" Greta snapped. "You're trying to get rid of Villains? In case you forgot—"

"I know that sounds shitty. But Quake? These assholes who want to destroy everything? Nobody wants that."

Greta's nostrils flared. She crossed her arms, gripping her biceps through her black leather jacket. "I told you about them for *your* benefit, not the Supers'."

"I know, and I didn't give up my source." Joan's fire bubbled under her skin in irritation.

"You see how I can't trust that something won't get traced back to me."

"I will never let anything happen to you."

"Even if that means lying to my face and disappearing on me?"

"You're the one who disappeared first," Joan pointed out.

"When you worked with Superheroes to take out three members of your found family."

"I never really thought of them as family. You know that."

Greta made her smarmy *Yeah, right* face that was so damn annoying.

"Sadie said she told you how hurt I was," Joan said.

"*You* were hurt?" Greta scoffed. "I'm losing my only true friend, but *you're* hurt."

"That's not fair. You know the situation. I'm doing the best I can."

"You're doing what's best for you."

Joan felt the angry sparks glinting in her eyes. "That's literally what you're doing."

"Mine is survival."

"*Mine* is survival."

"No, yours is wanting your sweet girlfriend and your cozied-up apartment and—"

"I'm having nightmares about what I did, okay?" Joan spat. "Does that make you happy?"

"No."

"I feel like shit about it. But you know what? I don't regret it. If that means taking a step back for a while, fine."

Tense silence settled between them. This was their relationship: everything was flowers and sunshine, then something happened and they got pissed at each other and didn't talk for a while. Still, it was their friendship on the line this time. That had never truly wavered.

Greta took a sip of her half-caf-whatever-the-fuck-complicated drink she'd ordered. She set her cup down. "Sorry you're having nightmares," she said in a calmer tone.

"I'm waking Sadie up. That's the worst part."

"What are they about?"

"Melvin and them yelling at me. Sometimes they have Sadie and I can't get to her."

"You're afraid that'll happen again."

"Every day," Joan murmured.

"You're a mess."

She met Greta's eyes, and they both laughed lightly. "I really am."

They quieted again as someone passed en route to the restrooms. Greta seemed wistful. Well, as wistful as Grets could get. She slid her cup off the table and stood. "Take care," she said.

"You, too." Joan touched her arm before she could breeze out the door, but Greta was already focused onward.

Her heart sank. Maybe this was just another speedbump. Or maybe it really was goodbye.

Nyah paused with a plastic bin filled with dirty dishes. "Did she take off?"

"Yeah."

"She does that."

Joan heaved a heavy sigh. "Yeah."

CHAPTER 14

Hot and Cold rocked this sunny Saturday afternoon. Friendship Park was playing host to a gathering of LARPers for a medieval fantasy card game. A lot of them were giving their spectacular pseudonyms, which was both fun and totally relatable for Joan and Mark (though with far more elf ears than in real-life villainy).

Joan leaned out the service window and called, "Order for Sir Maximilian Congrave, Lord Chancellor of Berntable."

"Berntableux!" several people called back.

"Apologies, my gentlefolk." She handed the two sandwiches to a white dude with a bushy brown beard and long maroon robe trimmed in fake fur.

Sadie wished him well as she passed an order ticket through the window. "This is the greatest day ever. A November Rain and truffle fries for Squire Finster Magentus."

"We're inviting all these people to the grand opening of Sadie's Café."

A bright, beautiful smile spread across her face. "I can't wait 'til Monday."

Joan smiled back before adding the ticket to the end of the row of metal clips. Sadie had an appointment to see the Knollwood Village property Monday afternoon. Joan couldn't wait to go with and tell her to sign on the dotted line if it really was the perfect spot. Her investors were ready for Sadie's Café.

"November Rain, Lord Markington," Joan said.

"Heard, Lady Joanie of Sparkland."

"I hope the other trucks are enjoying this."

"I'm sure they're getting a kick out of it. Except that artisanal wannabe with the ice cream truck."

"The *creamed dairy experience*," Joan drawled in a poor imitation of that irritating woman's voice.

They worked down the line of orders. She held out a cup of hot and spicy cider at the same time Mark grabbed the last order. "Squire Finster Magentus, your order doth be ready," he said. His grin grew at the thin blond guy in a long green tunic and tights.

Sadie climbed aboard through the side entry. She set the tablet down and grabbed her water bottle. "You guys need anything?"

"We're good," Joan said, scraping down the flat-top.

Mark finished flirting and leaned back. "I'd Finster his Magentus," he murmured.

After gulping down some water, Sadie said, "LARPers are the best. I love it when people are unapologetic for what they love. Like Nyah and Amit with gaming."

Joan forced a smile, her heart giving a tight pinch. *Like Greta with gaming.*

Sadie picked up on that and rubbed her back. "Sorry, honey. I didn't mean to bring that up."

"It's okay."

"I think you two will work things out."

"We usually do," Joan said, though she honestly wasn't sure this time.

Several people shouted outside. Man, they were really getting into it. "Must be time for another swordfight," Joan mused.

"Sounds like someone's been challenged," Sadie said.

A few more people shouted. Then there was a scream. And then a *real* scream.

"What the hell?" Mark peered out the window.

Joan scraped the burnt bits into the trash. The truck rocked a bit. "What are they doing out there?"

"Uh, I don't think this is part of the… Nope, that is not… *Shit.*"

She joined him to look out at the LARPers standing stock-still. They collectively watched someone leap onto a sturdy tree branch. *Prowl.*

She cackled menacingly. "Do you think you're tough with your plastic swords? Who wants to fight me to prove it?"

Someone must've said something because she dove down, claws first, and landed on a guy dressed in royal finery. The people around them screamed, dropped their fake weapons, and ran like hell.

Sadie gripped Joan's arm. Mark gripped the edge of the steel countertop. Joan searched the area for more activity.

Squawk's piercing yowl reverberated across the park. Joan pulled Sadie and Mark down to the floor. The truck rocked again. Oh, no.

"Is the ground moving?" Mark said.

"If Quake is here…" Sadie stared at Joan, eyes wide with concern.

SuperWatch alerts went off on their phones. At least the Supers would be made aware and could do something about this.

Her fire roared to the surface. Mark made a fist, ice crystals shimmering in his eyes.

A door banged open near the truck. Wren and Beth-Ann yelled to each other about locking their doors.

Powered by Plants. And Cajun Soul was parked to the north. Their friends. Those glorious nerds out there playing hero. They were all in harm's way. Shit.

"I can't just sit here," Joan said, taking her ballcap off.

Mark stood with her. "Me either."

Sadie got up, but Joan halted her. "Stay here."

"People need help," she said. "I'm going with you."

Joan started to tell her no, but Squawk screamed again. They pulled their aprons off while waiting for their ears to stop ringing.

She pushed through the back door into pure mayhem: the good gentlefolk running everywhere. A few truly brave knights trying to fight with Prowl. People lying around Squawk curled into balls, holding their heads in agony.

Quake stood in the middle of the field, palms facing the grass, making everything wobbly.

Dread mixed with the angry fire pinging around Joan's body.

A light blur knocked Quake over. Race stopped and said something to him. Flight divebombed Squawk but got blasted back with a shriek.

"There's Lunk," Sadie said, pointing to the left. He was trying to muscle his way through the horde of onlookers too stunned to move.

The crowd around the food trucks didn't know which way to go. Morris and Tenia furiously tried to shut their metal awning.

"We have to help these people," Joan said. Pandemonium created more potential for danger. "Sadie, get them out of the park."

Sadie nodded and waved her arms toward the street. "Everyone get out of the park!" she shouted.

She moved to a group of frightened LARPers and guided them behind Hot and Cold to safety.

Catch ran across the grass, throwing herself on top of Squawk. Apparently using Lunk's strength by how he dropped. Lunk tried to grab Prowl, only Prowl climbed up on his shoulders and batted at his face.

Quake moved the earth around him, making Zee tumble. No doubt he wanted to destroy the park created in the wake of his previous misdeeds.

"It's a fucking free-for-all," Joan seethed.

"They're not working together." Mark shook his head in short, jerky movements.

Her fire roiled, frustrated at not being released. "What can we do? We don't have our bodysuits."

"Fuck if I know."

A huge *kaboom* crashed, and a compact car went flying end-over-end into the park. A big dude in orange jumped on top of it roaring, "*The* Smash is back!"

"What the fuck?" Mark said. "They caught that guy."

Flight soared over the Villain, his face saying the same thing. "How did you…?"

"I got broked out on the way to jail!" Smash bellowed with glee.

Quake laughed loudly. "For the right price, you can pay prison transporters to do just about anything."

This was another ring of hell. Flight flew toward Smash, but he held his ground and tossed Flight aside like a ragdoll. Panic flared up as Joan searched for—

"I'm back here!" Sadie called.

Joan turned to blessedly find Sadie in the opposite direction. She ushered a terrified mom and kids quickly down the sidewalk.

"Be careful!" Joan called back.

She wanted to go to her, but there was so much madness. And Sadie was capable and smart and this wasn't her first rodeo.

Lunk tripped on discarded shields and swords. Prowl nimbly hopped off him as he went down hard.

Zee got up and prepared to run. Quake stomped on the ground and sent them rolling to the side.

Catch was close enough that if Joan could get to her, she could give her some firepower. Only Catch was focused on keeping Squawk from opening his mouth.

Through the chaos and the noise, a moment of stillness settled between Joan and Mark. He met her eyes, and they knew what they had to do. No hiding anymore, no pretending. This was their fight.

A glint of silver caught in the sunlight. A Viking-style helmet lying on the grass. She tugged Mark's arm and hurried over to it, plopping it on her brother's head. The long metal piece in the center covered a large portion of his face.

Joan scanned the discarded items and found a heavy, hooded

black cape. She whipped it on and pulled the hood as low as it would go.

Mark tossed a short purple jacket on. He quirked his lips and shrugged. "Goodbye, food truck."

They ran headfirst into the melee.

Mark threw a hunk of ice at Quake. Joan held her arm out and shot a fireball at Prowl. "Get out of here!" she shouted.

Prowl recovered quickly, realized Joan was winding up with another flame, and laughed. "Is that who I think it is?"

"I told you not to mess with my city." Joan blasted her, making people scream.

The Villain regained her footing and hopped onto one of those catapult contraptions. "You expect me to take you seriously dressed like that?"

"Leave these people alone."

"Or what? You'll cast a spell on me?"

A large fissure broke through the grass, zigzagging down the length of the park. Quake was the real problem here.

Lunk grabbed Prowl from behind, who promptly slithered out of his grasp. As they tussled, Joan raced along the cracking earth, directing a steady flame at Quake's chest. Quake stomped twice. The ground shimmied so hard, she stumbled.

Prowl yelled something, but Joan was focused on the man in brown and black. Mark jumped over a crack and used both hands to bathe Quake in sharp ice. Quake raised several large chunks of dirt to block the shards.

"Who the hell are you?" he said from behind the wall of earth. "The delinquent Villains?"

"Your worst nightmare, pal," Mark said, spraying ice at Quake's feet. Quake simply crumbled it with a wave of his hand. Then the chunks of dirt flew toward Joan and Mark. They sprang out of the way in the nick of time.

"I'm your nightmare, snow boy."

Joan tugged at the hood to keep it on her head. Mark got

distracted by something—Zee on all fours in obvious pain but trying to get up.

Quake looked past them, nodding and smiling. He gestured toward the street and said, "Does that belong to you?"

Joan did a quick double-take. Something was— Some*one* was standing on top of Hot and Cold.

Smash.

Prowl leaned over Lunk's shoulder and cupped her hands around her mouth. "That's the one."

Smash gathered his strength and jumped high.

"No!" ripped from Joan's throat.

Smash came down hard on the roof, collapsing the middle of the truck straight to the ground.

"Oh god, no!" Mark moaned.

Evil laughter echoed out of Prowl and Quake. "Oopsie," Prowl crowed in delight.

Smash punched through the sides, sending bread and condiments flying. He wrenched the hood off the grill and lobbed it onto the sidewalk. The fryers would spill hot oil everywhere, and—

"Watch the propane tank!" Joan yelled.

"What's that?" Smash punched through the metal shelves. Paper cups and trays spilled out.

"Something on the back that will blow you up." And everyone and everything around him.

"Oh, shit." Zee pushed off the ground and sped over to put a stop to the smashing.

Too late. Hot and Cold was… Their dream was…

"I didn't mean *Goodbye, food truck* literally," Mark cried.

Joan stared dumbstruck at the twisted pile of metal that just minutes ago was the source of so much joy.

"That's my friends' food truck, you jerk!" Kade-as-Lunk swung at Prowl, who used his thick arm as leverage to swing from. She did a backflip and flip-flopped away. He chased in hot pursuit.

Zee managed to speed around Smash and disorient him, but they were clearly injured. Where the hell was Flight?

Fury engulfed Joan. Fire glowing in her eyes, hot enough to smoke through her clothes fury. She fisted her hands and turned back to Quake. Flight hovered above him as Quake battered the Super with rocks.

"Can I smash something else?" Smash said.

"Sure," Prowl said, then slid between Lunk's legs. "Knock yourself out."

Joan stopped in her tracks. The other food trucks. *No.*

Mark mirrored her across the fissure as they raced back toward the sidewalk. Stopping Quake was critical, but protecting their friends was more important. They could be inside their trucks.

A Squawk cry rattled the loose metal and debris from Hot and Cold. Joan positioned in front of Powered by Plants, Mark in front of the creamed dairy experience. They blasted in one accord and created a thick blanket of steam.

She counted the seconds in her head. Her ears rang too much to hear what was being said around the park. Another rumble shook the sidewalk beneath her feet.

At thirty seconds, she and Mark stepped back. It had gone eerily quiet other than the ground crackling.

She glanced toward the park as the fog slowly dissipated. Quake was gone, but she couldn't make out much else other than a whole lot of mess.

Her heart ached as the slanted back end of Hot and Cold came into focus.

"Holy shit," someone said nearby. "Spark and Ice."

Murmurs of *Spark and Ice* rippled through the small crowd around them. Crowds meant prying eyes and cellphone cameras. Joan tugged on her hood and met Mark halfway.

"We gotta get out of here," he said.

"Thank you," said a feminine voice.

"Are you good guys now?" someone tentatively asked.

Joan opened her mouth. Praise? Thanks? She didn't know how to respond to that.

"But they're Spark and Ice," a third person chimed in with obvious disdain.

Sirens wailed and tires screeched. Time to go. "I need to find Sadie," Joan said.

"You go." Mark backtracked. "I'll catch up."

"What are you doing?" Their steam fog was letting up with every passing second.

Mark went to where Zee was sitting on an unconscious Smash. Zee nodded at whatever he said. Mark set a hand on their shoulder and said something that made Zee pat his hand. Joan just barely heard them say, "Get out of here."

Where was Sadie?

Footsteps ran up and stopped abruptly. A horrified gasp, then "Oh god!" was a familiar relief.

Sadie clasped her hands on her chest, fat tears rolling down her cheeks. Joan walked past her, murmuring, "I'll be right back." She hated having to leave but needed to protect their identities.

"Psst. Hey you!" someone whisper-called.

Joan fell into a fighting stance, searching the haze.

"Over here."

It was coming from behind Powered by Plants. Someone waved her over. Mark joined her, and the voice said, "Both of you" in a Scottish brogue. Wren?

"It's us." Wait, that was Beth-Ann waving discreetly at them. "Hurry!"

They walked cautiously until a strong hand grabbed Joan by the arm and pulled her into the food truck.

She blinked against the dim lighting. Beth-Ann closed the back door as Wren dragged Joan and Mark to the center of their truck. They'd shut the accordion doors over their service windows and to block off access to the front.

"Get back," Wren said. "We don't want anyone to see you."

"Uhh..." Joan started to raise her hands, not really sure what to do.

"It's okay, Joan," said Beth-Ann. "Your secret's safe with us."

"You saved our truck," Wren said. "All our trucks, except..."

Joan peeked up warily from under her hood.

"Did the Villains know Hot and Cold was yours?" Beth-Ann asked.

Mark pulled the Viking helmet off, revealing tousled blond hair and a grimace. "They did."

"So this was personal."

"Oh yeah, it was personal," Joan murmured. The gleeful grin on Prowl's face...

"How did you know it was us?" Mark said, taking the purple jacket off.

Wren gave him a look. "Two people dressed like you who just happened to be here and made an effort to stop Smash from damaging the other trucks?"

"Who never let anyone in their truck while they're cooking?" Beth-Ann raised her pale eyebrows. "I've always thought that was a bit strange, like you might be hiding something."

An incoming call rang on her cell. "They're safe," Beth-Ann answered. "Do you have her? Great, I'll let you in."

"Who... What?" Joan turned in a circle, not having a fucking clue about what to do.

The rear door opened to Morris, Tenia...and Sadie.

Joan shoved past her brother to fold Sadie in her arms. Sadie squeezed just as tight. "Oh my god, you're okay," she breathed, then jumped back. "Wait, what? Mark, what are you... Joanie..."

"It's all right," Morris said, making sure the entry was secure. "We figured it out."

"Thank you," Tenia said. "You saved our lives. We're so grateful."

The vibe was a swirl of relief, confusion, adrenaline. Mark yanked the hood off Joan's head. "We couldn't stand around and do nothing," he said.

Tenia undid the clasp on Joan's cloak. "You need to change."

"Here." Wren handed her a sage-green-and-yellow Powered by Plants hoodie.

Morris gave Mark his red varsity jacket, while Beth-Ann handed Sadie her white coat. Joan's brain spun with equal parts fear and gratitude as she slipped into the sweatshirt.

Picking up the helmet, Wren said, "We'll stash these for you and get rid of them."

"Why are you helping us?" Joan asked. "If you know who we are… What we did…"

Tenia smiled. "We know you're nice kids who've always helped us out. Doesn't matter what you did before. You did good today."

"We'll tell everyone that Spark and Ice saved us," Beth-Ann said.

"Thank you," Joan said, even though she'd rather no one say anything and let them vanish into the ether. Huh. Where was Ether? There had to be another step in their plan.

"I'm sure Joan and Mark want to see their truck," Morris said, lightly emphasizing their names. "And Miss Sadie. We saw you getting people to safety. Are you a superpowered?"

"No, I'm a norm," Sadie said. "That's what they call the rest of us."

"Nothing normal about what you did."

Sadie gave him a tight smile.

Joan reached for her hand and clutched it tightly. "You did really great out there."

"Me? You went toe-to-toe with Quake."

Buttoning Morris's jacket, Mark said, "Can we trust you not to share our little secret?"

"It's dangerous," Joan said. "Those Villains know who we are."

"Absolutely. We owe you big time," Beth-Ann said, and the others agreed.

"You're our friends," Wren added, which touched something deep inside Joan.

Friends. Friends who would protect them the way Spark and Ice had protected them.

Joan nodded in thanks. Sadie pulled her into another bear hug. "Your dream, honey," she whispered through her tears. "I'm so sorry."

"We're all safe." Joan rubbed her back. "That's what matters."

She caught Mark's eye, silently accepting there was no going back now. They were in the fight to protect their city.

CHAPTER 15

The crisp night air cooled Sadie's cheeks after the longest day ever. Even longer than when she'd been abducted by Trick. Remnants of thick rain dripped outside the parking garage at their apartment building. The sky was still a funky green, though it was fading.

Joan met her around the back of the car. Sadie looped both arms around one of Joan's, dropping her head on Joan's shoulder. Joan nestled her head atop Sadie's as they headed toward the elevator.

They'd been caught in the rain earlier at Friendship Park. Ether had made clean-up efforts more difficult and added to the destruction of the greenspace by turning the cracks and holes into muddy, mucky pools.

After unhooking all the potentially dangerous things, Hot and Cold (what was left of it) had been towed to the warehouse. Her heart lurched every time she thought about its bright-blue paint marred, the logo completely gone, all their hard work smashed to pieces. Joanie and Mark were in shock, or some kind of odd acceptance in a *This is why we can't have nice things* way.

Perry had arrived to help Sadie deal with Hot and Cold while the twins watched from afar, hiding beneath Cajun Soul trucker hats in the rain. They couldn't risk being recognized so close to the scene. She and Perry had used the "too distraught to talk" line with the press to be left alone.

The whole afternoon was a mental blur replayed over and over on TV, online, on SuperWatch. They'd all convened to the warehouse to scour the footage for anything that connected Spark and Ice to Hot and Cold or its owners.

"Anything new?" Sadie asked.

After quick social media posts that they were sad but safe, she'd had to turn her phone off. It'd been blowing up with concern from her mom, her family and friends, her sister Carrie, her mom. Mostly her mom.

Joan wrestled with her phone in the front pocket on her borrowed Powered by Plants hoodie. Spark and Ice had been the focus of most media coverage. The sudden return of the former Villains to fight the current Villains. What did that mean? Were they working with the Supers? Flight had given an interview where he hemmed and hawed about "consulting with Spark and Ice in an unofficial capacity."

Zee would've told the truth, but they were recovering at Superhero HQ. They had a few bruised ribs but were otherwise okay, which Sadie knew thanks to Mark.

Fortunately, Smash was in custody—again. Hopefully for good this time. The Supers had been unaware he'd escaped from his transport. Quake must've paid a hefty bribe.

The important thing was that Spark and Ice were being seen in a mostly favorable light. Of course there were dissenting opinions, but every single food truck owner—even the annoying ice cream lady—talked about Spark and Ice being the real heroes of the day.

The four colleagues who'd protected Joan and Mark had also done a pretty incredible thing. Sadie was proud to call them friends.

Joan cracked a tiny grin at the latest SuperWatch chat post. "The owner of that helmet is excited Ice used it but would like it back if at all possible. With an autograph."

Sadie forced a chuckle. Joanie didn't seem to want to dwell on her dream literally being crushed despite the pain in her amber eyes.

"I wish we could erase people knowing Spark and Ice were there. Where's Melvin and his mind control when we really need it?"

"Joan," Sadie gently scolded.

"It occasionally came in handy."

"Not funny."

She guessed by Joan not responding that she hadn't been joking.

"Why don't you want people to know you were there?"

"It complicates things. We lurk about unnoticed."

"You should be noticed for saving the day," Sadie said.

"It wasn't that heroic. We just didn't want anyone to get hurt."

"You're not giving yourself enough credit."

Joan busied herself with putting her phone back in her pocket as a compact car drove past.

Getting positive attention must've been so foreign to her. Her whole life had been people scared or angry at her for her abilities and doing crime. Today, she'd shown them Spark was more than that.

"Almost home, babe," Sadie said. She laced their fingers and pushed the "up" elevator button.

"This has been the longest fucking day of my life," Joan exhaled.

"I was just thinking that."

"I am ripping off all my clothes the second we get in and taking a long, hot shower."

"I hope I'm included in that plan."

"You are an essential component of that plan."

"Certainly the ripping your clothes off part," Sadie said.

She adjusted the handles of her rainbow tote on her shoulder. Miraculously, she'd been able to finagle it out of the truck. They'd lost the cashbox and tablet, but at least she had all her personal effects. A small win.

"Tomorrow when you're with the Supers, I'll go out and buy you another Vultures hat."

"That's okay," Joan said. "I have other ones."

"But that's your Hot and Cold hat."

"I don't have a need for a Hot and Cold hat."

"You will in the future." When Joan didn't respond, Sadie asked, "Won't you?"

"I can't think beyond what we have to do to…" She trailed off as two brunette white women exited the stairwell chatting about lentil soup.

Of course they'd get a new food truck. They had to so they could park in front of Sadie's Café.

Unless Joanie had bigger plans. Super plans. She and Mark were already committed to spending tomorrow at Superhero headquarters.

The elevator arrived to take them the few flights up. Sadie studied Joan's weary face in the fluorescent lighting. "How are you really holding up?"

"By a thread," Joan said. "I can't believe we got spanked so bad. I can't believe our truck is gone."

"It totally sucks, babe."

"And Friendship Park is all jacked up. That place is special. It's where we had our first date."

"Aww, that's right." Sadie leaned into her. "We had our first kiss there, too."

"It's also where you said you knew I was Catch, so…"

The elevator doors opened to the far side of the seventh floor. "Still my favorite date of all time. We'll make more happy memories there."

"I hope so," Joan said.

"I know so. You'll figure things out with the Supers. You're good at plans."

She gazed at Sadie with those sad eyes. "But we made plans."

"We'll get back to them when this is over."

They dragged each other around the corner. "Almost there," Sadie encouraged her girlfriend as much as herself. "That shower is within—"

The words died in her throat at the sight of her parents standing outside their apartment.

Mom unclasped her hands. "Sadie Jane Eagan! Why haven't you been answering your phone?"

"What are you doing here?" Sadie said.

"Checking on my daughter who was involved in a near-fatal incident." Mom heaved her into a tight hug. "You stopped replying to calls and texts, and I got scared."

"We just wanted to make sure you're okay," Dad said.

"I'm fine." She almost asked how they got into the building, but no doubt her hysterical mother had made some poor resident let them in.

Mom pulled back only far enough to grasp Sadie by the upper arms. Her chestnut-brown hair was getting long, brushing her shoulders.

Joan started a handshake with Dad that turned into a semi-awkward hug. "Hello, Mr. Eagan," she said.

"Hello, Joan." Dad wore a knit gray cap that coordinated with his houndstooth coat. "Nice to see you again."

Sadie reached as far as she could to pat her father's arm. "Hi, Dad."

"Where have you been?" Mom said. "When you didn't return my calls, we worried something more had happened. So we got in the car and—"

"I told you the calls and texts were getting overwhelming and I needed a break from my phone," Sadie said. She unlocked the door so they wouldn't bother their neighbors.

"Everyone has been watching the footage of that maniac crushing the food truck." Mom walked in beside her even though they didn't quite fit side by side.

"Luckily, we weren't hurt." Sadie slid her filthy blue sneakers off as Joan dealt with the alarm. "Mark's okay, too."

"Did you see Friendship Park? It's eerily similar to what happened the last time Big Quake…"

"It makes sense. He said he wanted to finish what he started."

"I can't believe you were there. I can't believe my baby almost…" Tears welled up in Mom's brown eyes.

Sympathetic guilt twisted Sadie's stomach. "Don't cry. I'm okay." She gave her mom a quick squeeze. "I shouldn't have turned my phone off."

Dad tugged on his hat, revealing his mostly bald head. "You always seem to be in the wrong place at the wrong time. First the coffeehouse, now the food truck being parked where there was a big attack."

Not to mention the little kidnapping you don't know about…

Joan joined them. "Hi, Mrs. Eagan."

"Joan, can you please tell me why my daughter keeps putting herself in these dangerous situations?"

"Uh…"

"I'm not putting myself in danger." Exhaustion from the day meant Sadie had no spoons left to deal with this.

"There's a lot going on in the city right now," Joan said.

"A lot of scary, unsafe things," Mom said.

Sadie ignored them and focused on setting her bag on the floor and taking off the coat she'd borrowed from Beth-Ann.

Joan cleared her throat. "I understand why you're upset. I'd be upset if I were you. Sadie's very special. I don't want anything to happen to her either."

Sadie shot her a look that said *That's not helping.*

"I've been protecting her as best as I can."

"We appreciate that," Dad said, and Mom agreed.

"I don't need you to protect me," Sadie muttered.

"You can't defend yourself against…" Joan paused. She couldn't say what she wanted: That Sadie was a poor, helpless norm at the mercy of the mighty superpowered, and Spark was the only one who could save her.

"I did pretty well by myself today," Sadie snapped.

Joan shoved her hands in her back pockets and turned away. Probably worried about sparking in front of Mom and Dad.

Her parents murmured to each other the way they'd done Sadie's entire life. Deciding what was best for her. And Joan agreed with them! She really was dating someone who wanted to shelter and suffocate her.

Sadie crossed her arms. "Stop it. You know I hate being told what to do. The more you push, the more I'll rebel and do the opposite."

"We care about you," Joan said.

That was a gut punch, coming from her. "You're the one person who knows how much a little support means to me."

"Of course I support you."

"You don't leave me alone for five minutes. You have to trust me." She looked at her parents. "Everyone's been telling me what I need and what I should do, and it's driving me up the wall. What I really need is for you to trust me and let me make my own damn decisions for myself."

Her pulse pounded, every beat urging her to get more off her chest.

"I know this is all jumbled and the last thing anyone needs right now, but I'm tired and frustrated and upset." She went over to the kitchen island, then turned to Joan. "If you're that worried about me not being able to take care of myself, why don't you teach me how to fight?"

Joan shot a look at Sadie's parents.

"You know how to spar from your old job. At the gym. Teach me a few things."

"You can't fight someone with superpowers," Dad said.

Mom started to say more of the same, only Joan said, "You're right."

Sadie started to say damn well she was right, only Joan's whole demeanor had softened.

"I haven't been giving you enough credit. You consistently show everyone how capable you are."

"Thank you," Sadie said.

"I'm, uh… This relationship stuff is new to me. At least a healthy relationship."

"Me, too."

"I'm not great with feelings." Joan glanced at Mom and Dad. "Sorry, I don't know if you want to hear all this."

They weren't bothered—they were a pretty open family about most things. "We love to see Sadie in a healthy relationship," Mom said.

"We're working on our communication," Sadie acknowledged. "I'm clearly still bottling things up when I should be expressing them."

"You know you can always talk to me," Joan said.

"Yeah, but you've been so busy lately with everything."

"I'm never too busy for you."

Sadie tried to communicate with her face *But Supervillains are attacking you.*

To her parents, Joan said, "Sadie helped a bunch of people get to safety today." A small smile tugged at her lips. "You were so brave. You did really good."

"Thanks." Sadie's frustration lessened in slow waves. "Joanie helped with the other food trucks. She saved lives today. I'm so proud of you."

"Thanks, honey." Joan walked over to her. "I'll teach you a few things. I didn't know that was something you wanted."

"I don't think I knew until I said it. But I would like that."

"Of course." Joan rubbed her knuckles against Sadie's. Sadie linked their pinkies. "Anything else you want to get off your chest?"

Yep. "Not tonight, no."

Eyebrows quirking, Joan said, "That's a yes. Come on. What is it?"

"No, it's been a long day."

"I can handle it. Tell me."

Well, she'd asked for it. "Can you maybe be a little more, uh, patient with me around here? I'm working on putting my dishes in the dishwasher and stuff."

Mom unzipped her quilted midnight-blue coat. "Oh, is she being messy? Leaving her art projects all over the place? She does that."

"Not helpful," Sadie grumbled. "And not your business."

Joan chuckled. "I'll be more patient."

"It's just..." Sadie stared down at their joined hands. "I live here, too. I mean, I moved into your place, but it's *our* place now. And I respect that it's your home too, so I'm trying." She looked up into Joan's gorgeous face. "I really am trying."

"It's okay. I know you're trying. I'm trying not to be such a butthead about it."

"You can be a little bit of a butthead." Sadie glanced at her parents taking off their coats. Guess they were staying. "As *someone* suggested, I have a habit of not picking up after myself."

Dad hung his and Mom's coats on the back of a barstool. "Habits can be unlearned."

Mom gave him a look. "Does that mean you'll stop leaving your gardening supplies in the back porch?"

"When you only have one basket of yarn next to the couch."

"It doesn't all fit in one basket. And where would I put what I'm crocheting?"

Sadie giggled with Joan. "We're looking into our future," she murmured.

"Fine with me," Joan murmured back. The warmth in her amber eyes said it truly was. She really was the most amazing woman. More amazing than Amazing Woman.

"You *are* my favorite butthead."

"You're my favorite slob."

Sadie gasped and pretended to punch tiny jabs at Joan's stomach.

Joan gently took one fist and readjusted her thumb so it rested over her fingers. "You don't want to tuck your thumb in so it doesn't get broken."

"Starting our lessons already," Sadie said. A twirl of excitement danced up her chest. "I love it."

She copied the proper thumb position on her other hand. If she learned a few moves, maybe Joan wouldn't worry about her all the time.

Mom straightened the pile of pink and red craft paper on the island where Sadie had planned on making a string of hearts for Valentine's Day. "Any self-defense training would be useful. Even if there weren't these Villains running around starting earthquakes, the city is still a dangerous place."

Dad rested a hand on her shoulder. "The superpowered people are the ones you're really mad at."

Mom snorted. "Those people. A menace is what they are. Every one of them."

Joan stiffened. That had to touch a raw nerve. How painful for her girlfriend's parents to think she was a menace. Had her own family said things like that around her when she was young?

"They're like any group of people," Sadie said. "Some good, some bad."

"Mostly bad," Mom scoffed.

"There were so many of them today," Dad said. "The ones we thought were gone came back."

"Spark and Ice? Yes. They were helping the Heroes." Sadie squeezed Joan's hand.

"That's all we need," said Mom. "More of them wreaking havoc."

"Spark and Ice stopped the havoc. They did this thing with steam to conceal the food trucks. And Race, the Hero? They stopped Smash from doing any more damage."

"I saw Lunk and Catch fighting off the Villains," Joan said. Her slightly pained expression spoke volumes about how hard it was to give them credit.

"Things would've been so much worse if Spark and Ice hadn't stepped in," Sadie said.

Dad's mouth twisted doubtfully. "So now they're reforming Villains?"

"Why not? Anyone is capable of change."

Joan looked like she wanted to make a break for the sliding glass doors and blast off into the sky. Sadie rubbed her lower back.

"Things are gonna be okay," she said. "Vector City will bounce back."

"I still wish you'd move," Mom groused for the hundredth time.

"I've built a life here." Sadie touched Joan's sweatshirt. "We're building a life in our slightly messy apartment full of love."

That made her girlfriend smile.

"And I'm seeing that place on Monday that's the perfect spot for my café. It's something to be happy about, even in uncertain times."

"I know, but…"

"This is my home," Sadie stated so there was no confusion. "It's where I've always wanted to be."

"We're excited about this possible café location," Dad said, giving Mom a look like *Say something nice.*

"We are," Mom said. "I liked that neighborhood when you lived there. It's quiet, and…"

And less likely to have Super activity.

Dad pulled a fairly genuine smile. "We want to hear all about it on Monday."

"Thanks," Sadie said, her heart warming from their support, even if it was a bit reluctant. "That means a lot."

"We know it's what you want." To Joan, he said, "And you'll recover from this setback. Sadie tells us you're very resilient."

Joan nodded. "It just sucks right now."

"You can get an even better food truck," said Mom.

"Yeah." Joan gave her a strained smile. There was something

odd about the way she reacted every time that was brought up. Obviously, she was hurting and in shock. But still…

"Unless you want to do something else," Sadie lightly prompted.

But Charming Joanie was back, putting on her disarming grin. "I'll be busy helping Sadie's Café get up and running."

Sadie smiled back and accepted the sweet kiss Joan dropped on her cheek.

The focus turned to a late dinner. A solid meal before Joan had to shower and sleep. Tomorrow she was planning on doing whatever it took, as Spark or not, to make the city safe for these dreams.

Sadie studied her strong, powerful, superpowered partner. Her dreams were coming true. What if Joan's were changing, and all of this was steering her toward what she was meant to do?

Perry always said Spark was a part of her no matter what. What if Spark could be as good as the woman inside the bodysuit?

CHAPTER 16

Joan flicked sparks off her fingertips onto the shiny lobby floor at Super HQ. Mark did the same with a burst of snow. Either the Supers were too busy to turn on that power-blocking thing, or more unlikely, they thought it was no longer needed. Once Perry got there, they were supposed to go over some new information the Heroes had gathered.

Her brother shifted his weight, drumming his hands on his thighs. "So Sadie's parents hugged you when they left last night. What's the big deal? Aren't they huggy people?"

"They like, really hugged me. Hugs that said they appreciated me looking out for their daughter. It was nice."

"I'm glad they warmed up to you."

"I think they like me." Joan rolled her eyes. "As long as they never find out I'm Spark."

"Yeah. Sades said that would be the worst thing imaginable for them. Good thing we'll get the truck up and running so you have a cover again."

And therein laid the heart of the problem.

She really did like working at Hot and Cold. She wanted everything she and Sadie had talked about since their first date.

But she couldn't ignore this strange pull to do something more. Something that would drag her back to the world of superpowers and secret identities and lying. But doing it for better reasons this time.

Only that could mean losing everything she'd built with Sadie.

Kade lumbered in with Darlene, both in their Super suits. Darlene pulled her facemask back so it dangled behind her neck. Kade did the same. He had a couple of short scratches around his eyes and mouth not unlike the one healing beneath Joan's eye. Gifts from his tussle with Prowl.

"My ears hurt," he said loudly.

"Squawk?" Joan guessed.

Yanking her blue gloves off, Darlene said, "We need to invest in something to dampen the noise."

Kade tugged on his right ear. "Where's Sadie?"

"My sainted girlfriend is at our warehouse dealing with the insurance company for the truck," Joan said. "And contacting our suppliers to cancel orders."

She could handle it, and was good at stuff like that, and Joan wanted to show her she trusted her. Sadie was totally right about needing to be cut some slack.

"I'm sorry about your food truck," Kade all but yelled. "I really liked your sandwiches."

"Thanks, buddy," Mark said, glancing at his phone.

"I'm going upstairs to change." Darlene narrowed her eyes in typical Darlene fashion. "I trust there won't be any issues leaving you here alone?"

Everything inside Joan wanted to conjure a great big fireball just to spite her. "No problems," she said instead. "We're waiting on Perry."

Mark tapped his sneaker toe against one of the metal suitcases sitting next to an angular armchair. "We brought our outfits so we don't have to borrow renaissance faire costumes again. Should we put them on?"

Joan held up a hand. "I don't want to go full Spark unless we have to. It'll draw too much attention."

"I will defer that decision to Flight," Darlene said.

The Super duo walked to the large staircase. Mark started to follow.

"Dude," Joan muttered.

"Kade might need my help. He's wounded."

"Quit trying to make Zee jealous."

He waved his hand. "Relax. I'm going to pee," he said, and headed past the stairs.

Joan checked her phone—not to police Sadie, but just in case she'd reached out with any questions. It was so thoughtful of her to handle all the crummy phone calls and emails for a food truck she didn't even own.

Sadie had said it'd be good training for what she'd be facing at her café. And besides, stopping these assholes from destroying the city kinda took priority over filing a claim that'd be tied up for months.

Footsteps clomped closer until Perry appeared...with Gus. Which wasn't all that surprising. The former Hero wore a cotton olive-green jacket and loose jeans, her hair in a ponytail.

"You decided to come back?" Joan said.

Gus nodded once. "There's still work to be done."

"I'm sure the Supers appreciate your help." She wasn't sure whether or not that was true. Judging by Gus's pursed lips, she wasn't sure either.

Perry swapped his sunglasses for his regular glasses. "Does Sadie need anything?"

"She has access to everything. She'll be fine."

"Are we meeting in the conference room?"

Gus shook her head. "I'm not sitting on my duff waiting for the next attack. We're going out to gather information."

Ward came rushing down the stairs with his trusty tablet. He looked like he'd slept in the same clothes at the conference table for days. He probably had. "Oh hello, Ms. Amazing Woman. I just wanted to make sure it was you who accessed the building."

"It was," Gus said. "And don't call me that. Gus is fine."

"Yes, Ms. Gus. Mr. Flight is waiting for you all upstairs."

"Tell him to put his cape on and meet us down here."

Poor Ward. His loyalties were pulling him every which way. "Mr. Flight has some video he wants to show you," he said. "And he was already on patrol today."

Gus grumbled to herself. "Show me on that handheld device."

"Er, well, I'd have to go get Mr. Flight, and he would have to… It really would be easier if you came upstairs."

"Let's at least check in with the others," Joan said, playing peacekeeper.

Gus complained some more, but walked with her upstairs. As they reached the landing, Joan glanced at the Amazing Woman portrait hanging to the right. Her blonde hair cascaded down her long-sleeved gold-and-red top. A faint tear arced over the bottom of the canvas, slicing through the white go-go boots.

"What happened to your portrait?" Joan asked. "Did it get ripped?"

Gus didn't bother looking. "I did that in a fit of pique before I left."

"Really?" Joan laughed.

"I always hated that portrait."

Otis exited the conference room in his Flight getup. "You painted it," he said.

"That's not how I wanted it to look."

"Thank you for coming back."

Darlene raced toward them from the opposite hallway, zipping up her suit. "I've heard stories about your artistic talents. I've always admired your portrait."

"Mine turned out exactly how I envisioned it," Otis said.

Joan studied the Flight painting. Huh. They were similar in color palette and technique. "You did his, too?"

"My second and last." Gus shooed Otis out of the way. "Show us whatever you have to so we can get to *real* work."

Perry had mentioned Gus was an artist. Clearly a good one. They probably sat around having spirited discussions about which Impressionist had the most revolutionary style. Per had opinions he stated as fact. No doubt Gus did the same.

"We'll wait for everyone," Otis said.

"Tell them to hurry up." Gus moved to a chair. Joan and Perry followed suit.

Ward hastily set a pad of paper and pen in front of Gus. He cast a frazzled look at Otis. "I believe Mr. Lunk is changing, but I'll go find Mx. Race."

"Mark's in the bathroom," Joan said.

"Just get started," Perry said, his whole body dripping with irritation.

"Fine." Otis nodded at Ward, who dragged himself to his laptop. He went to the center console and brought up a series of videos. "We've been scouring footage of Quake to find a weakness. We noticed his attacks are very short before he escapes."

"That checks out," Joan said. "He's thirty years older. His powers can't last like they used to."

"Exactly. We can use that to our advantage."

Darlene sat next to Gus, ever the kiss-ass. "Getting them all in one place proved unsuccessful. They're more dangerous when they're together." She didn't look at Joan, but the weight of blame hung heavy. "We have to take them out one by one by exploiting their weaknesses."

"And how's that going for you?" Joan couldn't hold in.

Gus stared at the TV screen, watching the video loops. "He can't bend down the way he used to. He could get that whole ground shaking when he set his hands on it. He must have arthritis in his knees."

"Then it should be easy for Lunk to overpower him," Otis said.

Joan caught a clip of her and Mark trying to fight Quake at Friendship Park. She looked like some kind of sorceress shooting fire from beneath that hooded cape. It was actually kind of cool.

Then Prowl pushing Lunk backward caught her eye. And Squawk angling away from the other Villains.

"They flank him," she realized. "See how they protect him? They keep you from getting to him. They didn't factor Spark and Ice into the equation."

"Yes, we noticed that as well." Darlene gave her a smug smirk. "Take out the sides and you get to the middle."

Zee zipped into the room, gingerly sitting across from Joan.

"How's the ribcage?" she asked.

"Been better," they said.

Perry adjusted his glasses as he peered at the screen. "We only see Quake with the others. The rest of them go out day after day. He needs a break."

"We do tire more easily with age," Gus said. "I speak from experience."

"He's weak," Zee said. "That's good."

Otis looked at Joan and Perry. "What would you have done to exploit a weak link?"

Joan snorted. "How much time do you have?"

"This is why you were brought in. Take it seriously."

She laughed harder and backhanded Perry's bicep. "Per can attest to how little Mark and I take things seriously."

Her brother chose that moment to join them. "Very little. But you can— Oh hey, Gus. Fancy meeting you here again."

"Hello, Mark," Gus said.

He slid into the chair beside Joan's. "What we did take very seriously was our food truck being crushed into oblivion. We'll do whatever it takes to bring these douchenozzles down."

"They're working together," Joan said. "We have to work as a team to defeat them. We took down three Villains at once last time. This has to be a group effort."

Otis gave the twins an aggravated glare not unlike the one

Perry usually gave them. "Then put your Villain caps on and tell us what you would do if you were in their shoes."

"What is their next move?" Darlene said.

Glancing at Mark, Joan said, "We'd split up and make a big fuss at one end of the city. Then the real crime would take place without anyone noticing, or before you could get there to stop it."

"But they don't think like us," Mark said. "They want people to see all the shit they're doing."

"True. These are different Villains."

"Think like them," Otis said. "What would you want to destroy next?"

"Well, they hit Friendship Park," Joan thought aloud. "That was personal. Everything else has been strategic to disrupt our everyday lives. Gus, was there someplace Big Quake targeted but never took out?"

"We stopped him from ruining Vulture Stadium."

"That could be another spot."

"No." Gus looked up from her notes. "It's not baseball season. It wouldn't disrupt anything." She looked down again. "I know what he wants to take out."

She scribbled for a few moments. Then she pointed her pen at the ceiling. "This building. Our headquarters."

"Did he ever try?" Zee asked.

"Oh, he tried. This is the most stable building in the city. It was quite literally built to be quakeproof. He gave up rather quickly."

Mark wagged a finger at Gus. "If he's got these new cronies, he might be able to take it out this time."

"We don't want them attacking our base of operations," Darlene said.

Joan shook her head. "No, that's perfect. Lure them here and turn on the power blocking."

Darlene gave her a look. "It mutes our powers, too."

"You think we can't take out an old man who can barely walk and two dudes who rely on their powers for everything? The only real threat is Prowl. She's just as nasty without jumping on people like a bobcat. But we can take her out." She had to force the last word. "Together."

Her former archenemy slowly thawed. The rest of the room looked at each other like *That's not a bad idea.* A prickle of pride flickered in her chest.

"There is one small problem with that," Otis said. "Ward, don't type this."

"Yes, sir." Ward dutifully clasped his hands.

"It doesn't have a very far reach." He hesitated to elaborate.

Gus huffed. "He means it only works within the confines of this building."

"It's like Wi-Fi," Zee said. "It has a certain radius that works best in an enclosed area."

"Ahhh." Mark nodded slowly. "That's why you never used it on us. You can't beyond these walls."

"Other than in specially-designed transport vehicles, not really."

Perry leaned back in his chair, crossing his arms. "Why haven't you perfected it?"

Otis made a widely exaggerated face. "What a terrific idea. Why didn't we think of that?"

"It's a highly debated topic in the Superhero community," Zee said. "How much we want the norms to know it exists."

Darlene shot them a glare that they smirked at.

"Like it matters what we tell them now? They're on our side." Zee continued to the former Villains, "If we used it in public, the people who have issues with superpowers would know there's a way to prevent us from using them."

"It's as much a way to protect us as to keep Villains under control," Otis admitted.

Kade came into the room with a big grin that morphed into worry. "Uh-oh. Am I late? I had to change my clothes. What did I miss?"

"Nothing, buddy," Mark said. "Just that we're luring the Villains here to take them out by turning off their powers."

"Oh, okay." Kade paused mid-stride. "But that turns our powers off, too."

Joan understood why this tech wasn't public knowledge, but... "It has to reach a little bit outside. Like how home Wi-Fi doesn't stop at your front door. We just have to get them right up to the building."

"It is risky." Zee shrugged like *But what's the alternative?*

"This is a prime target. It's worth the risk."

Darlene stood, almost knocking into Kade as he passed. "How are we going to get them to come here when we're ready and waiting for them?"

She gazed around the room. It felt kind of nice to be included. Then again, they needed all the fighting bodies they could get.

"We fake a news story," Mark said.

A smile tugged at Joan's mouth. One of their tried-and-true maneuvers.

"Yeah. We make up a story that the city's Superhero headquarters is extremely vulnerable to attack. It's unstable. These Villains aren't local. They won't know it's not true. Quake will think it's the result of age and wear and tear."

"We leak it strategically so it just gets to them," Joan said. "We don't want the public to freak out."

"How are you going to do that?" Otis asked.

"Can you leak something false just to the Villains?" Darlene said.

Joan and Mark shared a grin. "Remember the supposed armored car robbery a few years back?" Mark said.

"Or the warehouse allegedly filled with stolen art?" Joan added. "Or the break-in at the botanic garden that ended up being a false alarm?"

Mark sent the Supers a knowing look. "We know how to fake a news story for our enemies."

Otis and Darlene clearly didn't know how to react, and Kade was obviously confused.

Zee, however, burst out laughing. "You assholes," they said.

Mark chuckled in return. "Yeah, well, these assholes are gonna save your assholes."

This was a good plan. Joan adjusted in her seat, ready for action. She could have Greta spread the word among the criminal element—

Nope, that wasn't an option.

Gus set her pen down. "Big Quake knows how secure this building is. We can't get him here unless there's something he wants more than destruction."

Perry raised his eyebrows. "Revenge."

She nodded at him. "He wants me. I'll come forward as being back in Vector City."

"No. You don't have to—"

"Yes, I do. I'll appear on video first for confirmation. That's how you young people communicate these days. Then we'll pretend to schedule a press conference in front of this building. A fake one you can leak to…" She waved a hand. "Whomever."

"You could get hurt," Kade said. "Your powers will be turned off."

"We won't let that happen," Darlene stated.

This was a brave-as-shit move from a ninety-year-old woman. Literally putting herself out there. Probably why she'd come back —she was Quake's ultimate target.

"A press conference feels a little too on-the-nose," Joan said. "It sounds like a trap."

"Then think of something else," said Gus. "We'll work out the details."

"Are you sure?" Perry asked, worry coloring his voice.

"I've been living in seclusion so he can't find me. This is what Big Quake wants more than anything."

Oh. *Oh.* That was what all the secrecy was really about. Damn.

Mark released a long breath. "Wow, Gus. I'm sorry."

"It wasn't the only reason," Gus said. "I was quite done with a life in the spotlight. But it was certainly something I considered when relocating."

"We can think of an alternative," Darlene said. "You shouldn't have to—"

"Kiddo, my work isn't done."

That made Darlene smile. "You will get justice this time. For everything. I promise you."

Gus pushed back from the table. "Less promising, more doing. Where's my Super suit?"

Whatever Joan thought about Gus before had totally gone out the window. The old bird was still a hero.

Otis was flying over to Destine to get her bodysuit from the National Museum of Superheroes. It had to still fit—she'd only aged a little since retiring. The other Supers were preparing to go out and insinuate they had some big news to share very soon.

Since Spark, Ice and Breeze were not trusted sources, they were planning on splitting up and going to a few dive bars to spread gossip the old-fashioned way. Gus didn't want to sit around, so she was tagging along with Perry. Ward was staying behind to monitor any activity from the control room (once he escorted the guests out, of course).

"Come along, twins." Gus walked out of the conference room. "You too, Perry."

Mark hopped up. He glanced at Gus's notes, ever the Nosy Nelly. "Those are pretty."

It turned out Gus wasn't taking notes—she'd been doodling flowers. Irises, lilies, things with long, sweeping petals.

"These look like that painting in your bedroom, Per. The one of the field of flowers."

"They do," Joan said. Wait—the painting he said he'd acquired from some up-and-coming artist, signed *AA*. "Augusta Abernathy. Why didn't I pick up on that? Gus did that painting."

"She did." Perry pushed his chair in.

"You love that piece," she couldn't help saying. Perry never wanted art that wasn't a masterpiece and/or worth a lot of money. She'd never quite understood why he'd fancied that one.

"Is that a real place?" Mark had also picked up on the deeper meaning.

"It's near where she lives." Per headed for the door. "Let's go. She's not waiting for us."

"I bet it's outside her house," Joan muttered to her brother.

"Totally."

Ward couldn't resist checking out the drawings. "I'll bet it's a happy place for both of them. Somewhere with good memories."

They used the back stairs to get to the inconspicuous rear entry. Mark gave Ward a smile. "Go take a nap, man. We've got this."

"I wish," Ward mumbled, then quickly added, "I need to monitor all the activity feeds. Best of luck out there."

He did the slow fade-out, half watching them, half tapping on his tablet. Joan said, "When this is over, let's send him on a nice, long, tropical vacation."

Gus pulled a pair of black-rimmed glasses from her inside jacket pocket. "Time to go incognito."

Hmm. She was from a time when Supers and Villains only wore a simple eye mask. "Won't you be recognized?" Joan asked.

"This has always worked," Gus said, settling the glasses in place.

Mark screwed his face up. "You just put on a pair of glasses and *nobody* recognizes you? That actually works?"

"An unassuming woman gets overlooked all the time. Especially one of a certain age."

Swinging his gaze to Perry, Mark said, "Is that why you wear glasses, Per?"

"It's something I started doing when I became Breeze," Perry said.

The twins cackled at the simple solution to anonymity.

"I do need them. They're prescription lenses."

"So ridiculous," Mark muttered.

They stepped into the bright midday sun. Joan and Mark slid their sunglasses on.

Perry raised an eyebrow.

"It's not the same," Mark said.

"It's sunny," Joan added, though *touché, Péricles.*

As they walked through the alley, Mark said, "So how did you two patch things up?"

"Slowly," Perry said. "It took a long time to make peace with what happened."

"I'm sure," Joan said.

"Were you surprised when she reached out to you?" Mark asked.

One corner of Per's mouth curled up. "Very."

"Considering how we left things before," Gus said. "What with you blowing me off a roof and all."

Joan and Mark paused. "He did what?" Joan said.

Perry shook his head. "It's not as bad as it sounds."

"You blew me off the roof of a five-story apartment building. How is that not bad?" Gus looked more amused than upset.

"It's not like it was going to injure you."

"Slamming into concrete after a long fall does not feel good."

Mark clutched Joan's arm, thrilled at getting to watch the fireworks.

Perry turned to them. "She came over to explain that she regretted how things went down. I was on the rooftop patio of where I lived at the time. The conversation turned somewhat heated."

"And *whoosh*!" Gus swept her arms wide. "Down she goes."

"I vaguely recall it was something to the effect of really showing her my powers."

"I very much recall you said exactly that."

This was the Perry they rarely saw. Happy and joking. They were kind of cute together.

So weird. Like when your divorced dad starts dating after years of singlehood.

Mark was more interested in the after, but Joan wondered about the before. "What did Per do that got him on your radar in the first place?"

"He never told you?" Gus raised her eyebrows at him.

"He said it was nothing."

Gus tilted her head like she was surprised. "A tiny child stepped into a busy street. He blew him back onto the sidewalk before an oncoming city bus hit him."

"You saved a kid's life?" Mark said.

Perry made a vague shrug. "I wasn't always a Villain."

"Perry has always been a good man," said Gus. "A bit grumpy, but he has a good heart."

Did...was...Perry actually blushing?

They started walking again. A memory of running into traffic to scoop up that little white dog in front of Sadie came to mind. Doing something heroic even as a bad guy.

The apple didn't fall far from the tree, no matter how twisted the tree appeared on the outside.

Speaking of Sadie... Joan checked her phone. The love of her life had sent a text.

> Still on hold with the insurance company but canceled pending orders. Hope it's going well over there. Love you 🩶

She grinned as her heart warmed, but then it faded. What was she supposed to do about this situation?

They rounded the corner and headed along the side of the building. Gus fell in step with her as Mark harassed Perry for blowing her off a rooftop. "A message from your girlfriend?" she said.

"Yeah. Sadie's dealing with things for our no longer operational food truck."

"You really care for her."

Joan smiled again. "I really do. We'd still love to have you over for dinner."

"It's unfortunate you won't be able to have a lasting relationship with her. Or with anyone. Not in this line of business."

That was a rather shitty thing to say. "Why?"

"It's impossible," Gus said. "You'll always worry about her safety. She's already been put in harm's way because of your connection to this world. If you continue down this path, it will only lead to heartache."

"Mark and I are going to reopen our food truck," Joan deflected.

Gus didn't buy it from the way she smirked. "I've followed everything you and your brother have done for many years. It's clear you always wanted more for yourself." She waved up at the building. "I see it in those meetings, how you step up. You're a natural leader. You would make a good Superhero."

"But, I mean…" Joan's pulse roared in her ears.

"But you would lose your girlfriend."

"I don't think I would. Sadie's been involved. Really involved."

They hit the sidewalk and headed left on Leyton Avenue. Gus shoved her hands in her jacket pockets and slouched. Becoming invisible. "Have you noticed most Superheroes can only maintain a passing fancy with each other? They turn to one another for comfort because that's what they can handle."

Like Flight and Aura. Like Catch and Lunk. Even—ugh, like Spark and Prowl. "This is different," Joan said. "Sadie's different. She's known I have superpowers the whole time."

"That doesn't negate how difficult it is in the long run." Gus cast her a quick glance. "Forgive my being so honest. She's a nice girl, and she cares deeply for you. But I've been around long enough to know it never works."

Joan's heart pounded erratically. Now she knew how Darlene felt to be so let down.

No, fuck that. Gus was just some crabby old lady. What did she know about the strength of Joan's connection with Sadie? What did she know about healthy relationships? She was in a secret one, hiding from the world, not talking to any Supers for decades. Sadie was gonna learn a few basic moves to protect herself. She was the best person Joan knew and could handle it.

Her hands curled into fists. Gus was wrong. Totally, totally wrong.

Then why did it feel so horrible?

CHAPTER 17

Potential Sadie's Café was perfect.

Sadie stood in the middle of the open space on the homey faux-hardwood flooring. Trying not to get her hopes up had lasted all of three seconds before she knew in her heart of hearts this was it. Every square inch of the walkthrough had only solidified that.

Nyah strolled along the white counter, being more shrewd with her assessment. Lorraine from the management company stood off to the side in a black pantsuit that made her pale skin look extra pasty.

Sadie tugged on the back of her lucky green blazer. Pairing it with dark-wash jeans and a white tee said business casual. That she was serious but fun.

"Is it okay if I take a few pictures for my investors?" she said. "They had a meeting today they couldn't get out of."

"Of course," Lorraine said.

Sadie went to the counter to set her notes and the listing sheet down. Rent and utilities were absurdly high, but Joanie had told her not to let costs be a deterrent.

She gave Ny a smile. "I'm so glad my future manager could come with me."

"I wanted to see it, too," Nyah said.

"What sort of businesses does your group typically invest in?" Lorraine asked.

"Most recently, a food truck," Sadie said. "That's what they're working on today."

She'd told Nyah the same story. How dealing with pulverized Hot and Cold was tying up Joan and Mark and Perry. In reality, she'd done most of the work yesterday, going around in maddening circles with the insurance company. They wanted her to file a SuperWatch claim first and wait for word on that before making a determination. Good thing she had an in with the Superheroes.

At least all the paperwork was helping her get more comfortable with that part of running her own business. The part she'd always been scared of.

"I've been involved with every aspect of that truck since its beginning," Sadie added. "I've learned so much that I can't wait to implement at my own establishment."

Look at me, using all the big words.

"I think your coffeehouse would be a welcome addition to Knollwood Village," said Lorraine.

"Yeah," Sadie breathed, and snapped a few photos of the main dining area. Then the span of brown brick along the far wall. Then behind the counter. The faint hint of fresh produce still lingered from the former juice bar.

Nyah rested her hands on the right side of the counter. "Would you take orders here or the other side?"

"Hmm." Sadie joined her to visualize both options. "The other side. Pick-ups can be on this side, closer to the exit." She took a pic of the big front windows and giggled to herself. "My girlfriend will want to know about the windows."

She glanced at Lorraine for a reaction. The broker smiled politely. Okay, good, she passed the *I have a girlfriend* test. And Joanie would laugh about the windows. Hopefully. As long as she didn't think they were too much of a hazard. She was so bummed to miss this, but duty called.

A SuperWatch notification dinged on her phone as well as Nyah's. A verified statement from the Supers about the video Gus had posted that morning. How did she still look amazing in a red-and-gold bodysuit she hadn't worn in years? Well, she was *Amazing* Woman.

"I can't believe Amazing Woman came back," Nyah said, reading on her screen. "She's a thousand years old."

"Quake is her nemesis. She wants to finally put him away."

Lorraine tilted her head. "Amazing Woman? As in the Hero from a few decades ago?"

"Yeah. She posted a message earlier today." Sadie held her phone up to show the broker the replay.

Gus's short video had been shot against the wall in the lobby at Super HQ. She sounded so much like her old self and less the tired woman she'd become: "I failed you before, Vector City. Big Quake said he's come back to finish what he started. So have I."

"Love her throwing shade by calling him Big Quake," Sadie said.

People still wanted to know what was up with Spark and Ice, and if Breeze was also helping out. The Supers were keeping mum, not willing to own up to how much the three of them were contributing. It was kind of a dick move, but Joanie said she didn't want to confuse or scare people if they saw Spark running around town.

"Sorry," Sadie said to Lorraine, slipping her phone into her jeans pocket. "I'm just excited."

"That's all right." Lorraine gave another professional smile. "I'm glad you're not thinking about starting another food truck. That's a risky enterprise with so much Supervillain commotion."

"No kidding."

"Which reminds me. There's also the NSA rider attached to the lease you'll have to sign. Standard language. It's required for all our tenants."

"I'm sorry, which rider is that?" Sadie asked, picking up her small notebook.

"The No Superpowered Activity agreement. It ensures you won't willingly allow superpowers to be used on the premises. Nor will you host any events that feature Superheroes. Autograph signings, appearances, that sort of thing."

Sadie blinked. Surely, she'd heard wrong. "That's an actual thing?"

Lorraine's thin lips tightened. "As you can imagine, those people make working in real estate quite a challenge. Inviting them onto our properties increases the likelihood of damage, which decreases property value."

Nyah moved beside Sadie. Her furrowed brow said she didn't know this was a thing either.

"It's fairly standard these days," said Lorraine. "More and more lease agreements are including them."

"Isn't that discrimination?" Sadie said. *And crappy. And wrong.*

"It's not. It merely states what sort of events can be hosted at our properties."

"By excluding a certain group of people," Nyah said, giving Lorraine a *This bitch* face. Sadie loved her for it.

The broker made prayer hands, putting on a too-polite mask. "We appreciate the protection our Superheroes provide the city. We just don't want to invite trouble if it can be prevented."

This bitch! "Well, I for one don't agree with signing any document that says someone can't come to my café. My goal is to provide a safe space for everyone. That includes people born with superpowers." Sadie leaned forward for emphasis. "Which yes, Lorraine, they are *born with*. Where do you draw the line? Who do you get to say has to stay away next?"

Lorraine tittered uncomfortably.

Nyah crossed her arms. "Is that rider a dealbreaker?"

"It is required," the broker said. "It's for your protection as our tenant. It will also save you a good amount of money on liability insurance."

"I don't care if it makes liability insurance free," Sadie said, fury raging through her. Imagine a damn piece of paper telling Joan and Mark they weren't welcome somewhere. That Gus couldn't enjoy a cup of coffee after all she'd given the city.

She tucked her notebook in her blazer pocket, hands shaking. "I can't in good conscience work with your company."

Lorraine took a few steps toward the counter. "I'm sorry to hear that. This would be a perfect fit for your coffeehouse."

It's damn perfect, damn it.

"If you'd like to think it over—"

"Oh, I've thought it over," Sadie said, stalking to the door. She took a last glance at the space that was everything she wanted but was now tainted. "And you know what? You don't always know who has superpowers. What if I do, huh? What if I can read your mind or make it rain or shoot a great big fireball out of my mouth?"

Lorraine's eyes grew huge.

Nyah laughed and guided Sadie through the doorway. "Okay, Amazing Girl."

"Treat people with more respect, Lorraine!" Sadie shouted, pointing a finger for emphasis.

She pounded down the sidewalk, hurt and angry and very, very disappointed.

Nyah kept pace with her, chuckling all the way. "I've never seen you get that mad."

"That's total bullshit," Sadie seethed. "And it doesn't solve the problem. Most damage is done during battles. It's unexpected. We didn't wake up Saturday morning thinking Hot and Cold would get stomped into oblivion that day. It's not like *signing a rider* would have stopped it from happening."

"Well, I'm sad they suck. That was a nice space."

"It was," Sadie moaned. "It's perfect. But I couldn't do that to—"

Nyah watched her, waiting for more.

"I couldn't sign anything like that. It's discriminatory. Who knows what else they'd make me sign. That's not a landlord I want to do business with." She wiped at a tear that had squeezed out. "Sorry I wasted your time. You have to get to work anyway."

"It was worth it to see you tell that woman off," Ny giggled.

"People with superpowers have enough to worry about. They don't need to be told where they can and can't go."

Nyah just kept staring at her, amusement written all over her face. Hopefully this passionate Super defending came off more like Sadie fangirling than—

"Sadie," Ny said. "I have to tell you. I know Joan is Spark."

Sadie stopped short. The person on their phone behind her almost ran smack into her.

"What?" she said with a fake, breathy laugh.

"Don't bother pretending to deny it."

"What... But, um..." *Shit.* "How?"

"Amit figured it out when you got kidnapped by Trick. He told me, and then I couldn't unsee it. Especially when Spark disappeared just as Joan began a new career."

Shiiit. "Amit always knew Joan was hiding something," Sadie grumbled. *Shiiiittt.*

"We haven't told anyone," Nyah said.

Sadie glanced around the sidewalk, then pulled Nyah into a narrow alleyway. "Thank you. It's obviously a big secret."

"So her brother. He's Ice?"

Sadie nodded.

"Then Greta has to be Volt. She's cool but sketchy as hell about her personal life."

A small laugh managed to bubble through the knot of emotions in her throat. "No, Greta is not Volt. Volt's in prison. Greta's just Joan's good friend." Well, *was* Joan's good friend.

"Huh." Ny squinted at her. "Can I tell Amit that?"

"Tell him whatever you want. Apparently, everyone's figuring it out."

"Who else knows?"

"Never mind."

Sadie leaned against the side of a building and covered her eyes. Part of her was glad she wouldn't have to lie to two friends anymore. Amit would probably gloat. At least there were a couple of people she could *really* talk to now.

Nyah reclined next to her. "Are they working with the Supers? Did they become good guys?"

"Yeah. Sort of. They want to get rid of these really bad guys."

A boy of maybe eight or ten wandered by on the sidewalk, chomping on a candy bar. He stared at them, chewing open-mouthed.

Nyah shooed him away. "Get in school."

Sadie sighed, willing her racing pulse to chill out. It totally sucked to finally get her hopes up about her café and be prepared only to have it yanked away. Hard not to be discouraged.

Joanie was gonna feel terrible about the rider thing *and* that more people knew her secret identity. She really didn't need another thing on her plate right now.

Still, Sadie had to be honest with her. Joanie was such an amazing partner, patiently working through their communication issues. Mainly Sadie's communication issues. Not telling her would only make things worse in the long run.

"You want to come to VCC with me?" Nyah said. "Have a few laughs with Amit? Make some tasty drinks?"

"Sure." Sadie gave her friend a pathetic look. "Can I have a hug?"

"You absolutely deserve a hug."

They squeezed tightly. Sadie breathed in the familiar, comforting scent of Ny's coconut body butter. "Thank you for keeping Joan's secret," she murmured.

"I don't want anyone to know I know. You got snatched off the street. That's freaky."

"My new friends will rescue you."

As they pulled back, Nyah said, "Wait, you've met the Supers? Like their real selves?"

"Yeah. We're sort of friends with Lunk and Race."

"Dude." Ny slapped her playfully. "What's the deal? Are they hot? I want details."

"Well, I can't give you too many details. But yeah, they're both pretty good-looking. All the Supers are."

They headed toward the sidewalk. "So your obsession over Superheroes finally paid off, huh?" Nyah teased.

Sadie giggled. "It hasn't quite been how I imagined it, but it's definitely exciting."

"What's the situation on their dating lives? Any of them single and looking to mingle?"

"Maybe. Oh, but guess what? Mark has a huge crush on Race, and it's mutual."

"No."

"Yes."

"A Super and a Villain?" Nyah whispered.

"Former Villain," Sadie corrected, then smiled to herself. "It happens more often than you think."

CHAPTER 18

Joan toed her red sneakers off at the door. The beeps from resetting the alarm were the only sounds inside her quiet apartment.

Sadie lightly stirred on the couch. It was dark other than the dimmed floor lamp.

It wasn't even that late, but Joan was exhausted. A full day of helping with Gus's video (Gus hated being on camera), and leaking false stories about Amazing Woman being seen around town, and working with Ward to post on a few underground message boards the rumor that would lay the trap for tomorrow. Then the Supers had to deal with Ether making another humid, wet, flight-delaying mess at the airport.

Being a Villain was way less stressful.

She walked slowly toward the gray couch. Her heart lurched at Sadie snuggled in one corner under a fuzzy pink throw blanket. A coloring book and pencils rested in her lap. She'd had a long day emotionally. Their phone call that afternoon had been a tangle of tears and anger from Sadie about her meeting. Her kind soul and big dreams had taken a hit, all because of Joan.

"Hey," Sadie slurred, stretching her upper back. "How'd everything go today?"

The weight of what Gus said yesterday had been sitting on Joan's chest, threatening to crush what little sanity she had left. Every time she looked at Sadie, panic flared at the thought of not being in her life. Or her leaving. Or worst of all, something happening to her.

Sadie blinked over sleepy brown eyes. Joan had missed an important moment with her today. Hadn't been around to comfort her. Was Gus right? That no matter what Joan did, having superpowers would be the thing that drove them apart?

Tears welled up so forcefully, the only thing she could do was sink to the carpet and shield her face.

"Joanie?" Sadie sat up and tossed the blanket aside, pencils clinking. "Honey, what's wrong? Did something happen?"

Joan shook her head and hiccupped a sob.

"Babe. Come here." Sadie slid her feet to the floor and folded Joan into her arms.

Joan clutched at her T-shirt, burying her face in Sadie's chest. Her warm tears flowed and sizzled out like they always did because she was a fucking freak who couldn't cry like a normal person.

Sadie gently rocked her. "Shh, honey," she said, kissing the top of Joan's head. "I'm here. It's okay."

"No, it's not."

"You're safe. I've got you." She rested her cheek against Joan's temple. "I've always got you."

That only made Joan cry harder.

Sadie rubbed her back, murmuring reassurances that racked Joan with more tears.

After a minute or so, Sadie said, "Can you tell me what happened? Is this because of that thing with the management company? I told her off good about that disgusting superpowers rider."

"No," Joan snuffled. "Gus said… But it's not true. I don't want it to be true."

"What did Gus say?"

"I don't know what I'd do if…" She drew back from the security of Sadie's arms. It was too painful to say this while touching her.

Joan closed her eyes and admitted her single biggest fear to Sadie, to herself.

"I'm terrified I'm going to lose you."

"Oh, Joanie."

"I'm afraid what happened with Melvin will happen again. That's why I've been so clingy. I feel so damn guilty you had to go through that. I want to protect you from anything bad, even though I know I can't be there every second of every day. That doesn't stop me from wanting to be."

She risked opening her eyes to find Sadie's brows drawn together, sympathy written all over her face. "I'm not going anywhere," she said, touching Joan's cheek.

"We made all these plans. I'm supposed to park Hot and Cold in front of Sadie's Café. We have this perfect quiet life. But the truck's gone. You can't get your ideal location. You might not want to be with me if we don't have all that."

"Of course I want to be with you."

Joan chugged in a shaky breath. "You lost out on your café because of your connection to me."

"Honey, I wouldn't have signed that lease even if I'd never met you. I don't want to work with people who restrict who can come to what's supposed to be a safe space."

Okay, that was true, but… "I wanted to be there with you today, and I couldn't because I'm, well, *me*. Still Spark. Always and forever Spark."

"That's okay," Sadie said.

Joan dropped her face in Sadie's lap. She didn't want to lose her. Couldn't lose her. She looked up and whispered, "What if I want to do something else?"

"Do you mean work with the Supers? Like all the time?"

Joan nodded.

"I think that's wonderful."

"But it changes everything."

Sadie skimmed a soothing hand up and down her back. "You might recall I thought you were a Superhero when we first met. You were so kind, and looked out for everyone you cared about. As far as I'm concerned, you've always been a Superhero."

"Even when you found out I was Spark and had been lying to you?" Joan huffed.

"Okay, maybe not right then. But I knew you were a hero deep down." She gave Joan a beautiful, earnest smile. "I fell in love with *you*, Joan Malone. I want you to do what you truly want. And I think that's something bigger than running a food truck."

Wrapping her arms around Sadie's hips, Joan said, "Even if it might pull us apart?"

"Why would it?"

"It's something Gus said."

Sadie snorted. "I can't wait to hear this."

"She said Supers can't have relationships with norms because they never work out. I'd always be worried about your safety, which I already do. That it's too hard."

"Since when have you been afraid of a little hard work?" She rubbed Joan's shoulder. "And also consider the source. And she also didn't factor into the equation how absolutely head over heels I am for you. And also *also* I'm about to become a lean, mean fighting machine."

Joan loosened her arms, resting her hands on Sadie's thighs.

"I worry about your safety, too. You fought against Supervillains without your protective bodysuit on. That scared the hell out of me. But it's not going to stop me from wanting to be with you."

"What if it puts you in harm's way again?" Joan said. "I can't pretend that someone won't try to use you to get to me."

"I came into this relationship eyes wide open. I know there's inherent risk. But like, just living is risky. I could get electrocuted using my hairdryer, or—"

"God, don't say that."

"Or some other freak accident could do me in."

"You know what I mean."

With a shrug, Sadie said, "I'm not dwelling on the worry that something could happen. Isn't not dwelling your thing?"

"It's more Mark's thing," Joan said.

"Well, be chill like your bother."

"I'm just..." She made a face. "I'm not comfortable in any kind of spotlight. And I don't know if the Supers want help beyond this. We've been using one another as a means to an end."

"They haven't turned on that power suppression thing in a few days. And from what I can tell, it's been a collaborative effort." Sadie's mouth tilted in a smirk. "Even Darlene doesn't want to fight you every time you open your mouth."

"Only half the time now," Joan quasi-joked.

"You're always telling me not to sell myself short. Well, don't sell yourself short. I believe in you."

Her heart pulsed with relief. "Thank you. That means everything."

Sadie tugged on Joan's upper arms. "Come up here. I can't believe you think I can't have my café because of you. You're the reason I'm going after it in the first place."

Joan started to get up, then realized, "Oh shit, you don't have a job. If we don't reopen Hot and Cold, you're unemployed."

"Well, then I should really get on finding another location for my café."

"I'm serious. I'm so sorry."

"Don't worry about that."

"Of course I'm gonna worry." Joan squeezed Sadie's knees. "I unemployed you."

"Smash unemployed me. And I can always pick up some shifts at Vector City Coffee."

"No. I mean, of course you can if you want. But I'll support you financially."

Leaning down, Sadie said, "I'm a big girl. I can get a job. Besides, you pay for everything anyway. I have money saved."

"That's for the café."

"And it'll still be for the café. Now please get off the floor so I can snuggle you."

Joan slumped beside her on the couch, drained but feeling better. "We'll keep supporting one another's dreams," she said. "Always."

"Always," Sadie echoed, because she was the best.

"Jesus. I shouldn't have taken advice, however well-intentioned, from someone who hangs out with Perry. But I think I get them now. They both have the false belief that they can't have a normal or real relationship."

"Maybe now that Perry is making amends, they could be more open."

"I doubt it. They're weird."

Sadie giggled and scooted closer. She took Joan's hands. "You know what I just thought about? Your dream wasn't the food truck. It was to do something good. You told me that when you were a kid, you wanted to help people. What better way to do that than being one of the good guys? But on your terms. A real hero who doesn't take a bunch of free stuff. You're the one who can really turn things around with the Supers."

Huh. She had a point. Several points, really.

"And, maybe somewhat selfishly, but I kind of like being a part of that world." She glanced down with a small smile. "It's pretty cool."

"It's extraordinary," Joan murmured. The life Sadie always wanted.

"Yeah." She lifted Joan's hands and kissed the back of one. "So I can get a slice of extraordinary while we keep having a quiet private life, the way you want." She kissed the other.

Joan looked into the eyes of the woman she loved on a deep level she didn't know was humanly possible. "What did I do to deserve you, Sadie Eagan?"

"You were yourself, Joanie Maloney. The you you were always meant to be."

They hugged tight, swaying slightly. No wonder she'd been a

freak about losing Sadie. Only now Joan knew their love was worth more than whatever—or whoever—tried to get in its way.

———

They stayed in each other's arms for a while, Sadie resting her head on Joan's shoulder. Her sweet, sensitive Joanie. Always trying to protect her loved ones. She was meant to be a hero.

Sadie looked up with a teasing grin. "There will be other benefits to you becoming Spark again."

"Like what?"

"Like if you're shooting fire on a consistent basis, maybe you won't be so rampantly horny."

A slow smile spread across Joan's face. "You think that might happen?"

"It might," Sadie said, tilting her chin.

Joan moved her mouth a breath away from Sadie's. "I'm never not going to be at least exceedingly horny around you."

Sadie's grin deepened. "I can work with that."

Their lips met for the briefest moment. Then again. And again. Sadie reached up and touched Joan's cheek, pulling her into a deeper kiss. Joan shifted so she faced her more fully.

They kissed until the connection grew from a little light necking to *This could most definitely lead to more.*

Joan tugged on Sadie's hips, guiding her toward her lap. Sadie complied and straddled her, kneeling just above the zipper on Joanie's black skinny jeans. Their tongues met in a delicious tangle made better by Joan's throaty groan. Her hands slid to Sadie's butt, cupping and squeezing through the denim.

Her body radiated warmth—a surefire sign Joan was heating in more ways than one. Sadie kissed across her jaw to nibble on her earlobe, her neck. Joan hummed in appreciation, skimming one hand up Sadie's back to rest near the clasp on her bra.

She sat more fully and resisted the urge to immediately start grinding. Joan drew her closer, the growing friction sharp and delightful.

Sadie breathed out a little laugh. It was not going to be much of a foreplay night.

She tossed her hair and sat upright, giving in to the impulse to circle her hips just once. Enough to make Joan bite her lower lip. She did it again for both their benefit. Joan chuckled and leaned forward to kiss her.

"Oh, hi," Sadie murmured against her lips.

"Hello there."

"So this is happening, huh?"

"Looks that way."

She gave Joan an *Mmm* and looped her arms around her neck. Their kisses were slow, but Joan's hand pressing Sadie's lower half into her said *Let's go!* As did the other hand snaking beneath her white T-shirt to undo her bra.

As much as she wanted this, Sadie paused to check in. Joanie had just been so vulnerable and been on such an emotional roller coaster lately that this needed to be okay.

She sat back and sought Joan's focus. "Are you sure you're in the mood for this?"

"Yeah," Joan said. "I think we both need it."

"If you're ready, I'm ready." Sadie ran her hands down Joan's deep-purple shirt. "Let me take care of you."

Joan tilted her head knowingly. "You're still gonna boss me around."

"Obviously I am. While taking care of you."

They giggled together. Joan looked at her the way she did when she really needed connection, her eyes warming to a liquid amber flecked with gold. Sadie loved that. She might joke about Joan being horny all the time, but she recognized when Joanie's real need was to know she was loved.

She kissed the fading scar beneath Joan's eye, then slipped her fingers through Joan's hair to tug out the mini bun. The loose short waves cascaded down.

"I know what this means," Joan teased before kissing her.

"You'd better," Sadie said. Joanie absolutely knew she loved gripping that hair as she came.

She grinded more deliberately, Joan soon matching her rhythm. Sadie slid to grip her thighs around one of Joan's. It wasn't bad, but… "I'm taking our pants off."

"Yes, ma'am," Joan said, her low tone rumbling through Sadie's abdomen.

As Sadie worked on unbuttoning and unzipping, Joan closed her eyes and breathed deeply to contain her fire. She rocked side to side as Sadie tugged her pants and underwear off. Those strong thighs, those taut calves, never failed to ignite the throbbing in Sadie's core. She didn't even bother with Joan's black socks just so she could tear her own jeans and panties off that much quicker.

She climbed back up and sat where Joan had to be aching as much as she was. Her clit was wonderfully warm and slick. Sadie pressed into it with a moan. Joan gripped her ass, kneading as she bit Sadie's throat. Sadie swiveled her hips, gripping Joan's shoulders as she moved up and down.

Prickles of desire danced through her body. "I love the way you feel," she said.

Joan groaned and licked up to Sadie's earlobe. Their shared wetness felt so smooth and lovely, but it just wasn't giving the friction they needed. Sadie swung a leg over Joan's and moved her thigh up to Joan's folds. Joan readjusted so she could get better contact.

Sadie pulsed on Joan's thigh, sharing kisses mixed with tiny hums and sighs. She focused on rubbing her thigh up and to the right to hit Joanie where she needed it most.

"I love you so much, honey," Joan murmured. The thick emotion in her voice washed over Sadie like a tropical breeze.

"I love you too," she returned, meaning it so, so much. She wanted to come up with a better word than *love* to describe how she felt. She dropped her forehead to rest on Joan's.

She pressed her thigh more vigorously, more side to side to

spread Joan's folds and hit the magic spot. This was going to be all about her.

Joan clutched at her back, fingertips digging in. Her release seemed to surprise her, so Sadie caught the gasps with kisses.

"Nooooo," Joan lightly whined. "You're supposed to come first."

"Shh." Sadie kissed her. "Keep going."

She wrung the last bits of the orgasm out of Joan, even as her forehead wrinkled in frustration. Sometimes she wondered if Joan's insistence that Sadie be satisfied first had to do with Joanie's sense of self-worth. Like she didn't deserve it until she'd taken care of Sadie. Or maybe it was just what got her off, like she'd said more than once.

She dropped a tender kiss on Joan's brow, telling her she was worth everything.

Her own pleasure was reaching its high point. Joan gripped her hips and lifted her slightly so Sadie could better hit her thigh. Sadie gripped the back of the couch with one hand and stroked Joan's breast with the other.

She came quickly, the orgasm tearing through her and cresting just as fast. Definitely leaving room for more.

Joan kissed her neck and wrapped her arms around Sadie's waist. "Let me give you what you really want."

"What's that?" Sadie teased, 'cause they both knew damn well what she always wanted.

"You tell me."

"Hmm." Sadie screwed her eyes up and pretended that her clit wasn't screaming *Joan's mouth right now, you fool!*

Joanie's eyes swirled with hooded lust. What had they not done in a while? Lately, not much beyond morning shower sex. So something that required a soft surface and maybe lying down.

Ahhh, yesssss.

Sadie de-straddled and lightly commanded, "Lie down."

"Ooh." Joan's smile said she was excited for whatever was coming. "Your wish is my command."

She stretched out with her head against the armrest. Sadie shoved the throw blanket off the couch, smacking a few coloring pencils to the floor. Then she grabbed Joan's legs and pulled her a few inches down the cushions.

She kneeled over Joan and waddled up to her rosy lips. A golden burst flickered in her eyes, bright in the dim lighting. Such incredible eyes. Her hands went to Sadie's hips, guiding her down until—

Oh, *yesssss.*

Sadie sighed with contented pleasure at the familiar caress of Joan's mouth. Her tongue not hesitating to glide and tease. Her teeth gently tugging. She slid a hand up Sadie's shirt to fondle her hardened nipple.

"Oh god, Joanie," she breathed. She tossed her head back and rode the waves of tortuous pleasure. And then the warmth came —the way Joanie could get just enough heat to drive Sadie to the brink of ecstasy.

Her thighs quivered as she moved in rhythm with Joan's tongue. Fuck, the way she watched Sadie, eyes sparkling, and her sinfully hot mouth…

A sharp pang shot through her belly. She dropped forward to grasp the armrest, chasing another jolt with her entire being until it happened. Then another that made her toes curl.

Joan growled and rolled her nipple, dragging her legs up and clamping her thighs together. Sadie's eyelids fluttered closed. She bit her lip, trying not to lose herself just yet. It felt *so good.*

Stars shattered through her body and behind her lids. She cried out, then again as Joanie's teeth tugged at her sensitive skin. The release consumed her even as it renewed her and she fell helplessly into it. She came loud and proud when Joanie did this to her.

Vibrations of pleasure rolled through her, punctuated with shivers and shocks. Her moans subsided with her movement, though the struggle to regain her breath was very real.

Once the last of the tingles were a delicious memory, she scooted back slightly, still bracing herself on the armrest.

Joan held her up by her hips. "Good?" she asked in an oh-so-sexy gravel.

"You know it was, cocky-pants."

She pressed a soft kiss to the tattoo of four little flowers on the right side of Sadie's lower abdomen. "I know what my girl likes."

Sadie purred a grateful, "Yes, you do," and wanted to give Joanie exactly what she liked.

She found the strength to push back and wobble on her knees. She glided down, shoving between Joan's bent legs, bunching her shirt to kiss her glorious abs. Even without working out regularly, they were still spectacular.

She glanced up and smiled wickedly at the pure hunger on Joanie's face. "My turn," Sadie rumbled.

She kissed to Joanie's tight dark curls. Could've easily teased her, but she wanted to savor what had been building while she'd been getting off.

She lightly blew on Joan's swollen folds to watch her shiver. Apparently, Joanie had never shivered before having sex with Sadie. She never failed to be amazed at that.

One more gentle burst of air, one more shiver. Then she hooked her arms under Joan's thighs, hitching her up so she could touch the tip of her tongue to the top of Joan's clit. The little flicks tortured Joan as much as herself because she wanted it all.

Joan rested a hand on her shoulder as she tilted her head back in delight. Greedy now, Sadie licked all the way up her center. Her warmth, oh god, her salty and slightly spicy taste… Sadie eagerly drank it in. Her moan vibrated against Joan as she fought to keep the pace slow. To show Joan she deserved every second of adoration.

Joanie bent her legs further to wrap them around Sadie. Trusting her with full access.

Sadie caught her eye. "Do you want more?" she panted. Joanie didn't always want fingers inside of her, so it was good to check.

"That's okay," she said with a little headshake. "Your tongue is so good."

"Mmm. More tongue?"

"Whatever you want, sweetheart."

A thrill raced through her. She loved getting the go-ahead to take control.

She sucked and nibbled until reaching Joan's opening. She pressed into its unbelievable heat. Like liquid fire and the most delicious flavor imaginable.

Joan swore loudly. She pushed Sadie's hair back, fisting it so she could watch. Sadie dipped inside again and again, driving Joan wild. If she hadn't just had a mighty orgasm of her own, this would totally be revving her up.

Joan garbled something, then cleared her throat and said, "Oh god, I want to come just like this."

Sadie mumbled in agreement. She loved making Joanie feel this good.

Her thighs pressed against Sadie's arms, but she held her in place. That got a disgruntled groan that soon turned into moans of desire. Joan moved against her mouth, swiveling her hips, bucking when Sadie's tongue found the perfect spot.

She tossed an arm over her eyes and raised her ass off the couch. Sadie kept her tongue inside and let Joan ride it until she orgasmed. Waves of heat and wetness surged through her mouth, intense and indescribable. So clear Joanie was not a norm but so much more.

The climax was a lusciously long one. When her back returned to the couch, Sadie licked out and through Joan's folds. Her whole body shuddered. Sadie lightly sucked on Joanie's nub, getting a high, breathy pant in response.

She kept it up, igniting another small orgasm that delighted her almost as much as Joan.

Joanie's legs collapsed on top of her, and she patted her shoulder. "That's good, baby, that's good," she wheezed.

"But I'm still enjoying myself," Sadie said with a little nip.

Joan quivered and laughed. "You always get that last bit of—ah, yeah, *that*."

One of the absolute best things about being with the same partner for a while was knowing exactly when they were done. And Joanie usually had a little more left that was Sadie's treasure to discover.

A few aftershocks, then a contented sigh and Joan's legs flopping to the couch told her all was good. Sadie kissed her clit, her mound, moving up to deposit a few kisses along her neck before dropping one on her mouth.

They sat up slowly, grinning and feeling the love. Still wearing their shirts and Joanie with her socks. Damn, they had not wasted time.

Joan looped lazy arms around her. Sadie pulled her in, nestling tight as Joan tucked her head in the crook of her neck. Joan nuzzled her neck before resting her cheek on Sadie's chest.

Sadie cuddled her close, feeling the steady beat of her heart. "You're my favorite person in the whole wide world, Joanie Maloney," she murmured.

No matter what happened out in the real world, no matter what happened tomorrow, they had their home and their life together. They had each other. Nothing was going to change that.

CHAPTER 19

Nervous energy coursed through Joan as she stood in the second-floor lounge at Superhero HQ. It was rather comfy, like a windowless manor home library, all wood-paneled walls and rich colors and cushioned chairs.

The same room where not so long ago, she and Mark had stormed in demanding the Supers help rescue Sadie. Before they knew about technology that could inhibit their powers should it be turned on in there.

She scratched where her bodysuit rubbed against her neck. It was just bizarre being here in their Villain suits. Breeze sitting beside Amazing Woman, Ice giving Lunk shit for something, Catch and Flight bossing Ward around. They were waiting to implement their plan.

Kade had chosen some truly bad eighties hair band music to get them pumped up. Zee used their cohort being distracted to turn it off on Kade's phone.

Joan pulled up one leg at a time for a little stretch. Her muscles were sore from last night's couch activities. Totally worth it. She had Sadie's love and support to see her through any and every thing.

Thankfully, Sadie was safe at Morris and Tenia's house. There was a benefit to having a few people in on the Spark secret. She'd let them and Wren and Beth-Ann know today might not be the best day to park their trucks downtown.

The strategically leaked rumor was that Amazing Woman was doing an "impromptu" meet-and-greet outside this very building to reacquaint herself with the fine citizens of Vector City. Three o'clock in the afternoon, so there wouldn't be a lot of foot traffic to contain. Race and Flight were going out soon to be seen patrolling on the north and south sides in the ol' decoy maneuver. They could get back the fastest for the confrontation.

Something pinged on Ward's tablet that made him rush toward the doorway. "Ms. Aura has arrived. I'll let her in."

Otis nodded. He'd somehow convinced Aura to join them today. Joan did not want to think about how exactly he did so.

Mark snickered and looked like he was about to ask. Then he wandered over to Gus and perched on the curved arm of the couch. "Where are you staying? 'Cause I live next door to Perry, and—"

"You haven't been home," Perry stated.

"I've been home enough to not hear conversations through the wall."

"We can't hear through our walls, thank god."

"He has a guest room," Gus said. "And if you're neighbors, you know he snores."

"I don't snore," Perry said in a way that suggested they'd had this argument before. "It's the wind coming out."

"Which is snoring."

"Oh yeah, the wind-snoring," Joan said. She totally knew about the whooshing in and out of Per's throat while he power-napped.

"It's not snoring," he grumbled.

Darlene straightened into her *I like to pretend I'm second-in-command* stance. "Once Aura is ready, we can begin..." Her gaze crested over Joan. "Capturing our enemies."

Hey, she'd expected Darlene to get in a dig at the ex-Villains. Progress.

"I'll go out now," Zee said, pulling on their facemask. "I don't like standing around."

"Better to be seen longer," Otis agreed. "More SuperWatch sightings."

"Remember to listen for the signal," Darlene said.

Zee nodded once, then took a step. Then paused. "I hope this works," they said before zooming off.

"Why wouldn't it work?" Mark scoffed.

"Because we have to get all four of them directly in front of the building," Joan reminded him.

"Yeah, but if we don't, we'll just go after them and regain our powers. We outnumber them two to one."

"Plus one," Kade said, looking very proud of his math.

Gus raised an eyebrow at him. "I can't get injured, but these bones are old. I'm not fighting with anyone."

"We still value you, Amazing Woman."

Perry snorted and muttered to himself. Otis rolled his eyes and visibly tried not to clap back. Those two still hadn't decided to play nice, which was to be expected.

Irritation flared out of nowhere and Joan spat, "It would've been great if you valued her back in the day."

Darlene crossed her arms. "Maybe she pushed them away with her bad attitude."

Mark slid to his feet, saying, "It's easy to have a bad attitude around you jerks."

They broke into simultaneous bickering, pointing fingers and hurling insults. Joan wasn't even that upset, but it felt like the thing to do.

Ward entered with Aura wheeling a large suitcase behind her. She said something, then shook her head and waved a hand. A muted glow twinkled around her and flowed across the room.

Joan blinked as calm washed over her.

"My bad," Aura said. "I'm pissy 'cause of the freaking flight delay. I don't just get to hop into the sky whenever I want."

"I can't fly," Kade murmured. "I'm just a big, useless lunk."

"I thought your powers didn't work on Supers," Gus said.

"If the overall mood matches my mood, it sets off a chain reaction." Aura unbuttoned her thin, red, floral-print jacket that matched her flowing skirt. "It's been a long time, Gus. You look well."

"Good to see you, Sherrelle." For once, Gus really did seem glad to see someone from her past.

Mark rolled his head around. "Ah, dang it. That was weird."

Aura—well, Sherrelle—looked him up and down. "That's my thing, Iceman. I'm not going to pretend to feel great about working with the former enemy."

"To be fair, we never fought with you."

She wiggled her fingers. "Let's make things nice and truth-y. I came here to help an old friend and get that damn screamer locked away for good."

"Thank you," Otis said.

Sherrelle shot him a look. "You're not the old friend."

A small something passed through Joan but didn't linger. Sherrelle making things nice and truth-y?

"Gus was a mentor of sorts. We women Superheroes have to lift each other up."

Darlene's face contorted into so much internalized pain, Joan actually felt bad for her.

"I would have done more if not for how things were left." Gus directed this at Darlene.

"I really could have used that," Darlene whispered, then looked mortified. "Why did I say that?"

Sherrelle smiled and wiggled her fingers again. "It's best to cut through the noise and get to the heart of things."

Perry slouched into the couch cushions. "I hate everything about this, but I'm here for the people I care about."

"I'm sorry I never called you back!" Otis declared, throwing his arms back dramatically. "You're intense. It scares me. I like the rush, but it's a lot."

"About damn time," Sherrelle muttered.

Kade and Mark burst into giggles and high-fived. Joan took a step backward. What sort of crap would come out of her mouth if prompted?

Gus eased out of her seat, waving at her old friend. "You can stop. Things have been civil."

"Good. I'm out of juice anyway. That only works a little on the superpowered."

"I thought we aren't supposed to use our powers on each other," Kade said.

"*We're not.*" Otis crossed his arms, gripping his biceps so hard, you could hear the squeak of his fingers against the red spandex.

Gus tugged at the legs of her Super suit. "Review the plan with Sherrelle while I try to remember how I wore this contraption comfortably."

Ward bobbed his head and consulted his tablet. He went over Phase One: Misdirection.

Joan caught Perry watching Gus with concern. Too bad he didn't make his own declaration about what exactly they'd been doing all these years. It didn't matter if it was truly just a friendship or they boinked like grumpy rabbits, but it would be nice to know.

"Phase Two: The Trap is Set," Ward said. "Amazing Woman will take position directly in front of headquarters. Catch and Lunk will be on crowd control to keep civilian interaction at a bare minimum."

He went over Phase Three, where the Villains actually showed up. Greta's words flitted through Joan's head.

Did you just hear yourself? You're trying to get rid of Villains?

She glanced down at her Spark suit. The Supers must've had countless meetings about what to do to get rid of Spark. She didn't really know how to feel about it all other than this felt right.

"Phase Four." Ward proudly grinned. "And arguably the most important phase: The Signal. I will alert everyone to converge on headquarters. This is when Flight and Race will rush back. Breeze and Aura will come from the right side of the building, which we determined after several minutes of discussion is the right side *inside* the building, not looking at it from—"

"Yes, yes," Otis said, circling his hand. "Get on with it."

"Yes, sir. So they come from the right, and Spark and Ice will flank the left side of the building. You will all approach whichever Supervillains have arrived."

Sherrelle nodded. "I get the gist. Fight, contain, save the day."

Ward glanced up. "But there are five more phases, plus the three contingency phases."

"I'll get her up to speed while she changes," Gus said.

Reaching for her suitcase handle, Sherrelle said, "In the meantime, clear up the bad energy in here. Particularly you two." She pointed at Otis, then Perry.

"I don't have bad energy," Perry grumbled, arms crossed like the very image of bad energy.

"Yeah you do, Windy. Otis, you want to share with the class?"

Otis mirrored Perry's pose. "No."

Sherrelle leveled him with a glare. "Do I have to make you get truth-y again?"

Joan risked getting a read. "Former Villains, Superheroes. You said yourself you weren't thrilled to work with us."

"Oh no, Sparky. This goes deeper than that."

"Sparky?" Joan muttered.

Mark gestured toward both men. "Like perhaps how Otis exposed Perry, turning him into Breeze, who has made it his personal mission to be a thorn in the Supers' ass ever since?"

"Like that," Sherrelle said.

"And also how Otis was one of the Supers who let Gus be

thrown under the bus—like, literally? And Gus betrayed Perry after they had a little artistical tryst?"

"Yeah—wait, what?"

Gus headed for the door. "Lots to get you up to speed on."

She was at the threshold when Otis spoke. "I regret the way you were treated, Gus. I wanted to speak up, but I was young, and fighting for acceptance from the old guard."

"You were," Gus acknowledged. "It was a real boys club. They wanted to keep it that way."

"I would have done more if I could."

"Eh, that's all well and good. I'm too old to care any which way." She pointed at Joan and Mark. "You should be apologizing to these two young people you *did* let down."

Memories Joan preferred to keep buried rose to the surface. Being sixteen with seven dollars between her and Mark, trying to get a little assistance from Flight only to be dismissed as he turned his back to pose for pictures. Brushing off two scrappy teenagers angry at the world.

Then Perry coming across them a few nights later in a dark alley, recognizing they were at the mercy of their powers, offering to buy them dinner and a place to stay for the night. Then letting them invade his condo for the next few years and be the annoying children he never asked for. Being the parent they desperately needed.

"I want an apology for Perry," she stated.

"Yeah," Mark said. "That's who you really fucked over."

"I didn't—" Otis began, then wisely changed course. "We should have handled that situation differently. There was heightened vigilance with Big Quake around. Mistakes were made."

Perry didn't react.

"I don't blame you for hating us. I would if the tables had been turned."

A muscle twitched in Perry's jaw, but that was it.

To Joan and Mark, Otis said, "We could have done better with you."

Mark's eyes crystalized in sharp shades of blue. "We came to you for help, man. You could've done the right thing that time."

"By the time we tried, it was already too late."

"Yeah, well, you created the mess. I'm glad we made you pay for it."

Otis obviously wanted to say something that Sherrelle cut off with a loud throat clearing.

More memories flooded in. First Flight and then Race trying to talk with Joan and Mark about not having to be Villains.

The Supers really did try to get them to stop villain-ing. No— to give them the *choice* to leave. By the time Lunk and Catch hit the scene, it really was too late.

Perry may not have wanted what happened to him to happen to the Malone twins, but in the end, neither had the Supers. She'd honestly forgotten about that through the years and many battles.

Joan looked to Perry. The apology was well overdue, and he did enjoy carrying a good, long grudge. Forgiveness would come slowly, but Joan could see it for her and Mark. Hell, they'd all been working together and were still unscathed. If she wanted to join their fight for real, she had to trust them.

Kade clamped a hand on Mark's shoulder. "I wish we could've been friends sooner. You guys are cool."

"Thanks, buddy," Mark said with a small smile.

"Mr. Flight?" Ward said, eyes wide behind his glasses.

Otis shifted his weight and said, "What you have done these past few weeks has shown you've reformed your ways. As long as none of you go back to a life of crime, we'll leave you be."

"Bring back Hot and Cold!" Kade pumped his fist.

"Yeah." Mark sent Joan a look she couldn't really read.

"That wasn't so hard now, was it?" Sherrelle teased.

Ward waved his hand. "Guys?"

Joan caught movement from Darlene and stepped into a fighting stance by habit, but her hands didn't fist. And actually, her arms dropped on their own accord.

Darlene did the exact same thing.

They didn't want to fight anymore.

"GUYS!" Ward shouted.

"What is it?" Otis snapped.

Ward held his tablet so the screen faced out. A security camera feed showed it was eerily green outside. And standing in front of the concrete columns… "They're here."

CHAPTER 20

SuperWatch dinged from multiple phones and a small screen mounted on the wall. All four Villains had been spotted in the vicinity.

Joan crowded with everyone else around Ward as he brought up different exterior camera feeds. Prowl gleefully clung to one of the arched pillars while the three men called out something that looked like "Bring us Amazing Woman."

"Go to Contingency Phase Two!" Ward said.

Kade raised his thick eyebrows at Mark. "Which one is that?"

"Fuck if I know." He hastened to his mask and gloves on a side table.

"I can't go out there like this," Sherrelle said, dropping her suitcase to unzip it.

Joan's fire swelled. She switched to Spark Mode. "Otis, turn the power blocking on. Now. Everyone get downstairs and hit them from both sides. We're doing this our way."

Mark and Perry grinned. They knew exactly what that meant: fight dirty.

Darlene adjusted her facemask in place, then met Joan's gaze.

"Keep them near the building." Joan shooed everyone out.

"Gus, stay inside. We don't need you as a decoy, and I don't want you to get hurt."

Joan didn't give her the chance to refuse, hurrying to grab her own mask and gloves and jam them on as she ran down the hallway. Her heart pounded, exhilarated and anxious but focused. The rush she'd missed these past few months.

Then there was that odd muted tingle. She twirled her hand and, yep, no fire. This had better work on the Villains or else she'd truly learn what it felt like to be a norm.

She passed Perry and Kade on the main staircase. "You two come from the right with Darlene. Mark and I will take the left."

"Rock and roll," Mark said, giving her a fist-bump as she met up with him.

They exited into humidity and wind and an unusually overcast day. That irritating hum wasn't there. Hopefully turned off along with Ether's powers.

"We're here for you, Amazing Woman!" Prowl called, then shrieked.

Joan rounded the corner in time to see her fall off the pillar. Squawk opened his mouth, but only a tiny squeak came out. Zee ran from across the street at a normal pace.

She launched herself at Prowl, tumbling on top of her. Prowl batted at her, still a tough combatant. Legs and bodies tangled around them as they tussled on the sidewalk.

"What did you do?" Prowl said, clocking Joan's cheek.

Joan wasn't about to give away their little secret. Prowl got yanked off her—Darlene. The Super got her in a headlock, but Prowl just laughed.

"So you do have that capability," she choked out. "It's a go, boys! Engage counter measures!"

She touched a ring-shaped metal patch on her suit. It beeped, and then she snarled and flipped Darlene over her shoulder. Squawk released a faint wail that grew in strength the longer it went on. The ground shook. What was going on?

Prowl hopped up and dug her nails into a concrete pillar.

"Smash told us about how you prevent us from using our powers. So glad he got captured."

"What do you mean?" Darlene demanded.

"It was all part of the plan to gain intel."

Joan's fire wasn't burning, but her anger sure was. "He was in on this from the start?"

Prowl's teeth gleamed wickedly as Darlene struggled to pull her down. "I told you we had a plan. Well, *I* had the plan. The others are just pieces of it."

Quake said something to her that got lost in the noise.

Mark had been yelling as he grappled with Ether. "Ward has to turn it off!" came more clearly.

"Sidekicks don't have authorization," Otis said.

Squawk screeched again, bringing everyone to their knees. Prowl jumped on Otis.

Through the ringing in her ears, Joan made out Quake saying, "Bring us Amazing Woman or pay the price."

So they were blocking the blocking? Unblocking? Now the plan needed to be getting *away* from headquarters.

Joan glanced across the street to check out potential—

Oh, *shit*.

Sadie grasped the leather couch arm as she watched the mayhem unfold on TV. Her heart hadn't stopped hammering since the unexpected alert that the Villains had arrived early with their own agenda.

Beside her, Tenia fingered the small gold cross pendant she always wore. Morris gripped his knees on the far end of the couch. "Why aren't they fighting back?" he said.

The TV reporter with the aerial view in the helicopter asked the same thing.

The good guys struggled to recover from Squawk's scream. How had the Villains regained their powers? Something with those metal rings on their suits? Sadie couldn't explain it even if she wanted to.

A crowd was gathering in the street on TV, but it wasn't office workers. Weathered faces dressed in black, gloved hands ready for action. The criminal element that had been promised the city from the new Villains. And with the Supers' powers off…

Oh, no. *No.*

She lost sight of Joan. What was she doing? Was she okay?

Kade and Zee fought with Squawk while Mark and Ether traded blows. Perry was doing his best to distract Quake. Darlene struggled to get Prowl off of Otis.

Where was Joan?

Sadie couldn't sit any longer, restless and desperately wanting to help. But she was on the western edge of the city to stay away from all this.

She clasped her hands in front of her mouth, willing the camera to find Spark. Then she spied a woman in black and red running into the mob.

"There." She splayed her fingers at the TV. "There she is."

Joan shook her hands, probably trying to find her fire. She veered to the right, dodging punches, doling out a few. She really knew how to fight.

A deep rumble sounded through the whirring of the helicopter and the reporter's voice. The ground trembled, making Joan lose her footing.

Sadie gasped as Joan slammed into an office tower window. What was she going to do without her fire?

Joan blinked against the glass. The people inside the lobby startled and moved back. Norms who were worried and watching, unable to do anything about the situation.

She met the eyes of a short woman with curly dark hair. Saw her fear.

Determination welled up in her chest. She pushed off the window and gathered what little flickers of fire burned inside.

The gang was advancing on headquarters, so she got in there and sent heated strikes and kicks to the bodies closest to her. Narrowly missed a big-ass knife—not that it would do much to her suit, but still. She kicked it out of the dude's hand and tried to melt it, but—

A huge surge of energy shot through her. Flames blasted out of her palms. Yes!

She liquefied the weapon into the street, then stood tall. Ice shavings shot above their heads, and Otis soared into the air. Gus or Sherrelle must've deactivated the tech.

Prowl sprang onto Kade's broad shoulders. "Get them!" she yelled. "Vector City is ours!"

The guys around Joan hesitated. She flared roaring flames on either side, making them reconsider and go around her. Who wanted to fuck with the one who shot fire?

She used the moment to study the scene. The criminals were mostly going toward Quake. Flanking and protecting.

They flew backward, knocked off their feet and tumbling to reveal Perry blowing a strong gust of wind. It rustled the hair on Joan's wig and made her flames dance.

But it was Prowl jumping off Kade, calling for action. Prowl who'd said she'd had the plan. *She* was the mastermind, not Quake.

Darlene was doing her best to pursue Prowl. Exactly who Joan needed. She sent a wall of fire to block Prowl, who ran through it with an angry cry. Did it again, slowing her enough for Darlene to grab her arms and absorb feisty feline energy.

"Give her hell, Catch," Joan said.

Prowl swung around and went to scratch Darlene's eyes, only Darlene struck her palm into Prowl's chest and sent her back. She jumped high and took Prowl down to the ground.

A hard *thwack* hit the back of Joan's head. She stumbled, turning to see a scraggly-bearded, beefy guy about to give her another crack. "A sledgehammer?" she said. "Against a super suit? Really?"

She flared a flame at his hand, igniting the wooden handle and his glove. He screamed and dropped both. Then she shook her head and circled herself in a protective ring of fire.

The hostile group moved past her, but one person stepped out. Prowl.

"You're mine, Spark."

Joan caught a glimpse of Darlene trying to fight her way through. Prowl couldn't lead the goons if she wasn't there, so Joan waved out her fire circle and charged.

She grabbed Prowl under one arm and blasted into the air with fire from her free hand. She only got half a block away before Prowl slipped up her back and jerked Joan into a body roll. They crashed onto the roof of a dark town car, windows shattering.

Prowl climbed on top, pinning Joan to the dented steel. "I want you to watch as we take what's rightfully ours."

"It's not yours for the taking," Joan said, wrestling to get free.

"The superpowered are entitled to better things. We're evolved."

"We're genetic freaks."

"Evolved genetic freaks."

Joan concentrated fire into her eyes. She lasered twin beams into Prowl's suit to heat it up. Prowl bounced off her, patting her torso and going, "Shit shit shit, that's hot."

Sitting up, Joan said, "This was all your plan? Quake's not the real problem?"

"Joan." Prowl released a mean-spirited cackle. "Do you really think any of those dipshits could pull this together? Quake has the public image I needed. People are scared of who he once was. Now he's just some rich old dude with a vendetta I used to my advantage."

"So this has nothing to do with Amazing Woman?"

"I don't give a crap about some five-hundred-year-old woman."

"She's ninety-three," Joan gritted out.

"Quake's the one who wants her. He paid for Squawk's little invention in exchange for getting to demolish the city he hates." She tapped next to the metal patch on her chest.

Joan gestured at it. "Squawk made that?"

"He's a tech genius."

"No kidding," she couldn't help saying.

"We put up with his big brain even though he's a dick." Prowl curled up on her haunches. "Nice try with the fake rumor. We knew you were luring us to your HQ. Squawk's been working on this patch to interrupt the power disruptor. I'm glad to see it works. We'll make a fortune selling them to other Villains."

Damn it. The former Villains had lost their edge if it'd been so easy to see through their ruse. "Then how does Ether factor in? Constant, low-grade annoyances?"

Prowl shrugged. "Just a favor to a friend. I mean, he makes it rain. Whoop-dee-doo. But I treat my friends well, *Spark*."

A familiar figure in navy blue raced toward them—one that had come after Joan countless times. She kept Prowl distracted by saying, "Those kinds of friends will turn on you in a heartbeat. I should know."

"You're the traitor," Prowl hissed. "You *would* know."

Darlene leaped with what little of Prowl's energy she had left and yanked her off the car. Joan hopped down just as Prowl growled and slipped from Darlene's grasp. She was too slinky for the Super to get a good hold on her. Next best thing…

Joan grabbed Darlene's gloved hand and sent her a burst of fire. She nodded and understood the assignment.

They shot fireballs at Prowl as she deftly sprang and flipped to avoid them. But they were pushing her back toward HQ. Back toward reinforcements.

A golden glow sparkled across the mob. A moment later, everyone stopped fighting. A moment after that, the norms turned to one another and hugged.

Prowl did a double-take, muttering, "What the hell?"

She didn't know about Aura. Finally, a real advantage. Through a break in the crowd, Joan spied the Super at headquarters in her gold-and-white bodysuit with its fluttering cape, mask all askew, boots unzipped. Dressed in a hurry for sure.

Prowl snarled, then flung herself at Joan. Joan pressed a hot hand to her back as she held on tight. "Hey Catch, remember all the times I would cook your suit?"

"Yes," Darlene said.

"It's fun. Give it a try."

Darlene pulsed waves of heat into the rubbery material, making Prowl howl and claw wildly at them both. "You bitches!" she shrieked. "That really hurts!"

"Surrender now, Villain," Darlene stated in her Catch-iest tone.

The ground shook with massive force, cracking the street in the middle. Joan and Prowl jumped to one side, Darlene the other.

A burst of wind sent someone flying through the air—Quake. He guided chunks of blacktop to cushion his fall. Then he flung them at Perry.

Otis soared above him. Quake raised earthen debris and sent it straight up.

The Villain fiddled with something on his metal patch—a dial? It was different than Prowl's. He stomped the blacktop so hard, it made everything move. Joan had to right herself before she fell into the growing crevasse.

He sought out Prowl and gestured at her. "You're taking the credit for everything?"

"This is my scheme, old man," Prowl said.

"Don't disrespect your elders. Or count them out." Quake turned the dial as far as it would go. Short, quick beeps sounded. "Or discount how I can pay for upgrades that you cannot."

He slammed his palms downward. The whole street cracked and crumbled.

Screams and shouts came from all over—bystanders, the criminals who'd been reduced to hugging it out. Joan blasted into the air. So did Mark.

Quake swirled the chunks of blacktop and rocks and wreckage, creating a tornado of debris in front of him. Joan had to fly out of the way, heart in her throat. He was gonna use it to destroy HQ and whatever the fuck else he wanted to take out.

Steam and water shot out of broken pipes. Car alarms blared from where they'd sunk into the ground. The thrum of people running for their lives echoed up and down Leyton Avenue. Acrid earthy smells filled Joan's nose.

The debris-nado grew in width and height. The news helicopters backed off. Joan and Mark and Otis couldn't get near it. Perry flew up and blew on it, not making much of a dent. It was too densely packed.

Then the sidewalk crowd parted, almost in slow motion.

Amazing Woman appeared from a cloud of dust, staring straight ahead, on a mission.

She walked directly into a piece of hovering concrete, brushing it aside. Then a flying bicycle bounced off her.

Prowl pounced in front of her, swiping her nails at Gus. Gus barely batted an eyelash and said something clearly acerbic by the way Prowl reacted—stunned and a little taken aback. Kade grabbed her for another round of angry cat and gigantic mouse.

Gus stood at the edge of the cracked earth. "Big Quake," she called. "We have unfinished business to attend to."

The debris rose until Quake could see her. "At long last. I've dreamed about this day. The day I finally take you and your beloved city out."

"Best of luck with that."

He shot a line of rubble at her. Chunks of blacktop broke apart as they smashed into her, but she just took it. She stepped onto the newly created pile of crap, getting closer to him.

Joan roused out of her stupor and was ready for the next wave he shot at Gus. She blasted at it, hoping to break it up. A big trash fire rained down instead.

"That's not helpful," Gus shouted at her.

"My bad," Joan said.

As he lobbed fragments at Gus, Quake said, "How much can you take now? Still as indestructible after all these years?"

Perry blew some of the errant wreckage into the hole in the street. Mark and Otis pulled at stuff along the edges of the debris-nado. Gus kept advancing, taking the hits, never wavering from the man who held all her focus.

Joan couldn't help watching. "She really is amazing," she murmured to herself.

Quake condensed the debris and shaped it into a tall funnel. He slammed it in Gus's direction with a loud cry. Joan flew toward it, then was blown to the side. She grabbed onto a streetlight and held tight.

Perry floated in front of Gus, sending gale-force winds from his mouth, his hands, from every part of him. The rubble sailed into the sky but would have to come down somewhere.

Joan zoomed up and shot small fireballs at it all. Mark joined her to crack it with ice chunks. A helicopter hovered too close for comfort.

The remains floated down, ash and muddy wet splats. Messy but not fatal. Otis grabbed a large piece of blacktop and lowered it safely.

Messy. Wet and messy. "Hey," Joan said, waving Mark over. "Can we make it rain?"

"Ether style?"

"Try a different ratio of fire to ice and flood everything around Quake. He can't control water."

Mark nodded. They coasted down to the rubble pile in front of Gus and Perry. Joan ducked an incoming bunch of rocks, then watched Mark's steady stream of ice pellets. She kept the intensity of her flames low, just enough to melt the ice.

A blur circled around and around Quake, encasing him in a watery ball. *Zee.*

It was working—Quake couldn't find purchase through the water. The remaining debris in the air fell to the ground.

Otis flew into the water and emerged with Quake. He headed

straight for the river. Of course—drop him in the water to keep him contained.

Quake flung his hands, rumbling the ground one last time.

Joan and Mark stopped, as did Zee. They sped over to the twins. "About time," Mark teased.

"Busy taking care of the other Villains in attendance." Zee ran over to where Kade and Sherrelle had an unconscious Ether and Squawk under an archway at headquarters.

They said something to Kade that made him shake his head, make a pained face, and mime vomiting. Zee said something else, to which Kade reluctantly agreed. They wrapped an arm around their hulking cohort and raced off toward the river. The big guy needed to keep Quake secure. Moving that fast was probably a barfy trip.

Wait, where was—

Ah. Darlene stood with fists on hips, staring inside the huge hole in the earth. Prowl couldn't find her footing or grip to get out of it.

"Noooo!" she screeched from down below. "You cowards don't get to win!"

"Looks like we do," Joan said. She peered into the mucky pit at a very angry Prowl—no longer Ricki to her. "Told you this was my city."

The Villain caterwauled some more. Pride blossomed in Joan's chest. They'd done it. Vector City was broken but safe.

She turned to check on Gus and Perry. It had gotten sunny at some point, so…

Where were they? She stepped over holes in the ground and broken crap. Oh, there was Per, pulling a few errant chunks of concrete from a pile. The columns at HQ had been a little damaged.

Mark hurried past her, wobbling on the unstable ground. "What's wrong?"

"Help," Perry croaked. "Gus."

Oh, shit. Joan clambered over to where he was digging. Gus was probably fine. She was unbreakable. Just a little buried, right?

"The concrete fell," Perry said. "The last thing Quake did. Moved the earth under what was closest to her."

"She's okay," Joan said. "Maybe knocked out or something."

Then she got up to the heavy slabs. *Damn.* How were they gonna move them? They needed Kade for this.

"I can probably freeze them," Mark said.

"Don't hurt her," Perry stated.

"She can't get hurt."

"She's ninety-three. She's not as invincible as she used to be."

Mark set both hands on the biggest slab, concentrating so it froze slowly. Perry and Joan pounded on it, breaking off pieces. Gus was fine. She had to be fine.

Joan caught a flash of red and gold. "She's over here."

They broke more off until they saw Gus's arm, her blonde hair, her face. She was unconscious, and her eye mask had nearly fallen off.

"Gus!" Perry choked out. "Can you hear me?"

Her lower half was beneath a smaller hunk of concrete that Joan and Mark were able to shove enough for Perry to pull her out. He held her to his chest. "Gus. You have to wake up."

Mark shot worried eyes at Joan. Gus wasn't bleeding, wasn't bruised, but was unresponsive. That brave woman had walked headfirst into danger after swearing never to do that again.

A hero sacrifices for the greater good.

CHAPTER 21

Sadie followed Ward into the back entrance of Superhero headquarters. He'd had to come out and allow her through the blockade surrounding the area. A few texts and a quick call from Joan had not been enough to squash her nerves. She needed to see everyone.

"How's Gus?" she asked.

"As far as I know, she hasn't woken up yet. It's been…"

"I'm sure it has."

They passed the kitchen where a man and woman in pantsuits murmured over coffee mugs. The gray-haired man looked familiar—spotless in a politician way.

"Is that Mayor Thorpe?" Sadie said.

"Yes, with our liaison to his office. We have some other key civilians milling about. They have seen our Heroes without their masks but don't know anyone's real identities. Please refrain from using their names outside of where we're going."

Ward approached a closed white metal door. It led to a large hospital room with one empty bed and one surrounded by Heroes old and new in their civilian clothes.

Joan turned, her face softening. She took big steps across the room.

Sadie hurried to meet her, heart about ready to leap from her chest. "Oh my god," she exhaled, crushing Joan in a hug. "I'm so glad you're okay."

"Are you all right? And Tenia and Morris?"

"We're fine." She squeezed tighter. "I'm so proud of you."

Joan had been a force of nature. She'd worked with Darlene. Taken on Prowl. Did not back down from Quake to defend Gus.

"Is Gus doing any better?" Sadie said, pulling back.

"She's coming in and out of consciousness."

They walked to where Gus was hooked up to monitoring equipment. Perry sat next to the bed, holding her hand, looking more distraught than Sadie had ever seen. The whole group looked worried.

She gave Mark a quick hug, then squeezed Perry's shoulder. Glancing around, she asked, "Is everyone else okay?"

"Bumps and bruises, but otherwise fine," Mark said.

Her gaze lingered on the woman she didn't recognize in bright florals. Aura? "Hi, I'm Sadie," she said.

"Aura. Or Sherrelle, I guess. I heard you already know everyone."

"Your secret's safe with me."

Aura/Sherrelle studied her, then nodded. "You've got good energy."

Gus lightly stirred. Perry jumped to his feet and brushed the hair off her forehead. "We're here," he said. "We're all here, waiting for you to wake up and boss us around."

A smile tugged at Sadie's lips from his sweet concern. Then she got a good look at Gus's face. There were more wrinkles, or maybe deeper existing wrinkles? Her cheeks had sunken in a bit, too. And actually, her hands and arms were more gnarled, more aged. Even her hair appeared to be dulling.

Footsteps from a little desk nook startled Sadie. A brown-skinned man with short-cropped hair, maybe thirty-ish, in sky-blue scrubs. He gave Sadie a brief smile. "Hi, I'm Dr. Justin Devers. You can call me Justin."

"Hi." Sadie started to say more, then realized there were no masks, no…

Justin chuckled. "It's okay. It's in the oath I took not to divulge personal information. Plus, I have a vested interest. My aunt was a Superhero." He held up a smooth hand. "Can't tell you who or when or where. She's retired."

"He specializes in treating the superpowered," Joan said.

"Really?" Sadie leaned close and murmured, "You can ask him stuff."

Joan nodded. "Like about wonky menstruation."

"Superpowered people typically don't have a normal menstrual cycle or menses flow," Justin said.

Joan's face tightened in embarrassment. Guess it was too quiet in there.

"You didn't know that?" Darlene said.

"How would I know that?" Joan countered.

"Are you seeing new clients, Doc?" Mark said. "My sister needs to learn more about her menses."

Sadie smacked his arm and shifted the focus to the medical emergency. "Is something going on with Gus? She looks different."

Justin studied his patient. "Treating her has been a bit of a mystery. She doesn't get injured, but her body does experience wear and tear. My best guess is it's repairing itself after taking so many hits today. That could be drawing away from bone density, skin elasticity and the like."

"It's aging her," Otis said.

That's what it was. She was aging right before their eyes.

Joan laced her fingers through Sadie's. "We can't put an IV in her. Or do a blood draw."

"Yeah." Justin chuckled again. "Her skin bends needles."

"We took x-rays, though."

"So she'll be okay?" Sadie asked.

"Her vitals are strong. I'm optimistic for her recovery." Justin gestured back at the desk, which sported a small Trans Pride flag. "I'll be over here if you need anything."

The room quieted again other than occasional beeps and clicks. Joan had told her bits and pieces of what went on during the fight. Sadie would get the whole story later, but she had to know, "What were those things the Villains were using? Their powers came right back."

"Something that deflected the frequency," Zee said.

"Quake had one that boosted his," Otis added. "We have them in our possession. We're going to study them and then destroy them."

A small flame flickered from Joan's palm. "Just say the word."

Zee tilted their head. "Maybe no open flame near an oxygen tank?"

"Sorry." Joan mashed her fingers on it.

"Where are the Villains right now?" Sadie asked.

"Contained in the basement," Otis said.

"Here?" Her pulse jumped. "Like, *here* here?"

"They're secure," Zee said. "The power blocking is cranked up high down there. We're waiting for the team from the prison facility to come get them."

"I'm going with," Aura/Sherrelle said. "Make sure no shenanigans happen."

"Me too," Kade said.

Darlene crossed her arms. "And me."

"Is that a good idea?" Sadie couldn't help giving the norm perspective. "I mean, there was just a huge battle. Having half your Heroes leave town, even for a good reason...?"

Zee raised their eyebrows at Mark.

Sherrelle waved across the bed. "There's five of you. That's more than enough to start cleaning up this mess."

Sadie's breath stilled. Joan's fingers went slack. *Five Heroes. That includes Spark, Ice and Breeze.*

"You're right," she said, squeezing Joan's hand.

Joan met her gaze, brows quirked, asking permission. Sadie smiled and gave an encouraging nod. *Go for it.*

Joan cleared her throat. Looked at Mark, then Gus. "I want the city to know how much Gus has sacrificed. Her whole life. What she went through before, and hiding out all those years so Quake wouldn't find her."

"She's so brave," Kade said.

"Running headfirst into danger to help people. That's the sort of person I want to be." Joan paused, then added, "That's the sort of hero I want to be."

The energy palpably heightened in the room.

"I know that sounds cheesy, but..."

"That's what a hero would say," said Darlene.

Joan gave her a look. So did Sadie. *Darlene* of all the Supers giving support?

Drawing in a deep breath, Joan said, "I want to join you. Officially. I want to be a Superhero."

Sadie felt her brace for the response. It could be denied, laughed at, anything. She stepped closer to show her support.

Mark looked back and forth from his sister to Perry. "I do, too. It's nice to be the good guy for once."

Kade grinned and said, "That would be so cool!"

The others looked more skeptical, but not completely dismissive.

"What about you, Perry?" Otis asked, crossing his arms.

Perry gave him the stink eye. "God no."

Sadie leaned into Joan's side, telling her no matter the outcome, she'd be there for her.

"And I want Gus to paint my portrait," Mark said.

Otis tilted his chin down. "Let's not get ahead of ourselves. You assisted well with this latest Villain apprehension. You could contribute to society in a positive manner. However..."

"Come on, Otis," Zee said. "They have a perspective we don't. And they've proved they care. Give them probationary status or something."

"Is that a thing?" Mark said.

"It could be." Zee swung their gaze to the senior Super.

Otis stared at the twins. "It isn't easy. Villains get to pick and choose their battles. We do not."

"I know," Joan said.

"We wouldn't be in it for the fame or the glory or the free shit," Mark said.

Joan nodded in agreement. If anything, she was in it for people to not be afraid of her anymore.

"Gus?" Perry rushed out.

Gus's head rolled side to side. She smacked her lips and her eyelids fluttered.

"Doctor!" Perry called. "I think she's waking up."

He murmured close to her ear as Justin rejoined them. "Ms. Abernathy? Can you hear me?"

Gus coughed and struggled, but eventually said, "Did we get him?"

"We got him," Perry said.

She nodded faintly, then closed her eyes. "Asshole."

"Ms. Abernathy, I'm Dr. Devers," Justin said. "Can you tell me what day it is?"

"The day we beat that asshole."

"She's fine," Mark laughed.

Gus tried to sit up. Perry got all awkward like he wasn't sure if he should help or prevent her from moving too much. "I'm thirsty," she rasped. "Tired. So tired."

"Just rest," Perry said. "Sherrelle, hand me—"

Sherrelle passed him the plastic cup filled with water. Gus took a few drags from the straw.

"You need to stay hydrated," Justin said. "I'm not able to administer IV fluids."

"I break needles. I know that."

It was nice to see her grouchy because grumpy Gus meant healthy Gus.

After another sip, she said, "I assume since you're all here, we got all of them."

"We did," Darlene said. "I'm sorry you had to take the brunt of the assault again."

"I did my part. You got your justice, kiddo."

Darlene broke into a soft smile.

"Why am I so tired?" Gus fell back against the pillows.

Justin repeated his theory about her body repairing itself while Perry fluffed her pillows and pulled up the blankets. Fussing over her in a very un-Perry display of affection.

Sadie whispered to Joan, "He really loves her."

She raised an eyebrow. "Yeah."

Gus mumbled to Perry. He turned to the group and said, "Give her space. She wants to rest."

The Supers backed off with words of encouragement. Joan looked like she wanted to say something, but followed Mark instead. Sadie let go of her hand, quietly saying, "Thank you, Gus."

Gus regarded her before her eyes closed.

Perry returned to his seat as Sadie rejoined Joan. "I didn't talk to Per about this being a Superhero thing," Joan said. "I hope he's not mad. We made him open the food truck, and now…"

Mark shoved his hands in his back pockets. "Is the food truck totally off the table?"

"I don't see how we could do both."

"Yeah. For sure." A murky gray clouded his eyes for a brief moment. Aww, poor Markie. He'd really blossomed at Hot and Cold.

Joanie's worry lines deepened across her forehead. Before she spiraled out with her fears, Sadie rubbed her back. "Perry's gonna be busy helping me find another café location. And taking care of Gus."

"I'm glad she's getting better," Kade said.

Zee planted their hands on their hips. "Should we get back to discussing Spark and Ice's future?"

"Look, I know we have a long way to go to gain the public's trust," Joan said. "Especially me. Fire is so destructive."

"It's efficient," Darlene said.

Joan blinked, clearly surprised by that. "It is?"

"I've found it works well in short bursts. Efficient and effective."

"O…kay." She shared a *What the hell?* look with Mark. "We'll do what we have to do. Go to Superhero training or whatever. If that's a thing."

"We have media training." Kade rolled his eyes.

"Regimented workout programs," Darlene said.

"We love to work out," Mark said. Did he shift his eyes toward Zee?

"Mandatory weekly meetings," Otis said.

Sadie, Joan and Mark snorted. "We're used to meetings," Joan chuckled. "That's Perry's favorite thing."

"We could do with less meetings, more doing." Mark glanced over at Gus. "She was right about sitting around too much. We like to act."

"It would be probationary," Otis said. "You wouldn't be granted full access to anything. You would need supervision."

The twins nodded. Sadie wanted to wrap her arms around Joan and cheer.

Someone cleared their throat. Ward. The sidekick had been hanging out by the door. Panic practically vibrated off of him. "Will you be taking a formal vote? Are you—" He gulped. "—adding two more Superheroes to the roster?"

"Ward, buddy," Mark said. "We don't need a sidekick. We've done just fine without any help."

Ward's wide eyes said he wanted to believe that, but there was much more to the equation on this side of the Hero/Villain conflict.

Sherrelle wiggled a finger at Joan and Mark. "I wasn't sure creating an alliance was a smart move, but they proved me wrong. You've got two good ones here. One of them's even in a committed relationship."

She gave Otis a pointed gaze that he avoided.

Ward went over to a laptop on the counter. "If this is going to be an official vote, I need the exact wording for what you are proposing, please."

"That Spark and Ice join us on a probationary basis subject to terms to be decided upon," Zee said.

"That was good," Kade loudly whispered.

"I vote yes," Darlene said. She nodded at Joan. Joan smiled her gorgeous smile and nodded back.

"I vote yes," Zee said.

"I vote an enthusiastic yes!" Kade pumped his fist.

Everyone looked at Otis. He crossed his arms, very Superhero-y, and addressed Joan. "What changed for you?"

She turned to Sadie, the love in her eyes shining amber and bright. "I have something to fight for."

Sadie's heart melted. She was gonna fight just as hard for Joanie—for their relationship and their dreams.

Otis considered her answer for a long moment. "Then I vote yes."

CHAPTER 22

Joan paced around the small meeting room fiddling with the zipper on her Spark suit, quietly freaking the fuck out. They were holding the press conference on the steps of City Hall since there was currently no street in front of Superhero headquarters.

The past few days had been a blur of activity designed to prepare her for a life in the spotlight. A surprising amount of paperwork, and meetings to discuss what the Supers expected of her and Mark, and onboarding about expense receipts and insurance, and information requests for SuperWatch claims, and media training that she proved to be very bad at.

Where was Mark? The rest of the Supers were in the lobby warming up the crowd to the formal announcement of Spark and Ice becoming guardians of Vector City. Mark was supposed to be hiding in here with her so he could be all *"Everything's chill, sis."*

It still felt surreal, but good. No nightmares anymore, but she supposed those had been fueled by being scared for Sadie's safety. She couldn't *not* worry about her a little, but she trusted Sadie. And new friends were watching over her: Tenia and Morris, Wren, Beth-Ann. And Nyah and Amit, too. In retrospect, it totally made sense that Amit had figured out why Joan was so sketchy with the truth.

She shook her head. Her and Mark's new best friend Kade, who gave palm-stinging high-fives every single time they crossed paths, would take care of Sadie. Plus, there was Zee. Even Darlene wouldn't hesitate to do the right thing.

The door opened to a rush of weekday noise and Mark as Ice carrying two champagne flutes.

The second he closed the heavy oak door, Joan said, "Where have you been? I'm freaking out."

Mark frowned. "My face is breaking out. That's what happens when we don't wear our masks for a while."

"Where did you get those?" She pointed at the glasses.

"There was a little meet-and-greet for some head honchos."

"I don't want to do meet-and-greets. Otis said we aren't doing those yet. And hopefully never."

"Did I say I was invited?" Mark grinned, still her sneaky younger brother. "Here. Calm yourself."

Joan grabbed the offered glass and chugged its contents. The bubbles fizzled in her internal heat.

"That nervous, huh?"

She began her path across the room again. It was a beautiful, sunny day outside, but the thick wooden blinds were all closed. They'd replaced most of the windows on the first floor after Squawk blew them out.

The cracks of light around the blinds were strangely comforting. Like the old days at the warehouse when hiding was an option.

This felt just like entering villainy. "I've been thinking about the first time Perry took us out as Spark and Ice. Those early outfits."

"God," Mark groaned. "Those were terrible. I looked like I was in a boy band from outer space."

"I was terrified. You had to hold my hand to get me through it."

"I remember." He smiled. "But we got through it. We'll get through this."

Joan dragged her gloved fingers through her mask's flowing black wig. "Why can't we just go out and fight crime? Why the big press conference?"

"We need to start off on the right foot," Mark said, then sipped his champagne.

"People are okay, though, right? We've seen the comments on SuperWatch. Some people thanking us."

"The LARP community loves us."

"Yeah, they do. And everyone likes a redemption story."

"We've still gotta do the pressing flesh and kissing babies." He made a face. "I hope we don't have to kiss any babies."

Sadie had been relatively reassuring, showing Joan positive posts on social media from people relaying stories about Spark and Ice that weren't altogether bad. She'd posted on SuperWatch about Spark giving money to Vector City Coffee to repair Super damage. And Cajun Soul and Powered by Plants praised Spark and Ice's quick thinking that saved their trucks.

Sadie. The best person in the whole wide world. Joan stopped pacing and faced the door. "I need a Sadie hug. Can she come in?"

"We agreed to keep her and Per on the sidelines so nobody connects them to us," Mark patiently soothed. "She's here. They're both outside."

But I want a damn Sadie hug and her saying how proud she is of me like she did this morning.

Joan tapped her boot heel on the scuffed wood floor. "We're gonna be Superheroes, Mark."

"Yeah. Weird. Do you think…"

"What?"

"Nah, just…" Mark shuffled his feet. "Do you think Mom and Dad would be proud of us?"

"I don't care," Joan said.

"I mean, if things had been different, and we never became Villains…"

"We became Villains because of what they did to us."

Her brother stared at the floor. "I think they'd be glad we turned out okay."

Joan huffed and rolled her eyes. Mark still had that soft spot, but she couldn't give their parents the satisfaction of being proud of kids they'd kicked out. They'd probably be more proud of them running a food truck than anything having to do with their destructive powers.

"I really am sorry about Hot and Cold," she said.

"Me, too. I really liked it." He looked up with a grin that was maybe a touch too wide. "But like, *Superheroes*."

"Right? Good thing we never got tattoos."

"Yeah. You would've done something awful like get Sadie's name on your ass anyway."

"Why on my ass?"

Mark just shrugged.

The door opened to Kade's deep laugh and louder noise from the gathering crowd. Fuck, there were *people* outside waiting to scrutinize the former Villains trying to change sides.

Ward hustled in, dapper in a dark suit and deep-purple tie. Padma followed in a sleek red wrap dress. Their liaison to the mayor's office was full of energy (and buckets of caffeine) and loved using buzzwords that made Joan cringe. She was hot, though—Joan had always been a sucker for long, thick hair.

"Ward!" Mark cheered. "I thought we agreed you were taking time off."

"There's so much to do this week," Ward said.

"Not for us you don't. We're cool on our own."

The overworked sidekick gave him a grateful smile. "Thank you, Mr. Ice."

"Hi hi!" Padma sang. "Everything okay in here?"

"No," Joan answered very seriously.

She laughed merrily. "We're just about ready to get started. Now, we're going to have the other Supers go out before you." She consulted her tablet. "Flight will do a little light housekeeping. Give an update on Amazing Woman, assure our community of clean-up efforts, et cetera. Then he'll formally announce you both, and we're off to the races."

Joan swore under her breath.

"Remember to smile and stay positive and on point. There will be some pushback. It happens all the time. Nothing to be concerned about. Just stick to the talking points we discussed."

Talking points? Words? What were words? Joan jutted a thumb at Mark. "Ice is gonna do the talking."

Padma tossed her luxurious ebony curls over one shoulder. "Did you get the chance to look over the benefits package? Remember to set up an appointment with me to go over health benefits and our retirement plan."

"You bet," Mark said. "Hey, is it true that psychiatric services are available?"

"Absolutely." Their liaison grew serious. "We understand the unique stress of this job. All the Supers in the country work virtually with a wonderful therapist. Her information is included in the welcome binder."

He elbowed Joan in the ribs. "There really *is* a shrink who specializes in superpowered issues."

"What else, what else?" Padma referred to her tablet. "Oh, yes. I'm still waiting on the activation of your credit cards. Should be done by this evening. Since you're technically not full Superheroes just yet, there's a five-thousand-dollar monthly spending limit. If you have additional expenses like rent or car payments, let me know. I can get those approved."

"We have money from running our food truck," Mark was quick to defend.

"We pay our bills," Joan added.

"Of course." Padma smiled graciously. "You might find the transition a little strange. Just know that Vector City takes care of its Heroes."

That sat uneasily in Joan's gut. Years of griping about the Supers getting whatever they wanted, and here she was being offered just that.

Padma glanced at her smartwatch. "Oop. It's time." She touched the doorknob, then whirled around. "Did you have any more questions?"

"Is there more champagne?" Joan asked.

Padma giggled and shook her head. "You're so funny. I already like working with you. Welcome to the team, Spark and Ice."

She breezed out the doorway into the growing communal chatter. *Welcome to the team.* Ugh, so weird.

Ward clicked on his own tablet. "Did you get the fruit basket Blip sent to headquarters?"

"Yep," Mark said. "That was nice of him."

Ward nodded and clicked again.

"I didn't see it," Joan said.

Her brother finished off his champagne, then said, "Blip. Y'know, the Villain up in Canada who turned Hero?"

"Yes, I know. He sent a fruit basket?"

"The note said something like 'Congrats from another queer former Villain. Life is sweeter on this side.'"

Ah. Fruit. Sweet. Got it. "I didn't know he was queer," Joan said.

"Yeah, he's bi."

"Cool."

Mark snorted. "You know Vector City is gonna boast about having the most queer Superheroes now."

"Something to be proud of, I guess. As long as it's not exploited."

Applause broke out in the lobby. Joan caught sight of Otis waving to the office workers. Padma stuck her head back in. "Okay, you two. Let's go."

Joan's stomach churned. She could flee. Bust through a window and get out of there.

Her feet dragged like cement bricks. Ward gave Mark a fist-bump, then Joan.

The noise dipped the second they hit the marble-tiled lobby.

Faces pinched, eyes narrowed in suspicion. Okay, so not everyone was excited. To be expected.

Kade—bless him—came over and gave them his signature high-five, thankfully muted through their gloves. Zee smirked like *Get ready for this.*

Otis pushed through the double doors to the roar of the crowd. How many people were out there?

Darlene followed, then Zee, then Kade.

Joan couldn't make her legs move.

A hand slipped into hers. *Mark.*

He gave a reassuring squeeze. Joan squeezed back. They shared nervous smiles, and then walked into the bright light of day.

And promptly hid behind everyone else on the wide landing.

As Otis stepped to the podium and greeted the fine citizens of Vector City, Kade shifted and made room for them. Darlene and Zee spaced themselves so they could all stand in line. Together.

Then Joan saw the full magnitude of the crowd—the news cameras and microphones and rapidly clicking digital cameras and way too many people. Mayor Thorpe stood off to the side in a blue suit that made his spray tan really pop.

Beside him, Padma waved to get her attention. She moved her hands in front of her face and mouthed, *"Smile!"*

Joan clasped her hands and kind of wanted a Supervillain attack to distract them all.

"Before we begin," Otis said, "I am happy to share that Amazing Woman is recovering well. She sends her thanks for your support and well wishes. She has gone back into retirement now that Quake is no longer a threat."

Joan sought out Sadie and Perry. They'd been given VIP access so she could find them in the front of the crowd.

Ah, there Sadie was in her easy-to-spot lime-green trench coat, grinning from ear to ear. Joan's heart rate went down a notch.

Sadie winked at her and mouthed, *"Love you."*

Joan smiled back gratefully.

Perry looked too cool for school in his sunglasses and over-coat, but he couldn't hide the joy pulling at his mouth from his kids doing well. Gus was back at his condo, healed but weakened. Feeling her age and damn grumpy about it.

Otis went on with whatever talking points Padma had coached him to say about infrastructure repairs. He gestured back at City Hall with its boarded-up second-floor windows. "This building symbolizes that we may face adversity, but we always overcome it."

Someone staring very pointedly at Joan caught her attention. Off to the right, in the sea of faces…

Greta.

She tilted her head, dryly amused. But her eyes were sad. Joan lightly shrugged one shoulder. This was not a day either of them had ever expected.

The crowd clapping distracted her for a moment. When she turned back, Greta was gone. Doing what she did best and disappearing. Joan could only pray to whoever was in charge that she never had to face Greta on this side of the law.

She laughed to herself. Grets would never get caught anyway.

"And now, the reason we are here today." Otis glanced over his shoulder at the newbies. Oh, shit. "These past few weeks, Vector City has had protection from an unlikely source."

Joan lost the ability to hear through the roar of white noise in her ears. Otis was talking and gesturing, Mark was grinning, but oh god, she had to throw up.

She found Sadie in the crowd again. Her hands were clasped on her chest, tears running down her cheeks. The pure love radiating from her gave Joan the strength to breathe and stand tall.

"Therefore," Otis said. "And again reinforcing that it is on a probationary basis…"

Mark rolled his eyes at Joan.

"I'd like to introduce you to the newest members of the Vector City Superheroes squad, Ice and Spark."

The other Supers clapped and turned in to face them. Otis

vacated the podium. The crowd was lukewarm, but a few people whistled and whooped.

Joan moved to the podium beside Mark, who was waving to the crowd, enjoying this a whole lot more than she was. There were *so many people* and they were *all staring at them.*

"What's up, Vector City?" Mark said. "I'm sure most of you are looking at us and wondering what two former Supervillains are doing up here with the good guys." He glanced at Joan. "We know we have a lot of work to do to earn your trust. But we're here to make a positive impact and show you we really do want to make up for our past transgressions."

Murmurs rippled through the crowd. A lot of disbelief and "Yeah, right" and "I'll believe it when I see it." But at least one of them could remember talking points.

"I'm looking forward to getting to know you all and really working *for* you. I don't expect anything from you other than your trust. Which I will earn in time. I hope."

His charisma brought a few chuckles. Good. Mark could charm them so Joan wouldn't have to—

"Spark, would you like to add anything?"

She gave him a look. Mark just grinned at her.

Joan forced her torso to bend toward the microphone, half expecting the ear-shredding feedback that happened in the movies. "Uh..."

She cleared her throat. *Come on, Joan. You're Spark. Act like it.*

"Thank you for putting your trust in us. I'm going to do what I can to help the people who need it most. Everyone deserves a second chance. I'm really lucky to have been given this opportunity." She gave a solid nod. "Thank you again."

Relief flowed down her body as she stepped back.

"Oh my god, Spark is *hot*," some woman said, getting a ripple of giggles in response. "No, seriously, she's hot!"

The heat burning Joan's face had nothing to do with her abilities. She widened her eyes at Otis, telegraphing he could go ahead and wrap this up.

Otis resumed his place behind the podium. "Let's have a nice round of applause for Spark and Ice."

Joan could've collapsed against Kade's thick arm, only he raised it for a high-five. "Good job!" he stage-whispered.

"We have time for a few questions." Otis pointed toward the throng of press. "Yes, you there."

"Is Breeze also joining you?" a male reporter asked.

"Breeze has decided to remain in the private domain. He has, however, reformed his ways and no longer poses a threat."

Joan found Perry with an eyebrow raised above his sunglasses. Then she looked at Sadie again because she was such a comfort. A light in the storm.

"Next question. Yes you, madam."

A blonde woman held her digital recorder high. "Flight, what can you tell us about the rumor that the Villains had access to a technology that could block your superpowers while boosting their own?"

"Can you confirm that there's a way to inhibit superpowers from being used?" another reporter piped up.

Several others asked variations on that question. Otis looked a bit uneasy, then masked it with a smile. "We have possession of the items these most recent Supervillains were attempting to use. We're properly storing them to ensure they will not be of any harm."

"How can you assure us another attack of that magnitude won't happen again?"

"Flight," the blonde said. "Supervillains are unable to use their powers once they are apprehended. Can this sort of, let's call it power blocking, also be used to fend them off?"

Otis raised a hand. "I hear your concerns and want to reassure you we're doing all we can to shore up our defenses and protect our city. Adding two Superheroes is a big step."

Really dodging the question there, Otis. Though people sure were focused on that tech despite everything else that'd happened during the battle.

"I have a question for Mayor Thorpe," someone Joan couldn't see stated. "Where did you pull from the city's coffers for these additional salaries?"

Mayor Thorpe stepped toward the podium. "Ice and Spark are on a trial basis for now. No additional tax dollars are being utilized. Everything is well within our fiscal parameters."

"What are fiscal parameters?" Mark muttered to Joan.

"Pretty sure not a real thing," she muttered back. Just more buzzwords. Yeah, she was not going to talk in buzzwords. New and Improved Spark was about truth and honesty.

Otis set to concluding the presser (Padma called them pressers). If they had to go back inside and shake hands and possibly kiss babies, Joan would rather just go to HQ and get started fighting crime. Or go to Perry's and make a nice dinner for everyone.

Mark snorted as he studied her face—er, what he could see of it. "You totally want to get out of here."

"Can we just fly off and impress the crowd?"

"That would be fun."

"Thank you, Vector City," Otis stated with gravitas. "Our city."

The crowd woo-hooed. Zee and Kade nudged the twins to wave to the crowd. To be united as a team.

The woman who'd proclaimed Spark was hot and her friends cheered loudly for her. For Spark.

Joan acknowledged them with a nod, making them go all "Oh my god!" She couldn't help adding a lazy smile—she was supposed to be a queer role model now.

Then she turned that smile toward Sadie, the woman who got to have it whenever she wanted. As much as she wanted.

Sadie blew her a kiss with both hands and said, "Ice is so hot!"

Joan burst out laughing and did her best not to convey in front of the cameras how much she loved that beautiful redhead.

Tonight, though, she'd convey it thoroughly.

CHAPTER 23

Sadie wandered around the lobby inside Superhero HQ, smiling to herself. Her girlfriend was a Superhero. They both had access—though limited—to this building. To this world. It was just wild.

Ward had brought her and Perry back from the press conference while the Supers met upstairs. She wasn't checking Super-Watch or social media. Public opinion didn't matter because she knew Spark and Ice were going to do great things now that they'd finally been given the chance to shine.

She giggled thinking about the gaggle of young women who'd decided Spark was hot. The second Joanie opened her mouth and that sexy, husky voice came out, folks got a taste of what had first attracted Sadie outside an elevator on a warm summer night.

She flopped into an armchair with cobalt-blue upholstery and chrome legs and reached for her mineral water on the floor. Her upper arms and shoulders groaned in protest thanks to Joanie's boxing lesson at the warehouse yesterday. She could now somewhat throw a few different kinds of punches and knew how to properly balance and be light on her feet. It was a cool, powerful feeling. She hadn't expected to enjoy it so much.

Her phone bleeped with an incoming email. A reply from the bakery that had supplied Hot and Cold with its sourdough bread.

Sad to lose that mutually beneficial partnership. Maybe she could sell their pastries at Sadie's Café—if she ever got it off the ground.

She'd made a lot of good connections through the food truck. Friendships for sure with the four people entrusted with Joan and Mark's secret. They'd been joking in texts about getting Spark and Ice to endorse their trucks.

Perry rejoined her after stepping away to take a phone call. He eased into the chair beside hers as Sadie read from the email. "The bakery got our final payment and wishes us the best. They said if we decide to reopen to let them know."

"Maybe if you have food service at your coffeehouse," Perry said.

"That was never really my intention. I'd still like to have food trucks park in front."

He made a noncommittal hum. "That Knollwood Village property would have worked out well for you."

Sadie sighed. "Yeah."

"If it had a better landlord, would you have said yes?"

"Totally. I mean I would have freaked out and Joanie would've had to calm me down, but then I would've said yes."

He looked at her, afternoon sunlight catching on his glasses. "Good news. The owners are highly motivated to sell the building."

She turned to face him. "What do you mean?"

"They received a lucrative offer from an interested party on the condition the management company isn't retained after the sale."

Huh? "What does that mean?"

Perry's lips twitched. "Gus wants to buy the building."

"What? Why?"

"Because you want to open a café."

Sadie's heartbeat kicked up a notch. "I didn't think Gus liked me."

"She likes you fine. I told her about that lease addendum. She said it was, and I quote, 'utter horseshit.' She wants to support a woman-owned business. She knows how much this means to you."

What was… What? Gus? Gus thought Sadie was Joan's biggest weakness. She didn't like her. She didn't like anyone. "I don't understand."

"I said I was thinking about buying it." Perry grinned. "Revenge and all."

"Yes, your favorite, I know."

"But I'm too involved with the café. Gus said she'd go ahead and buy it if it was the perfect location. She lived in the Village for a time, so she's familiar with it."

Sadie leaned over her chair's arm. "I'm really not trying to… But like, really? Really really?"

"Really really," Perry said.

"Is it financially doable and won't put her in dire straits?"

"I've helped her invest her generous retirement package."

"You're good at stuff like that?"

He made a face. "I have an MBA. Why do you all keep forgetting that?"

"Oh, you never let us forget."

So Gus was actually doing this for Perry. To be more involved in his life here in the city. Still, this was a good thing. Like, a really good thing. Like, *Holy crap, Gus wants to buy the building so Sadie's Café can be the tenant.*

Perry gestured with his phone. "Should I make the call? It's up to you."

"For real?"

Irritation creased the skin between his brows. "Would I have brought it up if it wasn't?"

"Perry!" Tears rushed to her eyes. She leapt from the chair and crushed him in a bear hug. "Oh my god. That would be so amazing. Please let me call her and thank her. Oh my god. Thank you. Thank you thank you thank you!"

She pulled back to grin at him and babble, "It's going to be a safe place for everyone. The superpowered and the norms. And artists. Does she know I'm artistic? I'm gonna work really hard. I won't let you down."

"I've seen you in action," Perry said. "You can do this."

"*We* can do this." She held out her hand. "Partner."

"I'm just an investor. You're running it." He shook her hand anyway.

"You'll be as involved as you were with Hot and Cold. Please be as involved. I need you."

Sadie squealed, twirling from the pure joy running through her veins. It was happening! Sadie's Café where it belonged! Revenge did kind of feel good.

Time for me to be extraordinary.

She had to thank Gus. Make her a cute wreath or something. "I hope this means Gus will be around more."

"Not really," Perry said.

"She doesn't have to hide anymore."

"She likes the solitude. She does want to get to know Joan and Mark. And you, of course."

"Anytime." Her emotional tidal wave pushed her to hug him again. "I'm so glad you have her, and she has you. You make each other happy."

Perry patted her back. "I'm at my hug limit, Sadie."

"Sorry!" She straightened and grappled with her phone. "I have to tell my parents. And Nyah. This meeting better be over soon 'cause Joanie has to get her butt down here. I can't wait to tell her. She's gonna be ecstatic. Oh, wait—should we call Gus first?"

"I'll take care of that. Make your calls."

"Thank you, Perry. For everything you do for the people you care about." She'd almost said *the people you love*, but that was too much mushy stuff for him for one day.

"You're welcome," he said.

She twirled again, then scurried toward the kitchen. There was a little hallway there where she could have the privacy to scream and cry. She'd call Nyah first to tell her the incredible news.

Shuffling and bumping came from that direction. Sadie stopped short as her overwhelmed brain registered two bodies. Mark and Zee. Making out like horny teenagers.

She hopped back, then peeked around the corner.

Mark backed Zee up and pressed them against the wall. Zee groaned. "Watch it. My ribs are still sore."

"Aww," Mark cooed. "Want me to kiss it and make it better?"

"We need to get back."

"So the coffee run took a little longer than anticipated. Just giving Ward a break. He works too hard. The guy needs a vacation."

Zee growled and mashed their lips on Mark's. "Stop talking. You make this unbearable when you talk."

"You love it," Mark teased.

Sadie clamped a hand over her mouth to keep from howling with laughter.

They smooched a few more times before Zee pushed Mark away and tossed their straight black hair. "I'll go first. Don't forget your coffee."

With super speed, Zee zipped through the kitchen. Mark adjusted his baby-blue oxford shirt. His wry smirk morphed into a genuine smile. Aww, too cute.

She waited until he cleared the kitchen before dissolving into a fit of giggles. Now she *really* couldn't wait to talk to Joan. Life was full of surprises these days.

EPILOGUE

One month later

Joan opened her car door and stepped over a small puddle, not wanting to get her hot-pink sneakers wet. Or dirty. It'd been a risk wearing them with rain in the forecast (natural rain, not Villain-created rain). Taking little chances like this were helping her get more comfortable with being visible.

She locked her doors and took in Hampton Street. Knollwood Village really did have Sadie's vibe. The funky shops and art galleries. Older buildings mixed with carefully renovated structures. There was even a ramen place a few blocks down they couldn't wait to try.

She moved to the sidewalk, switching the hand holding the white paper bag filled with Mexican pastries. The ones Spark had acquired that morning because she was essentially always on call, ready to help whoever was in need. That was still taking getting used to. Hell, everything was in her new occupation.

The For Lease sign was gone from inside the window at Future Sadie's Café. Joan had only seen the space from the outside. With the sale finalized and the lease as good as done, Sadie now had possession.

Joan spotted her standing in the middle of the empty space, hands on the hips of a short, flowy purple dress. The overhead lighting highlighted her excitement but also her nerves.

She knocked on the glass door, waving when Sadie looked over.

Sadie skipped across the laminate flooring and unlocked the door. "Welcome to Sadie's Café," she said, then immediately started leaking happy tears.

Joan scooped her into her arms. "Congratulations, sweetheart."

Sadie tugged her inside. "Come look at your investment. I can't stop staring at everything."

She took in the exposed brick and all Sadie had been talking about over the past few weeks. Sketches and craft projects and Perry's paperwork were strewn about their home office, but that was okay. Not like Joan was using it anymore.

"A celebratory treat?" Sadie said, pointing at the pastry bag.

"Yep. Spark and Catch stopped a water main break from flooding a panadería. We sort of soldered the pipe back together. I didn't know I could do stuff like that. Non-destructive stuff."

"That's great, babe."

"Darlene suggested it." Joan made a face that caused Sadie to snicker. Darlene was her assigned babysitter that week. Neither would ever, *ever* admit to it, but they were learning handy tips and tricks from one another. "The staff was cool and wanted to thank us."

Sadie took the bag, then squeezed Joan's hand. "Was that hard for you? Getting free stuff?"

"I insisted I would pay for them. Then they admitted they were day-old pastries that would probably just get thrown out." Joan laughed. "They were honest about how people don't always give Supers the best stuff."

It'd felt good to help out a family-owned business and be able to talk openly with them. Spark and Ice were making it known they were not in it for handouts.

"Ooh, conchas." Sadie closed the bag and held it to her chest. "Do I get first dibs since this is my special day?"

"Of course."

"Thank you, my love. Look around. Tell me if you think a couch and coffee table can fit in that nook back there. I need to get to measuring."

Joan wandered over to the far corner. A wistful tug pulled at her heart. They'd been this psyched when they bought the food truck. It seemed like ages ago, but had only been months. So much had happened since then.

Sadie and Per had done the lion's share of tying everything up for Hot and Cold. Still a total bummer to go out like that.

With the coffeehouse, they had a perfect misdirection. On the food truck's social media, it now said that the owners *"have decided to focus on a brick-and-mortar café."* They'd changed the account names to the café and not ruled out the possibility of having signature sandwiches available in the future. Anything was possible.

Such as the owners becoming Superheroes.

"Let's take a selfie for my parents," Sadie said as she walked over. "They want lots of pictures."

Joan leaned into her and obliged. "Are we still telling them I started a restaurant investment group with Mark and Perry?"

"Yes, and this is your first venture."

"I hate that you have to lie to your family and friends again."

"It's not entirely a lie. You did invest."

"But they're gonna wonder how I'm making money," Joan said.

"If you'd like, we can casually drop the truth at Sunday night dinner at my sister's house." Sadie raised her eyebrows like *Not a chance.*

It would be kind of nice to let them know Joan was a good guy now. Maybe her own family even suspected it. Not that it mattered, but then again, what better revenge?

Sadie's phone buzzed with an incoming text. "Nyah's coming by in about an hour. She's bringing champagne."

"Nice. And yeah, a couch and table will fit here."

The door creaked open. A moment later, Gus moved through the entrance. Perry tried to assist her, but she batted him away. "I've got it," she groused.

Her healing had aged her about ten years, which she was none too happy about. Her mobility was back to normal, but she definitely had more wrinkles and a white streak in her blonde hair and aches and pains she'd staved off for a long time. Her sacrifice was still very much appreciated.

She peered through her glasses—ones she actually needed now. Sadie rushed over to give her a hug. "Welcome to your building!"

"Yes, yes." Gus patted her with both hands. "It's a big day."

Sadie showed her around, pointing out what she had planned. Perry joined Joan against the long white counter. She'd gotten to know Gus at a few homecooked dinners. She was as private as Perry, but they let things slip now and again. Weirdly cute ways she teased him about snoring, and him about her use of old-timey sayings like *dagnabbit* and *consarn it*. Joan had caught him holding her hand once in his condo, both insisting it was for additional support for her aging body.

Which was about as convincing as Mark and Zee saying they were just hanging out. Overnight. Arriving "separately" to HQ in the same clothes they'd been wearing the night before. Everyone had picked up on it, but only Joan and Kade were gleefully (and, okay, relentlessly) teasing them about it.

Sadie spanned her fingers along the back wall that blocked the small kitchen area. "On this wall, I'd love to feature work by local artists."

Gus nodded in agreement. "I like that. Perhaps I can paint a little something for it."

"Oh, I'd love that." Sadie slid a knowing look at Perry. "A landscape, perhaps?"

"Perhaps."

Perry pretended not to smile. He gazed at Gus like she was the most beautiful woman in the world. A few extra wrinkles hadn't changed that.

Joan nudged him and said, "You know you're allowed to be excited about this."

"I am." He pulled a thick roll of papers from his inside jacket pocket. "Sadie reads and discusses everything you and Mark ignored."

"I meant Gus. Her being here."

"I'm excited about that, too," he said quietly.

"Perry has a good eye for arranging pieces," Gus said.

Sadie glanced back at him. "I'll definitely consult with him because I'm more about vibes."

Turning toward the front windows, Gus crossed her arms and said, "I like this place and want to see it succeed. If there is anything I can do, just say the word."

"Thank you, Gus. You've already done so much."

"This could be a real neighborhood hangout."

"Where friends gather," Sadie murmured, getting that gleam in her eye that said a new craft project was brewing.

A SuperWatch notification jingled from Joan's phone. She checked that damn app more now than ever before.

Ice and Lunk had been spotted signing autographs for a group of tourists checking out what remained of Friendship Park. Mark had taken to being in the public eye like an ice cube to lemonade.

Good for him. And Joan, since he took the heat off of her—though not literally. He liked being in control of his public image, and she liked avoiding meet-and-greets.

Locals were still wondering about the power-blocking tech that Padma had coached all the Supers not to discuss. They didn't want to give other Villains any ideas, nor give the norms a reason to suggest all superpowered individuals should be barred from using their abilities. It was a hotly debated topic on late-night news programs, along with whether former Villains should be allowed to crawl out from the dark side.

Repairing and repaving what Quake had crumbled outside HQ had been a good distraction. And making good on a whole lot of damage claims. Plans were underway to bring Friendship Park back to its former glory. And seriously, what Villain would be foolish enough to come to Vector City now?

If they did, Joan was ready.

"Checking out all the comments about lesbian icon Spark?" Sadie teased.

"It's so embarrassing," Joan said, cheeks warming.

"It's awesome."

"Glad you think so."

Spark didn't discuss her personal life despite people wanting to know all about the two newest Supers. No Hero divulged that sort of information. She couldn't even remember when it got leaked that the Villains Spark and Ice were gay.

Sadie had assured her more than once that Joanie Maloney was very much her girlfriend, and they had a wonderful, safe, private life together.

"I need to use the restroom," Gus announced. "Dadgum bladder can't hold anything these days."

"This way," Perry said, leading her toward the two small washrooms.

Sadie not so subtly reached for the pastry bag sitting on the counter. "My arms don't hurt anymore after our workouts."

"You're getting used to it," Joan said, peeking at the large round treats. "And getting good at it."

"I don't know if I'll be up for it the rest of the week with everything going on here."

"Of course."

"I need to conserve my energy for a quickie or two in our busy schedules." Sadie waggled her eyebrows.

Joan sighed. "I'm gonna miss regular morning sex."

"Me, too. But I'm confident we'll find the time."

They laughed together. Joan kissed her cheek. There was a lot going on. Scary, yes, to both be starting new phases of their lives. But they had each other's support as a constant.

Sadie pulled out a strawberry concha, making yummy sounds. These had been given as a joke, really. It wasn't the same as expecting a freebie.

Things were gonna be different now. They were changing for the better, right? All good things from here on out: for Superhero Joan, for café owner Sadie, for them as a couple.

Right?

The norms sure are interested in this power-blocking technology. How will things go with Joan now fighting alongside the Superheroes? Can she and Greta repair their friendship?

Will Sadie's parents ever find out about that minor Supervillain abduction? And will Sadie's Café be everything she's dreamed about? Can Mark and Zee quit pretending they like each other already?

The trilogy continues in THE BRIGHTEST BLAZE, Vector City Supers Book 3.

A great way to celebrate a book you enjoyed is to leave a review. Dropping one at the retailer where you purchased this or on the review site of your choice would be super-duper appreciated.

Stay in the know with my bookish news by subscribing to my monthly author newsletter. There are cool perks just for subscribers. Membership has its privileges! www.kellyfarmerauthor.com

Happy Reading!
Kelly

ACKNOWLEDGMENTS

Huge thanks to everyone who read *Secret Spark* and was like, "Hey, I want to see what happens in this wacky world of Heroes and Villains." Writing this series has been a total blast. Thanks for going on the journey with me.

Endless hugs and gratitude to my awesome review crew, The Super Readers. You truly do rock.

To the reviewers, bloggers, podcasters, social media shouter-outers, and lovers of sapphic romance: Thank you. Sharing your love for the genre is a wonderful gift to the world and so appreciated.

Mackenzie Walton once again gave insightful and informative edits. It's a pleasure working with you each and every time, and I'm so glad no one reads my books before you work your magic on them.

Big thanks to Steve Buccellato for another banger of a cover! It exudes the love and support Sadie and Joan have for one another.

What would I do without Julie Cassidy fixing all my grammatical boo-boos? There would be...so...many...ellipses... So... Many..............

Thanks ever so much to Chandra Blumberg and Kelly Smith for the awesome beta reads. And love as always to the (reinvigorated!) Panera Supper Club.

Also, a shout-out to Tyler Florence and all the chefs who've been on *The Great Food Truck Race*. I so admire your hustle and dedication and want to eat all your specialty fries.

Thank *you*, reader friend, for spending your precious time on this spinning blue orb reading this book.

Fanning the Flames delves into some common fears when it comes to following your dreams. Joan has to literally step out of the shadows, while Sadie has to step into her power. It's scary! What if you fail spectacularly?

My self-helpery, woo-woo side will tell you that your heart's desire is on the other side of that fear. And yeah, some people will be all "You're a former Supervillain. You can't do this." Or a crappy lease addendum will set you back.

Do it anyway. Live your dreams. You're a damn Superhero.

ALSO BY KELLY FARMER

Vector City Supers:

Secret Spark (Book 1)

The Out on the Ice Series:

Out on the Ice (Book 1)

Unexpected Goals (Book 2)

Calling the Shots (Book 3)

It's a Fabulous Life

ABOUT THE AUTHOR

Kelly Farmer (she/her) has been writing romance novels since junior high. While the stories have changed, one theme remains the same: everyone deserves to have a happy ending. She is the bestselling author of queer contemporary romances with snarky humor and lots of heart.

When not writing, she enjoys being outside in nature, quoting from eighties movies, listening to all kinds of music, and petting every dog she comes in contact with. All of these show up in her books. Kelly lives in the Chicago area, where she swears every winter is her last one there.

To connect with Kelly, talk about current TV binges, and subscribe to her newsletter for access to free bonus stories, head over to:

www.kellyfarmerauthor.com